Thorne Grey and Darkness

The Phoenix S.

Book 1

FARRELL KEELING

1

Thorne Grey and the City of Darkness

Text Copyright © 2019

Farrell Keeling

ISBN: 9781980631453

(*Print Edition*)

*"The Phoenix can fly only
when his wings have
grown"*

Prologue

1,000 years ago...

Horizon is changing.

I tried to make the council understand, but they refused to heed my warnings. If they'd listened, Horizon could have prepared for the darkness that would soon overwhelm it. But what other end could have possibly been achieved? The council was besmirched with the foolish arrogance of Man and Warlocks, apprehensive Regals and self-centred Dwarves. But not even my own keen senses, gifted with potent Majik, could anticipate the immediacy of the threat.

It was on that day as I was riding through the Vales of Hrokomar that I saw the massed demon horde for myself. The screams of my townsmen carried across miles of open landscape, and the entire city – my home and throne – blazed like an inferno under the deceptively tranquil night sky. The three towers that pierced the heavens like giant glistening daggers, had crumbled; their devastated remains protruding from the ground like shards of glass. The roads and streets, which would have been all but invisible to the naked eye, were lit up with the blood red embers of battle that flowed across the cobbles like lava, devouring my city.

I closed my eyes, reaching out with my mind. My celestial form glided past the green landscape, through the crushed wooden gates, past the blood-soaked courtyard, the bodies of the city guard scattered around it. Having overseen their training personally, I knew all their names. I examined their ashen, ghost white faces, with their rolled eyes, expressions of pain and fear imprinted vividly across each one. Markus, Vant, Igor, Iris, Aphea, Vorn... I had to move on.

Despite the destruction that surrounded it, the clock-tower at the centre of the courtyard remained oddly untouched. Shaped like the fiercest dragon I'd ever fought, it rose to thirty feet, with gleaming scales and ruby eyes. It stood on its hind legs like a dog, its arms raised outstretched, in defence against an imaginary opponent. In its open maw and surrounded by a hundred, dagger-like fangs, the clock was held. A magnificent work of craftsmanship. The dragon's tongue burst through the centre of the clock and split into two, forming the hour and minute hands. It continued, blissfully unaware of the horrors around it, to tick away, counting away my peoples' final living moments. How time endures...

I passed into the streets, flying through the swarm of demons and the remaining soldiers who resisted them; each hopelessly outnumbered. I saw one man in a corner, with a long slash across his face and a limp, bloody left arm, fighting one handed against three demons. He managed to slay one, and slice through the horns of another, but his fatigue sowed the seeds of his destruction and he slumped onto the ground, his own sword buried deep into his chest. Immobilised by fear, women and children burned to death in their homes; their screams uniting together in one heart-rending crescendo, among the guttural cries of the blood-thirsty demons. Each street was consumed by unrelenting fires that burst through windows and blackened trees, their foliage set alight like giant funeral pyres.

I saw a boy, a mere infant, being chased through the street by a red skinned demon, its guttural laugh echoing within my ears. It would not claim another soul. Not today. I flew past the demon and into the child. The boy's thoughts were erratic, and he began to panic even more when he registered my sudden intrusion. *Don't be alarmed, I'm going to save you!* I told him. *Leave me alone!* His conscious screamed back. I informed him of my identity and intentions, but his fear prevented any form of rationality, his conscious screaming out all sorts of oaths and protestation. I continued to plead the nobility of my aims, wary of the quickly nearing demon, but the boy refused to acknowledge me.

I swept into his system, through the blood in his veins and arteries, working my way around the boy's body, and reluctantly, broke the seals of his mind. The crying voice that had screamed around my ears now became barely audible and completely unintelligible. I felt the flow of life within this new body of mine, and similar, yet completely different senses. My new heart pounded relentlessly against my fragile chest, my breath came in starts and stutters, the many blisters I felt on my feet hindered my movement.

I stopped in my tracks and turned to face the demon who had pursued me. I detected great confusion and terror emphasized by the tremors in the boy's voice, but I put them aside and prepared to fight. The demon glared at me with its dark eyes, something resembling a triumphant grin reaching its mouth, as it swung its sword in a sweeping arc above my head.

I ducked, but the creature swung again. Its sword had found its mark this time, and the boy's screams began to overwhelm my thoughts.

'No!' I bellowed out loud.

Channelling all the power I had into my new body, I caught the sword in mid-air, snatching it from the startled demon, shattering a cracked window as I threw it into one of the burning buildings beside me.

The demon roared, pounding a dent into the ground with its fist, and charged towards me. I felt myself lifted off my feet, the creature's sharp claws dug through my sleeves, drawing blood that trickled around its long red fingers.

My cries joined that of the boy's in my head, and tears began to curl from the corners of my eyes.

The demon roared again, straight into my ears, and then preceded to hurl my body across the street. I tumbled across the pavement, jagged rocks tearing into the back of my new flesh.

My vision had become a blur, the flames forming a fusion of red and amber that waved in front of my eyes like a desert mirage. I became aware of a dull ring in my ears that silenced the turmoil of others around me. I shook myself, my sight returning in time to warn me of the incoming creature.

I pushed my weight onto a leg, wavered for a moment, then crumbled. I'd spent much of my minimal reserves of energy to help this child, and for what? I could barely handle one damn demon! How would I help the boy manoeuvre past the entire horde? Let alone the hundreds of others I wished to save?

The air shrieked as the demon's claws pierced through the air towards my motionless body. I closed my eyes, begging the child's forgiveness, and then abandoned his body to ruin.

The sick unity of the despairing cries of my city and its people, mingled with the merciless roars of the flames and demons, accompanied my fleeing spirit at every street, alley, and house. The bodies in the square all seemed to be given new life as their eyes followed my spectral trail across the sky, accusing, and blaming. I could imagine the final moments of the men and women who had bravely, almost stubbornly, attempted to fight off the hellish horde. Tears streaming down their blood besmirched faces as the demons tore apart their compatriots. Brothers, sisters, cousins, sons, daughters, grandchildren. All gone. The most proud, strong-hearted, benevolent people I had ever known, all wiped out by an unrelenting horde of evil.

I returned to my body. My eyes shot open, and out burst from my lips an unintelligible howl of despair. It endured, seemingly forever, under the witness of taunting Gods.

My horse, startled by my outbursts, bucked suddenly and I was thrown onto the ground.

'My lord!'

Several of my personal guard jumped off their mare's and came to my aid. But any effort to console me failed utterly. My emotional unrest could, by no means, be tempered.

'A–all of th–them...' I stuttered through tears, 'all of them!' My fatigued body sank to the grass, my fists plunging into the ground. I had failed them all... But my pain was one which the men beside me, could not, would not, be able to understand. The consequence of an ancient oath that had been forced upon Räne's Golden Kingsguard that forbade them from pursuing love, marriage and the bearing of children, while under service.

'My lord,' one man insisted, 'we must make haste to dél Dręmăra! Horizon must be warned!'

He grabbed me, as firmly as he dared, to convey a sense of urgency, in a vain attempt to drag me to my feet. I would not rise, nor would I allow myself to tear my eyes away from the harrowing scene that lay before me.

As I closed my eyes, darkness overwhelming me, I could once again see the blazing fires that stole the lives of my people and the city, like a giant parasite. I could picture the final moments of the child I'd failed to save. I could hear those frantic thoughts ringing painfully in my mind as the demon performed the killing blow. I had failed them all.

It was then that it dawned upon me: I am the last king of Räne...

I rose to my knees, and with my head aimed at the starlit sky, I bellowed out a vow of revenge that shook the heavens above.

'MY NAME IS FIERSLAKEN! AND I SWEAR TO YOU: MY PEOPLE SHALL BE AVENGED!'

Chapter 1

It would be a horrible day. Not just because of the torrent of rain that pounded on the streets like drums, nor the winds that whistled through the alleyways but because a murder would happen tonight.

If you were misfortunate enough to be a beggar, you would most definitely consider your day ruined if the Baron paid a visit to the alley in which you happened to be. The Baron was known widely as a slave trader, which contributed, only slightly, to his abnormally cruel and foul manner. All the beggars despised him, although their immense fear of the Baron greatly masked their hatred. He'd been known to flog anyone who stood in his way; beggars were just practice.

On this particularly displeasing day, the Baron stormed into Wichin Alley, furious that he had to travel for so long in torrential rain and horrendous thunderstorms that raged and roared overhead. He looked up, scowling at the night sky which was set alight with forks of lightning.

His foot plunged suddenly, deep into a large pool of water that was cunningly hidden by the shadow formed by a rusted, ancient alley sign, its letters mostly displaced. The Baron swore, regarding his trouser leg and shoes with disgust. Both were brand new and made with the finest materials money could buy.

His horrendous temper already amplified, the Baron shook his sodden leg and strode into the alley, looking forward to venting his uncontrollable anger on some mindless beggars, who would undoubtedly be huddled together like rats. The excess sewage that poured forth from the gargling gutters, and moss-covered walls merely completing the scene.

A second thought played on his mind upon entrance into the alley: It had better be a bloody good meeting.

One meeting – it was the cause for the whole tiresome journey from the South – to Féy – to Dalmarra. Was it worth it? No, certainly not. But when The Shadow demands it, a man has no choice but to obey.

The Shadow: a man who uncannily resembled his name. The Baron had only seen him once, but it was enough to grasp the sheer presence he possessed. And yet, despite this, he had an unnerving gift to appear wherever he wished without the knowledge of those around him. Just an uttering of his name could make the heart of any man within earshot (who was brave enough to associate with him) palpitate.

He heard a sniffle. Turning to his side, he realized that what he'd first mistaken for a bundle of clothes was a person. Upon seeing the cloaked form of the Baron, the beggar shuffled back against the wall, dirt encrusted hands held up defensively in front of his pleading eyes.

With a look of the foulest malcontent, the Baron whipped out his cane and stepped towards the beggar, his shadow gradually enclosing the man in complete darkness.

The others had emerged from the piles of clothes and had immediately edged into the darkest recesses of the alley that they could find. All eyes were upon the Baron and his gleaming cane, as the beggars tried to anticipate what horror the tall dark-haired man would inflict upon their friend.

The Baron raised his cane above his head, pushing down the ears of the wolf-headed cane. With a sound like a knife being withdrawn from a metal scabbard, a thin but deadly looking blade emerged slowly from the bottom of the cane.

The beggar observed the blade with a look of terror, and although he was already pressed hard against the wall, he attempted to push himself even further, as though he held the hope that he may shrink into the shadows that had trapped him.

The Baron grinned sardonically, running two fingers across the blade, and then plunged it into the man's chest.

Despite their best efforts, the beggars could not avert their gazes from the shadows of the horrific scene that danced mockingly in front of their eyes. Blood spattered across the walls and turned the rain water running across the alley red.

The Baron's brutal attack relentless and unforgiving, the beggar uttered a single scream before he was abruptly silenced. His body was desecrated even further after death.

The Baron breathed a calm sigh and then ripped away the dead beggar's coat, whistling as he used it to wipe clean the blood from his blade, before throwing it back carelessly to the dead body and spitting on the ground by the man's feet. He withdrew the blade and strode through the streets, eyeing each of the beggars while muttering venomously under his breath, 'street rats.'

At end of the alley he was confronted by a wall blocking his path. A dead end, or so it seemed…

The Baron raised his cane again but this time tapped the eyes of the wolf-head. A second later, the eyes suddenly lit up, shining a bright yellow light upon the wall, highlighting three particular spots in a swirling ball of light.

The Baron tapped the eyes of the wolf-head again and the light disappeared. He then knocked with the side of his clenched fist on each of the three areas of the wall where the swirling balls of light had previously been.

In response, a slate that was at first unseen slid into view and a chubby-faced, bearded man peered through. He gazed questioningly at the Baron with his pair of piggy eyes.

'Who the 'ell are you?' the man grunted.

'I'm expected,' said the Baron, fighting back a retort whilst drumming his fingers impatiently on the end of his cane.

'Gonna have to give me something a wee bit more concrete than dat' replied the man.

'I'm the Baron' he replied.

'Sure.'

'Look whelp, if you don't let me in right now, I'll have you chopped *slowly* into pieces and sold to the nearest butch–'

The man raised a hand to interrupt the Baron, 'that's good enough. But I can't let you in w'thout the password anyway, so...'

'Even for the Baron?' he growled.

The man stared down at his feet and mumbled something incoherently.

'What was that?' demanded the Baron, 'Speak up man!'

'Shadow's orders,' he replied sheepishly.

Suddenly, time seemed to stop and the Baron felt the blood quickly drain from his face as the result of the man's words.

'He... He's come in person?' the Baron whispered.

'Yeah, he just arrived,' said the man, who had begun to tremble, 'he was very, uh... adamant... 'bout the security.'

'Of course,' said the Baron, stroking his long chin thoughtfully, 'yes he would be... very well then: *Ignisavem.*'

The man grunted and disappeared with the slam of the slate. After a few seconds of the grinding of locks being opened and the whirring of gears, a doorway formed within the wall and then opened. Sudden warmth flooded over the Baron, combined with the less pleasant mixture of stale beer and sweat. Once the Baron stepped across the threshold, the door slammed shut behind him and the many locks and mechanisms of the door were revealed. The multitude of such security gave him the impression that he was as much a prisoner as a guest.

Above the door was a sign, depicting an image of a spear embedded in a boar. Below, in red, faded lettering was the name: 'The Lanced Boar.'

The Baron turned and scowled. He recognised several of the men sitting ruggedly on the rusted metal benches, drunkenly banging their empty jugs on the mutilated tables. They were all well-known (though not in a good way), cunning thieves, savage cut-throats, and hulking barbarians. Their unshaven, dirty faces appeared more frequently in the newspapers and wanted posters than in a mirror. Even if slowed by the dimming effect of large quantities of alcohol, they were still, from personal experience, a threat to be watched carefully and closely. He coughed into his hand forcefully, his lip curling

15

when the crowd turned to face him with gormless expressions. He stroked the head of his cane, sneering at the men when they suddenly recognised who he was.

Beer sloshed onto the floor as the men closest to him dropped their mugs and hurried away awkwardly to the tables in the corners of the room, their heads bent and backs hunched. Even the others furthest away from the Baron had begun to edge their tables and chairs as far away from the slave-trader as they could.

A satisfied smile playing triumphantly on his lips, the Baron then paced slowly to the counter, where a bald man wearing a small vest that exposed his large belly stood. His attention was placed solely on a mug, which he was actively trying to rub clean with a towel that was so grubby, it looked as though it hadn't been cleaned in years.

As the Baron approached, the Innkeeper glanced at him, then began cleaning the mug much more vigorously, pretending as though he hadn't seen him in the first place.

When the Baron reached the counter, the man flinched, the mug crashing onto the floor behind him.

Snapping his cane on the quivering Innkeeper's hand, the Baron snarled, 'I believe I'm expected.'

The Innkeeper winced, still avoiding eye contact, and inclined his head in the direction of a pair of barrels, sitting beside the counter, their contents leaking slowly onto the floor.

Approaching them, the Baron noticed that the excess liquid didn't spread across the surface but into cracks in the floor. On closer inspection, he noticed, obscured between a pair of barrels, a rusty metal grip - a trapdoor.

After kicking the barrels aside, the Baron took off his right glove and carefully placed his thumb and index finger on the grip and pulled. There was a creaking noise and a breath of cold air greeted him. With a grimace, he pushed it open and clambered down the ladder that lay before him.

Why had The Shadow decided to come in person? On many occasions before an envoy had sufficed, what had changed this time? Perhaps this was a herald of good fortune for their organisation, or of trouble.

Something stirred by his feet when he reached the ground. Lashing out with his foot, the rat was launched into a wall before scurrying away into the darkness. It was here among the numerous dust veiled barrels and rats that the pungent smell had reached its sickening potential, clinging to the Baron's nostrils and throat. Standing entirely out of place was a large circular table positioned right in the middle of the cellar. A small candle, planted in the middle, illuminated the table and the men who sat around it impatiently, half-empty glasses of wine sitting in front. At his arrival, the servants who had been updating the fill of the glasses scurried away, and all the weary eyes of the table turned towards him.

'Ah, Baron!' exclaimed a man with an eye patch and an assortment of scars, 'we thought you would never come.'

'Unlike you Vervanis, I have had important matters to attend to,' the Baron sneered.

'Indeed,' said another, 'shall we begin?'

'No, not yet Reez, I can see that the Baron is practically bouncing in his seat to ask us something,' the man with the eye patch said with a mischievous grin.

The Baron glared at the man, 'you would not be so impudent were The Shadow here, Vervanis.'

Vervanis did not immediately reply. His one remaining eye twitched and he raised an eyebrow questioningly, 'and where is he? None of us saw him on our way here.'

'Presuming as always, Vervanis,' a voice rang through the cellar.

The room had suddenly gone silent, no one dared to blink. The Baron shivered involuntarily, as if ice had been caressed down his spine.

The Shadow stepped into the light, his arms curled behind his back. His dark, hooded robes that trailed behind his feet concealed his face completely. Under the candle's glow he looked, in the Baron's eyes, if ever so slightly, uncomfortable. He was a man who appeared more at ease in the embrace of darkness, amongst the other shadows, which dogged men in their every endeavour.

'My lord,' chorused the men, each bowing their heads as low as the table would allow them.

The Shadow then raised his pale hands in the air showing his palms to silence them, and said in almost a whisper: 'my *loyal* friends. Or, at least, mostly.'

'What do you mean my lord?' asked the Baron, surprising himself with his confidence.

The Shadow turned to him and regarded him silently, the lack of response causing the Baron to sweat unconsciously. It was remarkable how one could feel such a penetrating gaze without ever actually seeing his eyes, it was little wonder thus The Shadow was so greatly feared among his peers. For all you knew he could be smiling under the hood or fixing you with a glare so cold it would freeze your insides.

After what seemed like hours The Shadow responded, 'all in good time, my dear Baron, all in good time.'

The Shadow took the chair nearest to him, perching himself without so much as a creak of wood. Once comfortable, he pivoted his head to examine the men around the table in silent contemplation.

'I thank you all for coming tonight gentleman, as there are a few things I have discovered. There are decisions that I have made, which I will now bring to… light.'

The Baron chuckled. The Shadow, to his relief, ignored him and continued, 'Firstly, it has come to my attention – most unfortunately for the individual – that there is a traitor in our midst.'

There were a few murmurs of dissent and denial at the mention of these words, which were cut short when Vervanis asked in a tone of surprise: 'A… a traitor my lord?'

'Yes, a traitor,' repeated The Shadow, 'why so surprised? But do not worry, Vervanis, for I shall not hold you in suspense any longer. As it is you.'

There were a few seconds of complete silence and then every weapon in the room – including the Baron's rapier – was pointing at Vervanis.

The Shadow raised his hands again and said: 'Please, my friends, sheathe your weapons. There is no need for you to bloody them today. The matter has already been dealt with.'

After everyone sat back down, grudgingly putting away their weapons, Vervanis suddenly rose out of his chair.

'Leaving us so soon?' asked The Shadow in mock care, 'please, take a seat. Didn't you always say a man should die in comfort?'

Vervanis instantly paled and asked with a strained voice: 'What do you mean?'

The Shadow waved his hand at Vervanis' half-empty glass of wine and asked: 'Enjoying your drink, Vervanis?'

The man's face became a rainbow of colours, changing from white, to red, to blue and then green in only a matter of seconds. It would have been almost comical if his peers had not quickly reached the obvious conclusion.

'You...' gasped Vervanis, struggling to form his words, 'you poisoned me! How?'

'It's quite simple really' replied The Shadow in a tone so carefree you might use it to describe the weather, 'I had poison placed in each of your glasses just to make sure.'

'WHAT!'

Hands trembling, the Baron snatched his half-empty glass from the table, observing the red liquid swirling inside before dropping it on the floor for it to smash into shards by his feet.

'Be calm my friends,' boomed The Shadow, his voice echoing around the cellar. 'Once I realized it was only Vervanis who had betrayed my trust, I had my servants place the required antidotes to the poison in the glasses of all those who are still faithful to me.'

'You... you–' Vervanis began.

'Please Vervanis, over-exertion quickens the poison's effects.'

'You... will... regret... this,' Vervanis growled through clenched teeth, his hands were now clamped tightly on his chair, his knuckles the colour of paper.

'I'm afraid I won't, your time appears to be up. I believe our business together is concluded, Vervanis.'

Vervanis snarled, but before he could utter a final curse he gripped his throat, which had begun to swell and redden. The swelling continued to spread up into his face, enlarged his cheeks and nose to repulsive, and yet strangely amusing sizes. While Vervanis tried to claw aimlessly at his face, froth had begun to build up at his mouth and an obscene mixture of gargling and choking noises emanated from his throat. After one last violent convulsion, his body went limp and slumped back into his chair. Vervanis' swollen head lay flat on his chest and his arms dangled limply either side. Unmoving.

The Shadow placed a hand under his hood, circling the curve of his chin, as if disappointed with the efficiency of Vervanis' death. The Baron was not left to ponder this for long, as with a clap of The Shadow's hands, another round of servants appeared to drag the body away and replace their drinks. Not a single word was uttered or looks exchanged as one cleaned the shards of the Baron's last glass into a tray and then slinked back into the darkness. 'Thank you for your cooperation my friends, now, please, drink.'

The Baron hesitated, eyeing his new untouched glass with a newfound suspicion, but with the gaze of The Shadow upon him he instantly grabbed it and reluctantly slid the contents down his throat.

Once everyone had lowered their glasses, The Shadow began to speak again, 'I would like to bring something else to your attention. I imagine most of you would have travelled by horse and carriage here, and I'm curious. Have any of you experienced this kind of weather in Dalmarra? More importantly actually, do any of you know the significance of this storm that has raged for over a month… in the whole of Horizon I hear?'

The Baron frowned. Weather like this was virtually unheard of in Dalmarra, true. But what did The Shadow mean about the significance of the weather? Was it a joke?

The Shadow laughed softly – the Baron assumed at the confusion on all his disciples' faces. 'My friends, do you recall the discussion we had several years ago regarding a certain… 'prediction'?'

Of course, the Baron thought, 'the prediction',' The Shadow's fortune teller's prophecy.

'I remember,' the Baron said but he could, unfortunately, not hide the dubiety in his voice.

'Good, that is good,' The Shadow said, adding in a grave tone, 'but I sense you do not appreciate its legitimacy, Baron?'

The Baron hesitated, gripping his cane tightly for reassurance, 'I'll believe it when I see it with my own eyes, my lord,' he replied.

'And see… him… you shall, Baron,' The Shadow purred.

The Baron frowned, inviting another laugh from his master.

'As you are all aware, our line of business brings many conflicts with various organizations and races; Dwarves, Regals, Hunters, the Lycans or even the Warlocks,' The Shadow addressed the entire room, hisses accompanying each faction uttered.

'This month, as predicted by the daughter of Ozin, storms would arise in hail of the birth – the rise – of the great warrior, Fierslaken's heir. This child, this infant, shall mark the first day of our ascension to greatness. Soon, my friends, the world shall be ours!'

A great cheer rose up around the table and many of the men slapped their hands on the table in agreement. The only one not visibly pleased was the Baron.

'How will it work, my lord?' asked the Baron.

The cheering stopped and everyone turned to look at The Shadow expectantly.

'A valid question my friend. As I said, the child will play an important part in this plan of mine, and he will bring us control. One way or another,' explained The Shadow.

The Baron shook his head. Some of the men stared open mouthed at what he was doing – he was daring to say that The Shadow was wrong!

'How my lord?' asked the Baron, 'how will we find one child in thousands? It is an impossible task.'

'You doubt my plan,' stated The Shadow, seeing the hesitation in the Baron's eyes.

Suddenly, the table went silent again, as the men sensed trouble begin to brood between the pair.

'No... no my lord, I–I swear,' stammered the Baron, his short–lived surge of assurance failing.

'If my plan is to work I need everyone to have faith,' The Shadow said coldly, 'especially you.'

'M–me my lord?' asked the Baron surprisedly.

'Yes, you Baron,' replied The Shadow, 'I firmly believe your Skrunai will be invaluable in delivering my plan.'

'Of c–course, my lord, they will do whatever you ask!'

'They had better, Baron, otherwise...' The Shadow then pointed at the empty seat formerly occupied by Vervanis, 'you will suffer a far less pleasant fate.'

*

The woman cried out but it was in delight rather than the exasperation her brother had expected.

'Carmena! Are you alright?' the man rushed to his sister's aid.

'He smiled,' she whispered, tracing her fingers over the lips of her newborn.

He giggled, grabbing his mother's thumb with two hands and offered another smile, tempting her to make that wonderful sound again.

She smiled in return this time, she was tired and – she feared – nearing her end.

'Jonathon,' Carmena murmured.

'Yes?' he replied hesitantly, fiddling uncomfortably with his hands.

With a sad sigh, she gently moved her own hand free of her child's grip and proffered him in her weak arms to her brother.

'No,' the man said, taking an involuntary step back, 'I can't.'

'You must, please!' she pleaded, tears curling down her cheeks.

'I can't,' he repeated, but his protests had already begun to die down to the whispers of his sister. He would take the child, it had not been said but she'd accepted it from the look in his eyes. I will, they promised.

She smiled again for the last time, planted a kiss on the boy's head and closed her eyes.

'Not my name,' she whispered, the darkness circling around her, 'not my name... your choice Jonathon... yours.'

Within seconds, her head had turned to the side and she was gone, another victim of eternal sleep. A ghost of a smile displayed on her tired features.

His hands shaking, he reached under the bed and pulled out a small casket. The box was a dull gold colour, with mystical inscriptions shaped like vines darkening the case. That case... It had appeared by her bedside table a few weeks ago when the child had been born. No note, nothing. It had just... appeared, seemingly from nowhere.

She would want him to have it.

He brought the child up in his arms and looked into its innocent eyes, as it sucked on its own thumb, looking enquiringly back into his eyes.

'My name is Jonathon,' he whispered, the baby giggled again.

'What shall I call you?' he said, his voice cracking and tears beginning to sprout in his eyes.

The baby laughed again. However, his jubilation was to be short lived. There was a bang on the door.

'Who's there?' he said.

Another bang.

'Who is it?' he shouted, backing away from the door.

The third bang narrowly preceded a flash of light that illuminated the door before it was blown off its hinges.

A man burst through the smoke, his robes billowing in the air behind him. His staff, which was smoking at the end, was pointed straight at Jonathon.

The man's smoke stung eyes darted quickly around the room, remaining briefly on his sister's body, before snapping back to Jonathon. The Warlock stared at the child, held close to Jonathon's chest.

'That is the potential? Interesting...' the Warlock murmured, pushing away a strand of red hair that ran over his left eye.

'Stay away!' Jonathon said.

The man laughed, 'empty words scant, empty words. What hope could you have of stopping me?'

'This is not your child to take,' Jonathon said.

26

'Nor is it yours to keep, scant' the man sneered, raising his staff.

'ENOUGH! Let me through you fools.'

Another man, wearing a similar robe to the red-haired Warlock burst through the opening where the door had once been. He looked to be of a similar age as the other, in his mid-twenties but had a more authoritative presence and shorter, darker hair.

'Farholm,' the red–haired Warlock muttered, his lip curling.

'You had no right, Vey! The Masters shall hear of this!'

'As you wish,' Vey shrugged, stowing away his staff onto his back and then striding arrogantly out of the room.

The Warlock, Farholm, shook his head disapprovingly, turned solemnly to Jonathon and held out his hand. Jonathon looked at it once and took a step back, narrowing his eyes.

Farholm smiled solemnly and folded his arms behind his back.

'I'm terribly sorry for this intrusion of your privacy Mr…'

'Grey.'

'Mr Grey,' the Warlock said, his eyes then scanned the rest of the room, his expression saddened when they fell on the woman on the bed.

'Newly born?' he asked, nodding at the baby.

'Just over half a moon,' Jonathon replied, hugging the child more tightly.

The man sighed and bowed his head. He walked up to the woman's bed and leant over to examine her hand briefly.

27

'Is there anything you can do?' Jonathon asked, his voice cracking.

'I'm afraid not,' the man sighed, gently laying her hand back on her stomach, 'death has taken her from this world, my friend.'

The doctor slid to the floor, the baby, blissfully unaware of the on goings of the world around it, giggled.

'The child is a Majik potential?' Jonathon asked.

'I'm afraid so,' Farholm replied.

'How did you find him?'

'By luck my friend, by luck' said Farholm, 'we happened to be in the area and my colleague picked up on the rather unique scent. Unfortunately, his manners and etiquette are rather… lacking.'

'What do you want of the child?'

'It's not so much 'I want', as 'need,' if truth be told.'

'Why? Why can't he live a normal life?'

'I'm sorry Doctor, but if the boy is not given the necessary training, he will be unable to control his Majik. At that point, he'll be a danger to himself and others.'

Jonathon's brow creased, as he frowned at the Warlock.

The Warlock smiled and adjusted his robes so he could crouch on the ground beside the doctor.

'Hello,' he said to the child.

The baby instantly turned its head towards Farholm, looking curiously into the man's eyes. Jonathon gasped, surprised by their intensity, but the Warlock did not avert his gaze.

'This one is special,' Farholm whispered.

Jonathon nodded silently. For some odd reason, he couldn't question the man's conclusion, which appeared to ooze with sincerity.

'So, he must go with you?'

'All this talk of 'he.' What is the child's name, Jonathon?'

The doctor thought for a moment, not inquiring as to how the Warlock knew his name. 'He doesn't have one yet.'

'She asked you to give him your surname. Now a first name is all you need, correct?'

'Yes,' Jonathon replied, again not wondering as to how the man was, apparently, reading his mind.

Farholm smiled, and then glanced at the shelf by the bed. There were several unusually unattractive potted plants spaced unevenly. Each a different dull shade of green but all covered with long, fine... 'Thorns?' the Warlock enquired. 'Why thorns?'

'She liked them,' Jonathon blurted out, 'Carmena thought they gave the plants character.'

The man smiled sadly, patting Jonathon's arm reassuringly.

'You have your name now, I think.'

'Yes,' Jonathon sniffed.

The Warlock turned to the child, smiled and whispered, 'Your name is Thorne Grey.'

29

Chapter 2

Thud!

Thorne's eyes flashed open and he was almost blinded by the light that slipped through the parting of the curtains. He groaned as he pulled himself into a sitting position and rubbed his sore eyes furiously.

Thud!

'Alright, I'm up!' he shouted hoarsely at the door, realizing a second later that the sound had come from above, in the Majik rooms, where the raw and uncontrollable power possessed by trainee Warlocks was chained and then developed. It had only been a year ago when he'd first stumbled into one of the rooms at the age of eleven, eager and ready. Feeling dwarfed, not by the stature of some Warlocks but the powerful aura that trailed some, like cloaks. He still breathed a sigh of relief when he remembered his induction into the Order of Magi or Warlocks (as they were more commonly known) and the Sorcerers Spire (their home).

Thorne had little memory of his arrival in the order, he could only see cloudy glimpses into his past, then he remembered those years he spent with a quill and book, taking notes in the lower levels of the Spire with fellow potentials like himself.

He kicked away his covers and slipped out of the bed, flexing his toes in the soft carpet and gazed around his chambers with a sense of pride. His chamber was painted in a rich red. He possessed only a few pieces of furniture – drawers and a desk – where many of his prized relics and personal possessions were placed fondly.

One had no need for a wardrobe as a Novice, all Thorne had ever worn for years were robes, leather boots and trousers; although he wore a pair of black pantaloons, which the others didn't seem to mind.

He grabbed his set of dark blue robes with tight sleeves, which were separated at the front from the waist down. On the shoulders of the robe was the insignia of the Warlocks - a set of golden sparks, which he wore proudly. With a grin, he threw his clothes on and turned to the ornate mirror that hung precariously beside the door. He gazed at his dishevelled features; it must have been a particularly fractious dream to leave him in this state.

He had messy, long ginger hair. He had a misshapen nose from a fight in which it had been broken four years ago.

The feature that stood out most however, were his eyes, which were a dark grey and had a certain intensity that gave people the impression he had seen sights which would have caused an ordinary mind to crack and crumble. But surrounding his grey irises were a thin line of amber which flickered like a ring of flames. It was… unnatural… to say the least. None of the other Warlocks and Novices had the same condition, but despite the oddity of it, he revelled in the fact it made him unique.

He sighed, paced towards his window and pulled back the curtains releasing a flood of light into the room. But it was not what made him jump.

Standing… no… hovering in front of the window was a figure draped in a hooded, tattered black overcoat and holding a scythe. The scythe's handle was made of what looked horribly like a human spine and the blade gleamed in the sun.

To Thorne's shock, the skin of the figure's hands was gone, revealing the ivory tinge of bone. Thorne gulped, trying to urge his feet to move him away but it was as though he was stuck to the floor. However, it did not try to break the glass, which stood between the pair but instead inclined its head and descended.

His heart beating like a drum, Thorne ran to the window and pressed his nose against the glass, to see where the figure went. To his relief, the figure had disappeared completely, yet he still held his gaze open–mouthed.

He was on one of the lowest levels in the Spire, but it was at least a hundred feet from solid ground. Was he dreaming? Or had he actually seen the strange figure hovering in the air?

He shook himself vigorously and closed the curtains, as if in an attempt to shut out the memory itself.

Thorne half jogged, half sprinted to the other side of the chamber, thrust open the door and fled into the hallway.

The floor was covered with a beautifully weaved, violet rug embroidered with golden sparks on the edges. The walls were completely white, contrasting to the colour of the rug, and held brass torches with crackling flames. Along the seemingly never–ending corridor were a number of other doors, which led into the chambers of the Chief Warlocks.

Being only a Novice, Thorne had always wondered why he'd been the only one to be housed on the same floor as the Chief Warlocks. Perhaps they'd simply run out of rooms?

He briefly considered knocking on one of the doors of his superiors to ask about what he'd seen. Was it just a prank by one of the other novices? Surely, they would think him mad, that is, if they had bothered to open their door in the first place to a mere novice.

The bone had looked so real though....

With the encounter not quite diminishing in Thorne's mind, he hesitantly strode through the corridor his head turning at every door as though expecting to see the figure's head appear through solid wood.

As Thorne strode towards the arch, separating corridors, he was so lost in his thoughts, he failed to notice the large mass lurking in the shadows. He did, however, notice the smell, when it was too late to avoid walking into a troll. While many are inclined to run from such fierce looking creatures, presuming them to be a violent and ill-tempered species, Trolls were friendly and loyal. Just not particularly bright.

Looking up as he picked himself up from the floor, Thorne realized with some amusement that the troll was completely oblivious to the fact that he'd just bumped into it. The one who stood before Thorne was also perhaps the smallest one he'd ever seen, but it was still at least a few feet taller than him, and had to crouch to avoid banging its head on the top of the arch.

The troll had thick, scaly, grey skin, disproportionately short, muscular arms and legs that were the size of small boars. Its face was bloated and its long upper teeth jutted out at awkward angles around it dark lips. Its outlandish appearance was enhanced by the thick tuft of white hair that burst out the middle of its head. Completing the oddity, were two large bulging, green eyes.

Perched on its tuft was a violet cap. Embroidered on its hem was an image of a rope, with golden sparks surrounding it.

'Oh, 'ello,' croaked the troll, finally noticing him, 'why'd you fall over?'

'Good morning,' replied Thorne, his previous thoughts wiped away instantaneously by the comical appearance of the troll.

The troll grinned stupidly and showed Thorne a rope it was holding that hung in the air next to a large basket, big enough to fit a group of people inside. The troll's job was as a lifter, using its immense strength to lower or pull the rope to send anyone up or down the Spire. It was a frightening way to travel and Thorne preferred using the portals around the Spire. However, he still found it difficult to remember where each would take him, often ending up horribly lost.

'Where to Guv?' asked the troll.

'Just down one, thank you,' yawned Thorne, stepping cautiously into the basket and gripping a handle firmly.

The troll grunted and leaned over the gaping chasm between the archway and the basket and yelled: 'Oi! Down one!'

The basket shook briefly and then descended slowly in jerks.

After a few seconds of holding on to the basket for dear life, it suddenly stopped at another archway where another troll stood lowering a rope.

'Ho, sir,' said the troll, his hand in a clumsy salute.

Thorne nodded in reply, his hands trembling as he clambered out the lift. He had just set off at a trot, when he heard someone yelling in an adjoining corridor.

A boy, only in his late teens, rushed out of a training hall ahead of Thorne, with a trail of smoke billowing from the tail of his robes, yelling at the top of his voice: 'I'm burning!'

A Warlock trainer jogged behind him, calling vainly, 'really now, there's no need to panic.'

'Morning,' he grunted quickly as he raced past.

'Sir,' replied Thorne.

The man then stopped suddenly as though stung by a bee and whirled round to face him with a look of amusement.

'Ah, the 'late' Mr Grey. Aren't you due in class?' asked the man.

'Sir?' Thorne gulped. He had class?

'Not to worry Thorne,' the man chuckled, hurtling after the plume of smoke, 'as I recall you have a meeting with the Masters, do you not? A messenger was sent for you a while ago.'

Thorne frowned, 'I didn't get a message sir. Are you sure it was for me?'

'Definitely, I asked the man myself a quarter of an hour ago,' he bellowed behind him before disappearing past a corner.

With a gasp, Thorne jumped back in the lift and yelled at the troll with a measure of urgency in his voice: 'level 16, on the double!'

As the basket raced to the top of the Spire, a mocking voice whispered gleefully in his head: 'You're late! You're late!'

Finally, the basket shuddered to a halt. The troll stationed at this level, however, wore metal shoulder guards and had a large spiked club held in a harness on his back.

'Morning,' said the troll, in a tone that suggested boredom, but Thorne was feeling too sick to notice. The rapid lift ride had caused his face to turn a sickly shade of green and he had to lean over the basket in fear of a sudden violent bout of vomiting.

With the feeling of nausea subsiding, Thorne pushed himself off the basket and stepped gingerly through the archway into a splendid entrance room. The tiled black and white floor was polished to a perfect sheen to the point where you could almost see a reflection of yourself. On the blood red walls hung portraits of the past Majik Masters, the paintings capturing their magnificence perfectly.

At the end of the room were two large oak doors, so huge, they dwarfed the heavily armoured, monstrous sentinels that were standing immobile in front of them. Their bronze armour shimmered in the light, given off by the torches held in the walls. As Thorne neared, he could see arcs of blue light ripple across the sections of armour. Sentinel Spire guards were beings of pure Majik. They were not to be tricked, not crossed, and, as far as Thorne was concerned, not to be approached. Ever.

Nobody knew what these figures looked like underneath their mass of armour. The suits might even be empty. In living memory, they had never removed their helmets – in fact, as far as Thorne knew, they had never been known to move from their posts. The nearer he got to them, the slower Thorne moved.

He came to a halt, two metres in front of them and coughed quietly, 'erm, I've been told to come to the Hall of Majik. Could you let me in.... please?'

Without looking at Thorne, the guards swivelled on the spot, in a fluid movement, rotated their lances, plugging them into the similarly shaped holes in the doors. The heavy, riveted wooden doors swung open slowly.

His jaw dropped after he stumbled inside.

Inside, the floor was similar to that in the entrance but was engraved with the names of the current masters in bold, curling writing. The walls were made of marble, like the gargantuan statues that acted as pillars in the centre of the hall, supporting the beautifully painted, sloping ceiling. The frescos adorning the ceiling depicted the greatest heroes of the Order of Magi, golden halos circling their heads. The statues eyes and staffs contained glittering and glowing jewels, which sparkled in the embrace of sunlight from the opposing windows.

Finally, at the end of the hall was a large glass table, positioned perpendicularly to show its extraordinary width. Behind it, and much to Thorne's dismay, sat the rather decidedly disgruntled Majik Masters. In front of the table was a solitary wooden chair. He wondered how their intense gazes hadn't burnt numerous holes in its frame already.

Were Thorne not quite so focussed on his impending doom, he would have taken in their appearance. They cut an impressive sight, with their flowing, togas embroidered with golden sparks and a variety of other strange and yet interesting symbols. In their hands, they held wondrously crafted, white ceremonial staffs.

When Thorne reached the table, he bowed his head and almost whispered: 'Masters.'

'Thorne,' said Master Vey, 'you are *very* late.'

Thorne's eyes twitched and he replied apologetically, 'forgive me Master, but I was only just informed of your summoning as I arrived at class.'

'Of course, running a little late there too then?' Vey replied, in a tone that Thorne was sure was both accusatory and unsympathetic.

Thorne then gulped and unconsciously folded his arms behind his back, his sweating hands gripped firmly together. His eyes, wishing to look at anything but back at Vey, switched to statue behind him. Thorne glanced along the row of Masters, pausing at an empty seat.

Meydar, a very elderly master followed his gaze and he explained, 'Unfortunately, Master Farholm had treaties to discuss with the guilds in Féy, you understand, yes?'

Thorne nodded solemnly; he had been looking forward to seeing Master Farholm particularly.

'But let us not stray from the current matter at hand,' interceded Master Saymir, a man who had a distinctive hooked nose, 'please, sit.'

Thorne mumbled his thanks and sat.

Meydar then turned to his colleague, Master Dezan, indicating that the floor was his.

'Thorne, with great discussion, it has been decided between us and your mentors that it is time for you to leave the Spire,' Dezan said.

'What? M–masters, I swear I won't be late ag–'

'Not permanently,' Master Dezan chuckled.

'Only temporarily,' Master Vey added, with a hint of regret in his voice.

'It is time to put your skills to the first of many tests,' said Master Saymir.

'Tests? Masters?' Thorne, whispered, his fingers loosening on the arms of his chair.

'We wish you to go to the City of Light, Thorne.'

'Wh-what?' Thorne's mouth fell open; the City of Light was weeks away, and why of all places was he to go there?

'Of course, you will not be going alone, your role in this should be purely observatory,' added Meydar reassuringly.

'Masters?'

'You will be accompanied.'

Meydar then clapped his hands twice and the doors behind Thorne opened once again to reveal another Warlock. A man who stood six–foot–tall, was bald, had a trimmed beard, and prominently upturned eyebrows.

'Grey?' the man remarked in surprise. He then strode next to Thorne and after bowing inquired, 'you chose him?'

'Yes,' Vey grinned, 'why so displeased, Rozenhall?'

The Warlock's face contorted slightly and he glanced at Thorne anxiously before replying, 'I'm not Master, it's just that… he's too young.'

'A little fresh air won't do him any harm.'

'Masters, I–'

'Rozenhall!' Vey growled.

Rozenhall closed his lips before he could utter another word, and with an expression of utter reluctance, he turned back towards the door, beckoning Thorne to follow.

'Wait!' the pair twirled around to see Vey standing in his seat, his lip curling.

'Master?' said Rozenhall.

'Forgetting something Rozenhall?' Vey asked.

'I don't believe so, Master,' Rozenhall's eyes narrowed.

Vey grinned and turned towards his colleagues with open arms, 'my friends, surely such a test would require certain... precautions.'

'Precautions?' Dezan frowned, 'what do you mean Vey?'

'He means a Binding, Dezan,' Meydar said, 'why would that be necessary Vey?'

'This is a test is it not? Should there not be an element of realism to it?' Vey replied, his lip curling even further.

'He is... right,' said Saymir begrudgingly, 'after all, the event where such a precaution would be needed is highly unlikely.'

Thorne frowned too. What was a binding?

'Masters?' Thorne began.

'Silence!' Vey hissed.

'Vey!' Saymir growled.

'Apologies,' Vey muttered, correcting himself.

All eyes fell on Meydar, who sat with his head bent, his hooded eyes hidden by shadow. He tapped his fingers methodically on the table, contemplating.

He sighed and then lifted his head, his eyes flickering to Rozenhall and then finally resting on Thorne.

'Very well, if Rozenhall and Thorne consent to it, a Binding may be undertaken,' Meydar said.

Vey grinned and sat down, folding his arms together triumphantly, 'well, gentleman?'

'Do we actually have any choice in the matter?' Rozenhall growled.

'As always,' Saymir replied.

'But you would do well to watch your tone, *Chief* Warlock' Vey added, placing particular emphasis on the man's rank.

Rozenhall turned back to Thorne, 'have you been taught about Binding's in your lessons yet, Grey?'

'No, sir,' Thorne replied.

'If he bothered to turn up on time for them,' Vey muttered under his breath.

Rozenhall glanced back at the Masters, Meydar nodded for him to continue.

The Chief Warlock gulped, 'we must be bound together by Majik. A Binding serves purely as a bond between an apprentice and a higher Warlock. Basically, we would be able to find each other if we happened to be separated. However, there are… other implications as well.'

Thorne licked his lips nervously, inquiring hesitantly, 'such as, sir?'

'Nothing that should concern you, Thorne,' Vey said tersely.

'Master,' Thorne hung his head.

41

'Take my hand, Thorne,' Rozenhall said. Thorne placed his hand in Rozenhall's and lifted his head. The Warlock avoided his gaze.

The Chief Warlock closed his eyes and began to mutter words incoherently under his breath. Within seconds, a blue light began to pulse from his veins, spreading from his hands to Thorne's causing their skin to glow brightly. Thorne felt a sudden warmth flood around his body, from his chest to his head and toes, and then it vanished, the light dissipating along with it.

'We are bound,' Rozenhall muttered, quickly releasing Thorne's hand.

Thorne stretched his fingers and looked down upon his hand, his skin was normal, no scars or change of colour, but that was not what bothered him…

'And now we have already wasted enough time in talk. You must leave now. Horses will be awaiting you in the stables.' Dezan stood up, 'may Ozin be with you, my friends.'

Once the pair had left the Hall, Dezan shifted uncomfortably in his seat.

'I don't like this…,' Dezan muttered.

'We have no choice,' Vey returned curtly.

'We should have warned Rozenhall at least!' Dezan pleaded.

'Rozenhall?' Vey scoffed, 'he will be no great loss.'

'Vey!' Meydar reproached the Master, 'this is not a matter to be taken lightly'.

'This is a day for shame,' Saymir murmured through his hand, 'to send one trained into the dark is one thing but a mere boy...'

'We have no choice, we gave our word,' said Meydar.

'Precisely!' Vey slammed his staff in agreement, 'Masters, what is the life of a child against the lives of thousands?'

*

Thorne paced around his chamber furiously. He was only twelve and was being sent on errands around the whole of Horizon, while most other Warlocks, let alone novices, sat safely in their chambers, reading books and cutting their toenails. Still... he supposed it would be nice to get out of the Spire for once, even if it meant weeks of travel.

His eyes caught sight of the casket in front of him which lay untouched and dusty.

He began to place his hands above it but pulled away hurriedly. No, he daren't open it. The casket itself had been an old family heirloom, nothing too significant he had been told by Master Farholm. No, it was what lay inside that, perhaps, posed a great danger. He couldn't quite place a finger on it, but the item inside... unsettled him.

But then, said an unbidden voice in his head, the journey could be dangerous. Why not take it? It could be useful.

He gulped, hesitantly placing his hands on the lid, wondering whether he had the courage to open it. It was too late to stop now he decided, pushing the lid open and hearing a dull thud

43

as it banged against the wall. He gulped, feeling a small sense of dread at the thought of seeing the object again. He leaned over cautiously, examining the contents, as though afraid they might suddenly explode. Inside, surrounded by a jumble of trinkets, lay a metal rod, its features not disturbed after months of rest. The rod was engraved with strange but beautiful runes, so intricate that Thorne held the opinion that they couldn't have possibly been carved out by a human smith. The workmanship was too... perfect. And yet its shape was unusual; curving to a sharp point, like a horn or a fang.

The moment Thorne had laid his hands upon the rod, it emitted a single bright green pulse, illuminating the runes, and began to vibrate violently.

In that instant, a splitting pain erupted in Thorne's head, bringing him to his knees.

Strange images flashed through his mind, too jumbled to make sense. But one word managed to burn through in a deafening roar...

THIEF

The pain faded suddenly, leaving Thorne panting and gasping for air. Though it was not what had disturbed him greatly. He could have sworn that he'd heard that voice before.

'Who's there?' he demanded.

He looked frantically around the room but found no–one. His only answer being the awkward silence that had befallen the room.

He groaned and pulled himself to his feet, and as he did so he noticed that the rod was no longer shaking and had returned to its normal colour.

Carefully, he stooped over to pick it up but stopped, his hand hovering in mid-air.

Thump!

This time he was sure, the noise had definitely come from his window. Thorne snatched his staff from his desk where it lay, holding it out in front of him like a spear, and tip–toed slowly to the windows.

Thump!

The cloaked figure! Who else could it be? Well, he would find out. With a mounting sense of dread, he grabbed a curtain and ripped it open.

Outside the window, glaring down at him with a shadowed face, cracked bones curling round a bloody blade was… no one.

Outside only the calm breeze disturbed the ominous silence.

Thorne pulled his face away from the window. The noise *had* come from there. But even as he took a step backwards, the certainty faded, Thorne breathed a sigh of relief, spun on his heels and froze, feeling the blood drain from his face. Sat in his armchair, scythe lying on the lap, was the hooded figure.

Chapter 3

'GOOD AFTERNOON' the figure boomed, his voice immense and echoing around the room, which felt so suddenly small. Each word carried so much weight that Thorne felt he could be crushed by it.

Now that he was closer to the figure he could see for certain that the scythe's handle was indeed shaped like a spine of sorts. The blade, much to his horror, was composed of faces, each clearly in distress, their faces squeezing and writhing against each other and the edge of blade.

The figure, noticing Thorne's expression, casually tapped the blade and the faces vanished.

'HEH HEH, SORRY ABOUT THAT,' said the figure, placing the scythe behind his back, 'THEY WERE... AHEM... RECENT ADDITIONS.'

Thorne stared open–mouthed, frozen in his half–turned position.

'YES,' mused the figure, looking up and down at Thorne, 'I GET THAT A LOT. THEN AGAIN, RUNNING OR SCREAMING ARE BOTH PRETTY POPULAR TOO.' It scratched, or given the sound it created, scraped a bony finger across its chin, 'OR A COMBINATION OF THE TWO.'

'Maybe it's the stress of the day,' Thorne mumbled, not taking his wide eyes off the figure's hood. Thorne could feel his palms sweating heavily, 'but I'm not used to hallucinations.'

'OH, I'M QUITE REAL... IN A SENSE,' said the figure, suddenly standing up, 'ERM, YOU MAY FIND THIS... SLIGHTLY DISTURBING.' It threw back its hood to reveal a skull with flames burning in its eye sockets, a long, thin, black tongue that danced around its rotten teeth. Thorne backed slowly against the window. For the first time in his life, he was truly afraid.

The figure fiddled with the hem of his sleeve, casually flicking a flake of ash off with a bony finger. 'YES. NOT UNCOMMON. RELATIVELY CALM EVEN.' He glanced at Thorne, 'HOWEVER, I'M NOT COLLECTING TODAY.'

'No?' Thorne spluttered.

'NO, NO,' muttered the figure, 'BUT I DO HAVE OTHER PURPOSES.'

It snapped its fingers together and the room went ablaze with fire.

Thorne watched in horror as he saw his chambers burn. He then saw images of Warlocks running through the corridors fighting off bizarre monsters. The scene changed. There were corpses – the Majik Masters! Their skin pale, faces bloody.

Finally, he was back in his chambers facing his mirror, the sight offended him so much he almost screamed. He saw himself but a twisted version. His hands and face were covered with blood, his clothes torn and his face... his face was dark and scarred and he wore a vicious, sardonic smile. 'BURN! BURN IT ALL!' the twisted version of him screamed in delight, as flames began to crawl up his body.

'Stop it,' begged Thorne, 'please!'

The figure snapped its fingers again and the chamber turned back to normal, the fires extinguished along with the cruel replica of Thorne. The figure then pulled its hood back up and sat down, observing Thorne with what, he thought, was mild interest.

'What was that?' demanded Thorne, placing his hands on a chest of drawers to steady himself.

'THE FUTURE,' replied the figure in a matter of fact tone, crossing a leg over his other, 'OR PERHAPS ONE OF MANY POSSIBLE OUTCOMES, A GIFT FROM MY FRIEND ZAKAR–'

'That was foul sorcery,' retorted Thorne, leaping to the door, 'and I... I-!'

At a complete loss for words, Thorne pulled opened the door, rushed outside and slammed it shut, only to come face to face with the figure again.

'YOU FORGOT THIS,' the figure said, handing him the rod.

Thorne grimaced but took it. 'Who are you?' he asked, 'and what do you want with me?'

The figure chuckled, 'YOU MIGHT NOT FIND THE 'WHO' PART *ENTIRELY* HELPFUL...'

'Why would I be scared of a name?' replied Thorne.

The figure sighed, 'I AM CALLED BY MANY NAMES, SEVERAL OF WHICH ARE REALLY QUITE RUDE. BUT IF YOU MUST, YOU WOULD KNOW ME AS... DEATH.'

A slow chill crept up Thorne's spine and he started to back away to the door.

'LOOK, I'M JUST HERE TO GIVE YOU A WARNING,' said Death, holding his hands up defensively.

'I'll bet!' stuttered Thorne, raising the rod.

Death sighed, 'SO YOU'RE THE HYSTERICAL TYPE THEN? VERY WELL…'

Death then paced back towards the opposite wall, 'THIS FAR AWAY ENOUGH FOR YOU?'

'Just say what you have to say then!'

'AS YOU WISH,' said Death, taking a mock bow, 'I HAVE COME TO TELL YOU OF BETRAYAL AT THE HIGHEST LEVEL OF YOUR ORDER.'

Thorne froze, the words hitting him like a giant brick, 'how can that be possible?'

Death rubbed his jawbone as if to show he was thinking: 'I CAN SAY NO MORE. I AM BOUND BY RULES THAT CANNOT BE BROKEN, BUT YOU MUST UNDERSTAND – YOU AND YOU ALONE,' Death stressed, 'HAVE THE POWER TO RESOLVE THIS.'

'How can THAT be possible?' Thorne repeated confusedly.

'ALAS, THAT QUESTION, OF WHICH YOU SEEM SO FOND, CANNOT BE ANSWERED,' Death paused, mulling the words over. 'HOWEVER, IF YOU DO NOT HEED MY WARNING YOUR ORDER WILL CRUMBLE AND THOUSANDS OF INNOCENTS WILL PERISH.'

'But you're Death. Don't you enjoy your job?' Thorne stuttered.

Death hissed, the reply sounding like metal being forged in a furnace.

'IT'S A BIT OF A DEADEND, ACTUALLY,' Death chuckled, 'SORRY, SELF REFERENTIAL. MICTLANTECADES WORKS ME TO THE BONE...'

Death paused as if to grin at the irony of the statement.

'So, the Death God is real,' said Thorne.

A sudden silence filled the hallway, which was broken abruptly by the sound of Death slapping a fresh dent onto his bare skull.

'DAMMIT,' he said, and then dropping his voice to almost a whisper, 'YOU MUSTN'T BREATHE A WORD OF THIS TO ANYONE, UNDERSTAND? OTHERWISE...'

Death then twisted his head to glance briefly at his scythe and then snapped it back to face Thorne, 'I REALLY WILL HAVE TO ... COLLECT YOU.'

Thorne felt the blood drain from his face, 'you... you can't do that! I-I thought I wasn't supposed to be taken yet!'

Death then rummaged within his pockets and withdrew a large roll of parchment, it was yellowed with age and gave off a faint, dark glow. He started to scan down the apparently long list.

'ACTUALLY...' began Death, smartly tapping the parchment, 'YOU ARE DUE TO HAVE AN UNFORTUNATE LIFT-RELATED ACCIDENT AT ONE O'CLOCK THIS AFTERNOON.'

'What!' exclaimed Thorne, fumbling in the pockets of his robes briefly before pulling out a pocket watch, 'but that's in a few minutes!'

'EXACTLY,' said Death, 'SO BE GLAD I'M WILLING TO OVERLOOK THAT MINOR INCONVENIENCE.'

'Minor?' said Thorne, his mouth agape in shock.

'EVERYTHING'S RELATIVE,' Death shrugged, and turned to leave.

'Hang on a minute!' shouted Thorne, 'why should I trust you? How do I know if this is even real?'

Death stopped and turned to face him, 'YOU HAVE THREE POSSIBLE ALTERNATIVES AVAILABLE TO YOU,' explained Death, raising three fingers to illustrate the fact, 'ONE: YOU ARE STILL DREAMING.'

'TWO: I AM REAL. AND YOUR LIFE IS ABOUT TO GET VERY COMPLICATED.'

'OR THREE: YOU'RE QUITE INSANE.'

'One,' said Thorne hopefully.

Death shook his head, shrugged again and then pointed a boned finger down the corridor, 'MESSENGER.'

Thorne whirled round, but there was no one there and, when he turned back, he saw that Death had disappeared as well. 'A dream,' muttered Thorne, without conviction.

Before Thorne could even begin to gather his thoughts, he was interrupted by hurried footsteps of a new individual, who Thorne realised to be – to his dismay – one of the Spire's messengers.

The messenger wore a red tailcoat, pinstripe trousers and a lime hat, and appeared to be balking under the pressure of the two bulging bags that bumped against his thighs.

'Ah, Novice Grey,' said the man brightly upon noticing him, 'the stable master says that he has your horse ready for departure, and… is something wrong?'

Thorne shook himself and put on a weak smile, replying, 'no, no everything's… fine. I'll be there very soon.'

The messenger nodded and made to leave but then Thorne grabbed him. 'By the way, you wouldn't happen to know who was supposed to bring me the message from the Masters would you?' he inquired.

The man blushed a deep crimson, mumbled something about having letters to deliver, and sprinted off into the corridor.

*

Thorne attached his satchel and staff to the saddle of his horse and then clambered clumsily onto it.

The supposed visit from Death still haunted him. His effort to convince himself the whole thing was a hoax, some kind of ridiculous prank, failed to calm his mind.

Thorne was awoken from his troubled thoughts by Rozenhall, patting him sharply on the back, 'all set?' inquired the Warlock.

'Yes sir,' Thorne replied.

As soon as Rozenhall mounted his steed and set off from the stable, Thorne's mount began to march behind. He gripped the reins tightly. As eager as he was to discover what life outside the Dalmarra had to offer, his heart longed already to be home. He spent much of the first few hours of travel with an eye behind his mount, focusing on capturing in memory every stall, tavern and street sign he could spot. Smells that were commonplace, such as those of the spices sold by the merchants or the ale spilled into the street crevices from the night before, filled him with a new vigour.

He placed a closed fist to his forehead, and made a silent prayer to Ozin, in the hope that it would not be the last time he would gaze upon his home.

Chapter 4

Thorne pulled his horse to a stop and grimaced at the sight before him.

The Silent Forests spread for miles in length and breadth. The trees stood tall and menacing, armed with thick needles. A thick wall of emerald blades.

While generally safe to the wary traveller, it was known that many creatures inhabited the forest, none of them particularly friendly. Yet he couldn't hear a sound from where he was sat. It was unnerving.

Suddenly, the trees began to shake and a powerful blast of wind blew from within, like a cork from a bottle. The forest seemed to scream, as the blast cut through the air like a knife.

The horses neighed wildly. Rearing suddenly, catapulting the Warlocks off their backs before galloping away to Dalmarra.

'Wretched animals!' Rozenhall barked at their rapidly retreating rears, brushing dirt off his robes.

Thorne picked up his satchel, took out his rod and sighed, wishing the horse had dropped his staff as well.

He turned reluctantly to the forest before him as the cold breeze whipped around his robes.

Thorne twisted his head around to examine the landscape behind him, Dalmarra now appearing as a hazy shape on the horizon. They were nowhere near their destination, and yet home seemed as distant as it ever would, like the fleeting memory of a dream.

'Must we go on sir?' Thorne inquired, desperately hoping the answer would be 'no.'

Rozenhall put his hands on his hips and lowered his head. It seemed that even the Chief Warlock was conflicted on the issue at hand. He glanced briefly at the forest looming ominously behind his back, the wrinkles by his mouth hardening as he scowled.

'We camp tonight!' he said, 'we'll head through the forest in the morning.'

*

Thorne threw the last twig into the smouldering pile of wood, the flames hissing gratefully in response as they devoured the new entrant.

He sat down, the Chief Warlock, Rozenhall, following him soon after.

Thorne hugged his knees to his chest, his eyes observing the dancing flames.

'Boy.'

He looked past the flames. Rozenhall sat cross-legged, his hands lying on his lap, his staff on the floor beside him.

It may have been perhaps a mirage of the flames, but he was certain he'd seen a flicker of sympathy from the Warlock, before he'd managed to bury it deep within him. Out of sight.

'I believe you are owed an explanation in terms of the purpose of this trip,' he said.

55

'I– there's no need, sir,' Thorne lied.

'Perhaps the Masters feel that way, Grey but I do not,' Rozenhall replied curtly.

Thorne gulped, averting his gaze.

Rozenhall sighed, got up and then sat next to Thorne. 'You are aware of the Shadow War, yes?' he whispered.

'Yes, sir,' Thorne replied. What did that have to do with anything?

'Then I assume you are aware of the Portals?'

'Portals?' Thorne frowned.

'Yes, the Dark Portals, it was believed that the Necromancer Lord had used them to move his armies with speed around Horizon,' Rozenhall explained.

'They were all destroyed,' Thorne recalled, 'Warlocks were used to search for the dark energy coming from them, weren't they?'

'Yes, we provided a great service to this land, although our role in the war is often minimized... However, one still remains untouched in the City of Light.'

Thorne gazed at the Chief Warlock, mouth agape, 'It wasn't destroyed?'

'No. It stopped releasing energy near the end of the war and became dormant, and so it was... left,' explained Rozenhall.

'Left?' exclaimed Thorne, 'but they were transporting the army from the Foglands all around Horizon!'

'Keep your voice down!' Rozenhall hissed, glancing anxiously behind him, 'the forest never sleeps Thorne.'

Thorne pursed his lips, refusing to look back, trying to drown out the fear-induced thoughts that were circulating in his mind.

Rozenhall leant in closer. Thorne could now make out the tiny wrinkles by the corner of his eyes and the perspiration shining across his forehead.

'Being dormant, the Portal posed no threat to the city,' Rozenhall explained, 'however, unfortunately it has become active once again.'

Silence wove into the camp after the Warlock's words, Thorne sitting back in disbelief.

What if demons still roamed the Foglands in their vast hordes? The City of Light could be ripped apart in merely a few hours by the creatures of the Foglands.

'You must understand Thorne, what I am telling you is incredibly secret. Only on a need-to-know basis,' said Rozenhall, 'but we can't take any risks. The darkness must be purged.'

'But how, sir?'

'The forests are... far different to how they were several years ago' Rozenhall remarked with a sigh, paying no heed to Thorne's question, 'far different.'

'Sir?' Thorne said.

'You can feel it, can't you? The darkness that has spread inside, swarming whatever remnants of light remain,' whispered Rozenhall. 'Listen. Close your eyes and reach out with your Majik.'

Thorne frowned but did as he was told. Darkness greeted him and he thought: *okay, reach out.*

How?

What did Rozehall mean by 'reaching out with Majik.' What was he supposed to do?

'Be calm boy, just picture the forest as you see it. Imagine you're in a dream, forget where you are now and imagine yourself roaming the outskirts of the Forest. Feel your Majik flow through your veins, your eyes, and your mind.'

Thorne scrunched his eyes together and clenched his fists. He pictured himself, anxious and scared, walking straight into the forest. Why would he have wanted to go in the first place?

'Focus on the image Thorne, your hands drifting through wood and leaves,' Rozenhall's voice guided him.

A flash of colour, Thorne grunted and opened his eyes. But Rozenhall was gone, the camp was gone, and there he was standing in front of the forest, and the dark trees that ominously beckoned to him.

He closed his eyes again, but when he opened them the camp had not returned. In fact, he could not spot the flicker of the flames wherever he looked. The camp had disappeared to be replaced by a vast empty expanse of fields.

He wanted to turn back, but his legs suddenly had a mind of their own, pushing him forward through the barrier of needles.

He was through, but darkness once more surrounded him, and Thorne began to panic. His mind wandered and he began to imagine strange things brushing past his legs. Ominous beings laughing raucously as he stumbled in the dark.

Am I blind? He thought. Where's the light? In the name of Ozin, let there be light!

A flash of white and a path was illuminated for him. Thorne rubbed his eyes and looked on ahead.

Something stood ahead in-between the light of the path and the darkness that encircled it. He could have been wrong, but he detected a shimmer of gold.

Thorne couldn't speak or move. He was forced to watch.

A hand emerged from the darkness. The gold thing beckoned with its gauntlet. Was it a soldier?

But why wouldn't it let him see its face?

The golden figure beckoned again, and Thorne's legs were forced into action once more, moving him closer to the golden figure.

But as soon as Thorne got anywhere close to the figure, close to possibly finding out its identity, it suddenly vanished into the shadows.

Wait! Thorne screamed with his mind. But he was unanswered and again, horribly alone.

Thorne heard a splash and his head snapped to the illuminated ground where a dark liquid had stained the grass red. Blood.

He could even taste it now. That distinctive iron tang.

Thorne moved, slowly retracing the blood. A drum began to pound a slow rhythm in the background. It was quiet at first, but as the speed of his steps increased so did the pace and heaviness of the drumbeat.

DA DA DUM!

The blood was in larger quantity here, forming sickening pools in the ground.

DA DA DUM! DA DA DUM!

Something laid out on the grass, a man! Not the golden soldier, the clothing was different. He wore dark robes, he was bald and there were… golden sparks on his shoulder… a Warlock!

DA DA DUM! DA DA DUM! DA DA DUM!

The man turned over suddenly, the light illuminating his bloody face, and Thorne screamed. It was Rozenhall!

Rozenhall grinned, blood trickling from the corner of his mouth. He then moved his hand to his mouth, pressing a finger to his lips.

'SHHH!'

Then his eyes were ablaze, and the corpse came upon him, bloody hands clawing at him.

A flash of colour. Thorne opened his eyes and gasped, collapsing to the floor, sweat dripping heavily from his forehead.

'Thorne!'

Rozenhall sat by him, padding his forehead with cloth.

'Thorne are you alright? What did you see?'

'Such darkness…' Thorne muttered, 'no… no…'

'Thorne!'

'Darkness… Blood… Death...'

*

Thorne burst through the bushes, wincing as the spiny needles scratched against the skin of his face, drawing blood.

Discovering that he was no longer being followed with a quick turn behind his shoulder, he sighed in relief and collapsed to the ground.

Rozenhall wandered into the clearing after Thorne. He was in an equally bedraggled state, twigs were stuck in various parts of his hair and torn robes.

For what seemed like weeks (more than likely only a couple of days at most) they'd been running around the forest, avoiding the numerous predators that lurked there. The forest seemed endless. Thorne had come to the inevitable conclusion that they were horribly lost.

He failed to understand how Rozenhall didn't seem to know where to go. The Chief Warlock looked confused and had muttered repeatedly every few hours: 'changed, so changed.'

'Hopeless,' Thorne muttered quietly to himself.

'Excuse me?' Rozenhall said.

'Nothing sir,' Thorne replied quickly.

'Changed, so changed,' Rozenhall whispered.

'Sir?' said Thorne.

'The forest… it's more different than I could have ever anticipated. Things have changed, for the worse, I fear,' Rozenhall muttered worriedly.

Thorne sighed and turned around, bumping into something solid.

He scrambled away, holding his rod defensively in front of him, breathing a sigh of relief when he realised what he had first mistaken for an attacker was actually just a wooden pole.

'Sir, what's this?' Thorne inquired.

Rozenhall walked past Thorne and peered closely at the pole.

The pole was coloured exotically, with strange and remarkably ugly creatures mounted crudely on top of each other. Each leering aggressively. Thorne turned to Rozenhall to ask him what the pole was for but was taken aback by his expression. Rozenhall had clearly seen these carvings before. Much to his horror, he realized all the carvings were goblins.

'Not good,' whispered Rozenhall, 'we appear to have entered sacred territory, and, er, the goblins do tend to take that very badly indeed.'

'Oh no,' Thorne mouthed silently.

Before they could move, Thorne felt the ground tremble slightly. He could hear the pounding of feet. A lot of feet.

'Whoopee!' screamed a gleeful little voice in the distance.

'Come to Raz Raz,' cried another.

'Damn it,' groaned Rozenhall.

Thorne didn't need telling twice. He urged his already tired legs into a sprint, Rozenhall directly behind him, hearing the thud of a spear embedding itself into the ground, a mere few centimetres from his heels.

As he sprinted through the undergrowth, he noticed a crop of light, leaking from a tightly grouped circle of trees. He was unable to explain why, even later he was still at a loss for a viable justification for his decision but there was something... familiar about the grouping of the trees. The light fell in the centre, reminding him strongly of the shape of a lantern. It was almost ethereal in appearance but surely it was safer than outside among the mob of starved goblins.

'In here sir!' he shouted behind him, his legs screaming for a reprieve. Thorne and Rozenhall clambered between the unnaturally tightly-packed trees and fell into the centre.

Thankfully, it seemed that they had managed to lose the goblins, at least. The creatures hadn't managed to track them into the tree circle.

Thorne laughed weakly, turned around and jumped. In the centre, where a sharp beam of light penetrated the canopy of trees, lay a man. His arms and legs were spread out at awkward angles and his face was buried in the ground. Soaking his back and visible amongst his long, dark hair was what looked very much like blood.

Had he led them both into a trap? How could he have been so stupid?

Rozenhall didn't waste any time, immediately rushing to the man's side and prodding his shoulder with the edge of his staff.

Before he could check whether the man was still alive, however, he heard a low growl. Rozenhall and Thorne both spun to look for the source of the noise, their eyes darting around frantically at the trees.

Slowly, a large pair of glowing, yellow eyes appeared, its gaze locked onto them. Thorne gulped, and stepped back involuntarily, his legs moving with a mind of their own.

More eyes appeared. The creatures stepped out, into the light, moving their bulky forms into view. They were alpha wolves – lion-sized monstrosities with thick, white fur. Extending from each paw, three curved knife-length claws. Their legs were beefy and muscular, their faces long and pointed, with large fangs jutting out from the sides of their frothing mouths.

He'd only ever read of such things in the Spire, confronting them rarely in hellish nightmares. The goblins had avoided the tree circle for a very good reason.

Rozenhall jumped to his feet and took a step forward, twirling his staff in the air.

'No, no, no, this isn't right,' Thorne heard the Warlock mutter under his breath, 'here? So far from the Plains?'

The beasts growled in unison. Sensing Rozenhall's discomfort, one of their number swiped a massive paw at thin air, inviting a flinch from the Chief Warlock. With savage roars, they pounced, each vicious and unrelenting in their attacks.

Thorne could only watch in horror. His body was paralysed as he observed the savagery of the attack.

'HELP! HELP ME!' Rozenhall screamed. His bloody arms and legs flailed hopelessly in the air. His staff let off a brief steam of flames which singed the fur of one of the wolves causing it to leap away from its prey but did little to stay the aggression of the others.

His cries were silenced after several dreadful seconds but continued to resonate in Thorne's mind. He had seen this before, he had foreseen Rozenhall's death, and he had failed to warn him.

The beasts greedily patrolled the pools of blood that had gathered from Rozenhall's corpse with their thick tongues. Thorne uttered a faint gasp when the last beast moved away from the mutilated body revealing the pale bloodless face that stared at Thorne, he thought, accusatorially. You led me to them. You!

He wished he could escape the stark – and rather bloody – reality he had found himself in. He wished he'd warned Rozenhall of his vision.

'I'm so sorry...' Thorne whimpered.

The one nearest to Thorne looked up at him with bloodshot eyes, its fangs dribbling with a gruesome combination of saliva and blood.

Thorne pressed himself back into the tree, praying it would lose interest in him, knowing it was hugely unlikely. However, instead it went over to the body of the other man. As it lowered its head, the 'dead' man suddenly leapt up. With a mighty slash of a previously concealed dagger, he decapitated the wolf.

The other wolves roared in fury and bounded to him. The man drew his sword, the metal gleaming in the faint light and the ruby embedded in its pommel sparkling, almost blinding

Thorne where he lay. The wolves stopped in their tracks, glaring at the man's sword.

The one nearest to the man, seemingly ignoring all sense in Thorne's view, lunged at him, fangs bared. The Swordsman punched the creature's face, whilst in mid-air, breaking its neck with a resounding crack. In a continuous fluid movement, the swordsman wheeled around to slash the second with his sword, opening a deep wound. The wolf howled with pain and limped out of the circle of trees, along with the third wolf, who growled venomously at the man before fleeing.

The Swordsman wore a black, thigh-length, sleeveless leather overcoat, his bare chest was covered by a network of scars, burns and bruises. He wore a pair of matching black, baggy trousers that were tucked into his mud coated steel greaves. His right hand was encased in a bloodstained, dark leather glove, with intricate skeletal metalwork protecting the knuckles and fingers. A cracked, dark green pendant, like a carved piece of crystal, hung above his chest. He grunted in apparent satisfaction and then turned slowly to face Thorne, who had backed away, nearer to the edge of the circle.

The Swordsman's face was concealed. Not by a helmet, but by musty bandages with holes for his eyes. Raven black hair plumed from the top of the man's head, falling to his shoulders.

However, it was not the man's scars or appearance that concerned Thorne but his eyes which glowed bright silver. He had heard something of these people before… read about it in a book at some point? He was sure but for the life of him he couldn't quite seem to remember it.

The man gazed at him questioningly and asked gruffly, 'are you alright?'

Thorne bit his lip nervously, trying to rack through his brains to find an appropriate answer. After a few long, silent and unsuccessful seconds, he nodded.

Although he was terrified by the sight of him, Thorne found that he could not tear his eyes away from his former master.

'Rozenhall...' Thorne muttered.

The Swordsman strode towards the body and then crouched beside it.

Thorne knew it was hopeless but he couldn't help but wish that by some miracle the Warlock had survived the vicious attack. He had to have.

Thorne arched his head towards the sky. Please he begged the dark, green expanse above him. Please let him be alive.

The man shook his head and sighed.

'Dead,' he announced, removing his gloved hand from Rozenhall's neck.

Dead? Thorne gulped. As his mind considered the gravity of the man's words, he became acutely aware of the blood pounding in his ears and his legs suddenly began to shake uncontrollably.

Dead?

Vey's words stuck out tauntingly at him in a red haze in his mind. *A little fresh air won't do him any harm.* Had the Masters known more about the dangers of the forest than

Rozenhall was aware of himself? Surely, he should have been warned?

Before he could speak further, however, he heard a high–pitched howl escape from outside the tree circle, and, as he imagined, echo around the forest, causing the hairs on the back of his neck to stand up sharply.

In that same moment, the Swordsman jumped to his feet and dropped his blade in its sheath. 'We have to go, now,' he said, grabbing him by his shoulder.

After a brief moment of hesitation, Thorne followed. He knew that if he stayed, he would be killed by the wolves, but if he went with the stranger who would say that his fate would be any better? Could he really trust him?

The Swordsman then snapped his hands onto Thorne's shoulders, 'Listen to me, this is no time for games,' he began, 'if we stay here we're finished! Understand? We're dead!'

'My master, you knew we were there...' Thorne whimpered, 'why didn't you do something?'

'We don't have time for this now, Warlock, you want to die here, fine, be my guest!'

There was another howl. Much closer this time.

Thorne glanced around worriedly. As much as the idea of running off with a complete stranger with the ability to sever heads off of giant wolves with ease didn't feel like a particularly great idea, he couldn't argue with the man's logic. The way he saw it, escaping the dark of the forest with the Swordsman was his only viable option, provided that the man didn't on a whim decide to sever his head.

The man had already begun to set off ahead.

'Hey! Wait!' Thorne cried, lunging after him.

As soon as the Swordsman had turned to face him, his hand had flown to the pommel of his sword, unsheathing it slightly so the brim of the blade was visible by his waist.

Startled, Thorne stumbled back, almost tripping over his own feet. The man snatched his arm and dragged him behind. 'Hey! What are you–' Thorne protested but paused mid-sentence as he realised what had set the stranger on edge. A blue light had begun to emanate from the clearing, beyond the Swordsman. Thorne leant by the Swordsman's side and his eyes widened. The light was coming from Rozenhall's body. Had he survived after all?

Within seconds the light began to disappear from the bottom half of his body and slowly collected around his head. A blue smoke drifted from the Warlock's open mouth into a shapeless mass. Without warning, the smoke suddenly shot forward, engulfing Thorne, seeping into his pores, sending an odd tingling feeling across his body.
The light now burst from Thorne's skin and he began to feel the same warmth he had experienced in the Binding, the sensation spreading quickly throughout his body.

But within seconds the warmth and light had disappeared, from all but his hands. Looking down, Thorne gasped. The palms of both his hands were a maze of blue scars that spiralled all over his skin. They pulsed a vivid blue for a few seconds and then faded.

'What's happening to me?' Thorne wondered out loud.

The Swordsman grabbed Thorne's right hand and examined it briefly. 'You've been branded. You undertook a Binding?'

'Yes!' Thorne said, a sickening feeling rising from the pit of his stomach.

The Swordsman shook his head in dismay, dropped Thorne's hand and began to walk towards the furthest edge of the circle of trees. The Warlock looked confusedly at his hand, and then sprinted towards the Swordsman. 'What does it mean?' he asked in exasperation, 'tell me!'

The Swordsman paused in his tracks, and looked back at Thorne, his eyes revealing nothing. 'It means that whatever task your Masters bestowed upon your guide, has now been passed to you. And, as I'm sure you have now surmised, you cannot return to your Spire until it has been completed.'

Chapter 5

The Shadow - a man who truly epitomised his name. It was a thought shared by many who knew him, or rather, survived the encounter. He seemed to have the ability to appear wherever he wished, unseen and unheard.

His feet bonded soundlessly with the soft grass, while his cloak trailed behind him, like a silhouette, as he emerged from the shadow of a larger oak tree. As he continued to tread through the glade, the wind seemed to hold its breath and the branches became motionless; a deep silence, broken briefly by the chirping of a small bird.

With the trees thinning, he paused briefly to observe the sight before him – the City of Light. It lay, surrounded by high walls and a single gated entrance. Etched into the gate's weathered metallic façade, in a language long forgotten, were the words Nậrr Dúrừm dél Drẹmăra - the City of Dreams.

At night, the city was just that.

Light flickered around the huge crystal statues that poked up – waist-upwards – above the walls, highlighting their every carved nick and the symbols etched in the swords they held with measures of pride in their weathered faces. Although, all this was dwarfed by the grand walls that towered over the highest peak of the city, ascending into the starry heavens above. He wondered if the people truly appreciated what beauty they had been gifted. Such a shame that the city would soon fall into ruin, its beauty lost; its grandeur forgotten.

He turned to survey the graveyard that lay only a few strides away from him. Here, the darkness resided, although, to those lacking the intuition, it would not seem unusual.

He could feel the strong fluctuations of Majik that bounded uncontrollably around the area, like a rabid dog. Compared to the dusky haze of night, here, it was not merely the absence of light – it was as if it had been consumed.

A large boulder blocked the entrance. Looking around, The Shadow could make out the jagged outline of the *robber fencing* – metallic, curved, unscalable, jagged-tipped poles – surrounding the graveyard. However, due to the fact that the graveyard had clearly been neglected for several decades, some of the poles were heavily corroded and had snapped in places.

Upon approaching the boulder, a voice like thunder boomed, 'who goes here?'

As far as The Shadow could see, there was no-one to whom this imposing voice belonged. It was as though it was part of the darkness itself.

'Who goes here?' repeated the voice, the poles vibrating under the weight of the words.

'A friend of fog!' shouted The Shadow.

The voice paused, as though contemplating The Shadow's words. Suddenly, the boulder began to shudder, and a crack burst through, rising from the base of the rock. As The Shadow watched, the boulder began to crumble into smaller pieces, which rolled aside, allowing him entry to the graveyard.

The graveyard before him was silent and empty, aside from the haphazard rows of gravestones that lay undisturbed. Yet The Shadow was not to be fooled. He was certain that he was being watched closely by eager eyes.

The Shadow began to walk through the pebble-scattered path formed by the crumbled boulder. As soon as he had entered, the boulder began to reform, the pieces circling in the air before crudely piecing back together like a jigsaw.

The Shadow smiled grimly and continued on into the heart of the graveyard, leaves scattering with every step.

'Ah, there you are,' he muttered. He came to a halt in front a gravestone, standing slightly apart from the others in the row. It was split through the middle, separating the sentence etched upon it: No light without darkness.

He then took a step back and whispered, 'Darkness lies in us all.'

Immediately after the words had left his mouth, the grave began to tremble and then rise with the sound of the grinding of stone on stone, dirt sliding off the edges like sand. With the grave hovering above, a large hole was revealed. Light shimmering around the edges.

Without a second thought, The Shadow slid himself into the hole. Dropping a few feet, he grimaced as his feet met more stone. The Shadow looked ahead to observe a descending, twisting corridor. It was lit by burning candles that floated near the walls, the wax dripping onto the floor like droplets of rain.

As he walked through the long corridor a strange smell began to drift to his nose. The further he went, the more unbearable it became. Much to his repulsion, it was becoming increasingly apparent that the smell was that of decaying flesh. Something had died down here.

When he reached the end of the corridor, a small circular room lay in before him. Sitting with his back to the doorway was a hooded man, gazing intently at an odd painting. The painting seemed peculiarly ordinary, thought The Shadow. A generic piece, depicting an open plain that was full of small, unrecognizable, figures. But wait, The Shadow glanced back at the painting. He must have been wrong, but he could have sworn that with every blink of his eyes, the figures moved.

When The Shadow dragged his gaze from the painting he saw that the man had stood up and was looking directly at him.

'So, you came alone?' the man asked. His voice surprisingly silky, in stark contrast with his dark demeanour.

'Don't I always, Xalem?' replied The Shadow. The smell was at its worst here and probably would have felled The Shadow were he an ordinary man.

The other man made a 'humph' sound and then pulled down his hood.

Xalem had a chalk white face with a seemingly mischievous look that a played across his features. His eyes were completely black like small, dark gemstones, giving him a cold, almost lifeless look and his long silvery hair was plaited, falling to his waist behind his back.

Xalem smiled, 'one must be sure.'

The Shadow returned the smile and then pointed at the painting asking, 'how long?'

Xalem grinned viciously and then walked towards it, caressing the painting with a long, hooked claw of a finger, 'centuries, and I plan to keep it that way – he is of no use to anyone now.'

Centuries. Just the thought of it could make a man mad. How had his spirit endured?

'Such a cruel way to leave a man,' The Shadow said.

The other man laughed, 'has age mellowed you, my dear Shadow? I have heard many stories about your methods, which make mine look very kind indeed.'

'I assume you did not summon me to discuss our methods,' The Shadow replied curtly.

Xalem's lip curled, 'no,' he admitted, 'I summoned you to discuss the boy. He is the last of his... kind, correct?'

'Of course, you of all people should know that.'

Xalem smirked, briefly glancing at the painting behind him before replying smugly, 'naturally. But where is he now?'

'I believe he is just leaving the Silent Forests.'

What appeared to be annoyance flashed across the man's face, disappearing as quickly as it had come.

'Well, if that is all…' The Shadow began, turning to leave.

Xalem suddenly appeared in front of the exit to the passage, his eyes alive with malice. 'No! It is not all. I tire of my pointless role. I tire of waking every morning with my heart pounding the same deathly chorus. I am tired of it all!'

Bemused, The Shadow replied. 'A heart? I was not aware you had one?'

Xalem's face contorted with rage. 'Do not play the fool with me,' he snarled. 'I know you understand what happens when my hunger goes for so long unsatisfied.'

'I'm sure you'll enlighten me,' answered The Shadow.

'This!' Shrieked Xalem, gripping his glove with his other hand and ripping it off. Underneath it was repulsive. The skin of the hand was sallow and missing from the fingertips, revealing bleached bone. The veins were black and writhing sickeningly in his pale flesh.

'So, it has begun already,' murmured The Shadow.

'Yes!' Xalem snapped, still fuming with anger, 'I am deteriorating.'

'I would not worry, my friend. With the boy gone, our Lord will soon return, and you shall have all you seek.'

Xalem's features softened. 'I had better, or one of these days…'

'Noted.'

'And before you go, I require one further thing.'

The Shadow stopped, and turned back from the exit, 'Go on.'

'All this time, and I still do not know who you are. You claim you come under the banner of fog, but I find it difficult to trust a man whose hides his face.'

'I'm not sure if I understand what you mean, Xalem'.

'I think you know exactly what I mean: your hood, remove it if you please.'

'My identity is of no importance.'

'It is to me, Shadow. At the very least, it is a common courtesy performed by even the most debased in this land. And believe me, this time, my curiosity will not be abated.'

The Shadow paused, resting his hands on his hips.

'Very well,' he replied, after a moment of deliberation.

The Shadow placed both of his hands on his hood and pulled, letting his face bask in the light and the cool breeze that circulated around the room from the grave opening.

Xalem's eyes drifted up and down, his stern expression unchanging. His eyes then latched onto something uncovered by the hood... something white... with what looked like golden sparks etched onto the shoulder of the material.

'Ah,' said Xalem, a flicker of a smile touching his lips, 'so, it all makes sense now. Warlock.'

The Shadow's eyes narrowed. 'No,' he replied, 'Master Warlock. But you may call me Vey.'

Chapter 6

The Swordsman had to be wrong, Thorne was certain of that. They'd been walking for what seemed like hours, and despite the painful protest of his legs he could not bring himself to ask the stranger to stop and take a break. This was partly because he was (at least slightly) terrified of the man and the fear that, if they did stop, a gruesome death inflicted by some foul creature was likely to befall them.

He trudged on after the Swordsman, panting heavily. When he noticed the state of his boots, he could not prevent a moan from escaping his lips. He had such nice boots once. If the others in the Spire could see them now – stained with the fruits of his labours – mud, old leaves and some colourful fluids of dubious origin.

What a disaster this excursion had been. Damn Vey, Thorne thought. Damn him for planting the suggestion of the forest in the other Masters' minds, and damn them for listening to him! He still couldn't believe that they didn't know about the dangers of the forest.

He pulled aside his robe and unhooked the rod from his belt. It was still pulsing a luminous green from the symbols etched in its frame – it had been doing that for days now. Why? He simply did not know and he preferred to use the little energy he had left to focus on keeping awake during this long, daunting walk.

He sighed and slid the rod back onto his belt, his eyes returning to the Swordsman's back. Who was he? Some sort of knight? No, silly, he'd, surely, wear more armour? A special Council bodyguard then? They always took the best, even if not the most mentally stable. Some rumours went as far to say that they hired reformed vampires; could he be one? Perhaps, this was all part of his plan. Take him out of harm's way and then feast on him when there were no beasts to distract him.

No. He had to be over thinking it all. But why would he be out all this way from Dalmarra? And in the Silent Forests of all places?

The way he had killed those beasts... Thorne could have been wrong, but it seemed so... natural. Not simply as though he'd done it several times before but almost as if he'd been trained to do it all his life.

Thorne groaned as he strained his mind for a conclusion. There was something about his eyes, he thought, perhaps something he'd read once in a book or heard in a lesson? He did occasionally turn up for them after all. But by Ozin's beard, what was it?

The Swordsman chuckled, 'you Warlocks are a restless bunch, aren't you?'

Thorne jumped, 'What? How did you know?' he asked, Banging his head on a branch.

The Swordsman smiled, or at least Thorne thought he did from the way his cheekbones raised under the bandages.

'Well, I thought the attention seeking robes and sparks would have been a bit of a giveaway.'

'Erm..' Thorne mumbled, fiddling with the belt of his pantaloons, 'well, I–'

However, the rest of Thorne's words became muffled as he bumped headfirst, straight into the Swordsman's back.

'What–' Thorne began, before he was suddenly silenced by the man's hand.

The Swordsman stood, as if frozen to the ground, with a finger to his lips, observing the area in front of him.

'Can you hear that?' he whispered, his gaze unmoving.

'What?' replied Thorne, the sound of his voice stifled by the man's thick glove.

'Exactly,' the Swordsman answered. His voice almost a whisper, 'not the whisper of wind or the scuttle of leaves. Something's... amiss.'

Abruptly and now unsettlingly aware of this fact, Thorne felt his palms sweat and his heart pound uncontrollably against his chest, turning his head in all directions looking for an unseen foe.

Strangely, the Swordsman was still notably calm.

Thorne swallowed back the lump in his throat. 'Shouldn't we...uh...go?'

The Swordsman nodded, 'yes, yes we should.'

He then removed his hand from Thorne's face, grabbed the hilt of his sword and slowly pulled it upwards, the sound of the two metals of the sword and scabbard scraping together piercing the silence of the forest like a knife.

Thorne's eyes flew to the sword, an odd brew of fear and comfort bubbling inside him. Comfort from the fact that this weapon could very well save his life, and fear from the opposing fact it meant imminent danger would be lurking near.

'You're not going to have to use that, right?' Thorne asked hopefully.

'You'd best hope not,' the Swordsman replied, disappearing under the shadow of the trees.

'Wait!' shouted Thorne, sprinting to catch up and bumping into him yet again in the process.

'Oh, Gods dammi–' Thorne began, only to be halted in mid-speech again by the man's glove.

'Ssh,' he hissed, 'what do you make of this?'

The Swordsman held up his sword and prodded a throbbing red vine that curled around the tree like a snake. With his luck, it probably was a snake.

'Some sort of vine?' he replied, shrugging his shoulders.

'Hm. I'd say we're reaching the end of the forest, follow me.'

Thorne shook his head in dismay. 'You said that about four hours ago,' he mumbled.

The man did not reply.

Thorne sighed and followed the man into a thicket of trees. Seconds later, the Swordsman came to an abrupt halt. Thorne was rubbing his sore head, having ploughed into his back.

'Why are you stop...?' Thorne's words were cut off by the sight before him.

Thorne pointed, finger trembling at the tree in front of him.

'Poor soul...' muttered the Swordsman.

Entangled in the mysterious red vines and hanging upside down was a young man. His face still bared the remains of life with a lopsided grin but from the smell it was clear the man was long dead.

There was something not quite right with this man however. Upon closer inspection of the corpse, the Swordsman pointed out that the grey pallor of his skin and the cut of his jaw resembled that of a Regal.

'What's he doing here?' Thorne asked, 'alone?'

'Regals tend to spread their numbers wide when travelling, to get an idea of the lay of the land,' the Swordsman said, adding ominously, 'we may find more of them.'

'More?' Thorne said, a lump forming in his throat.

The Swordsman sighed and closed the eyelids of the other man with two fingers. He then held his hands together in what looked like prayer.

'What did this?' Thorne asked.

Strangely enough, this question seemed to unsettle the man, but all Thorne could get out of him was: 'I have a number of ideas.'

Perhaps it was too soon to judge, but from his limited experience in the stranger's company, anything which rattled the man's composure was surely not an encouraging sign. He shuddered to think what lay ahead.

Just before they passed the tree, the Swordsman paused and turned to face Thorne. 'What?' asked Thorne.

'We had best be extremely cautious.' The Swordsman gestured at the thicket of trees in front of him with his sword, 'whatever did this is probably lying in wait for us ahead.'

'Probably?'

The man shrugged, 'well, I say 'probably.' Really - it's 'most definitely.'

'So?' Thorne replied, trying to sound braver than he felt, and to ignore the clamminess of his hands.

'If you'd rather we turn back–'

'Back through the forest?' Thorne stammered, feeling his face go pale at the thought.

'A valid point,' the Swordsman conceded. Although Thorne couldn't see anything through the bandages, his eyes had narrowed in thought.

'Onwards then…' The Swordsman bent until his face was close to Thorne's, 'but be particularly vigilant, young Mage.'

Thorne continued to look firmly into his eyes and nodded. The Swordsman began to head into the thicket, shaking his head.

Thorne grunted and followed, putting his hands up to defend his face from the multitude of needle-like branches that concealed the path before him like a green wall.

It did not take long for Thorne to regret this path. Of course, turning back wasn't really an option but he did miss his soft warm bed, with only nightmares to threaten his blissful serenity. He had no wish to remain in such a forsaken place where his nightmares became reality.

As they progressed further, Thorne noticed to his disgust, more bodies strapped to trees, wearing bizarre mixed expressions of fear, anger, sadness... Almost every emotion he could think of.

Suddenly, each of the bodies' eyes suddenly flashed open. Thorne stumbled back in surprise and tripped, falling back onto the floor.

'All hail!' the voices moaned together.

'Wha–what?' Thorne blurted out.

'All hail he, second to the flame, bearer of the immortal fire!'

'All hail he who shall lay on the flames of old unto Horizon's darkest dawns! Unto the rise of the Phoenix!'

Their speech fading into murmurs, the corpses fell into silence their heads hanging against their chests.

'Wh–what was that?' Thorne cried.

'I think the question, Warlock' the man began, pulling Thorne back onto his feet, 'is who would employ such ghastly Majik?'

A giggle echoed around the forest, the trees shaking in harmony.

Thorne jumped and searched frantically around the forest for the source of the voice. He knew it had to come from some individual... one... thing. Yet it sounded like it was coming from everywhere at once.

'Who's there?' the Swordsman demanded, 'show yourself!'

The giggle grew into a laugh, which rose into a terrifying crescendo, causing the bones in Thorne's body to shudder.

Then, without warning, a blur of a form suddenly dropped onto the ground within a flurry of leaves.

'Oh, Gods' Thorne whimpered, as the leaves settled.

'Oh,' the Swordsman muttered worriedly, 'a blissgiver.'

The creature had the body of a shapely woman, its skin was a mixture of pink and white, and it wore a dress of leaves. It had claws on its hands and feet like smooth metal nails, eyes that swirled maddeningly with colour, and horns that sprouted from its forehead and curled to its cheeks. It also wore a smile that seemed to mock and yet soothe at the same time.

The creature grinned and then began to emit a bright light from its belly until it completely engulfed its body. Thorne slapped his arm over his face to shield his eyes from the blinding light. However, when the light dimmed and Thorne removed his arm, it was not the creature that stood before them but a young man wearing a leather overcoat, steel greaves and…

He jumped back in surprise. Aside from the blonde, spiky hair the other man was almost identical in build and dress to the one who stood next to Thorne.

Thorne looked at the Swordsman beside him, noticing that his shoulders had sagged and his grip had loosened on his sword.

'Dez,' he whispered.

'Dez' grinned sadistically and, with another flash of light, changed into another man. The clothing was similar except for a bright red bandana that covered the bottom half of his face. This still failed to distract attention away from the gruesome maze of scars, which looked like they had been hacked into his bald head by an axe. The man himself was a monstrosity in every sense of the word, standing a clear couple of feet above the Swordsman beside Thorne.

In a matter of seconds, with the appearance of the scarred man, the Swordsman had become drastically more tense. His hand gripped the pommel of his sword so tightly Thorne thought it would snap under the pressure. The bearded man was clearly not too happy to see him either.

'ZAINE!' the man boomed, spitting out the words with venom, 'YOU ARE UNFIT TO RULE!'

Thorne noticed the stranger's hands and arms were shaking uncontrollably now.

The words cycled over and over again, booming around the forest.

'WORTHLESS! USELESS! DISGRACE! ABOMI–'

'ENOUGH!' the Swordsman yelled, a knife arcing from his hand towards the other man.

The bearded man smirked and disappeared with another flash of light.

Thorne swivelled his head around, but he could not find the creature. He turned to the Swordsman, whose breathing had become heavy and his teeth were grinding against each other. At that moment, Thorne wasn't sure of what he should be more afraid of – the creature? Or the Swordsman's rage?'

But at least now he had his name.

He risked another glance. The Swordsman, Zaine, was still fuming, so Thorne decided it was probably in his best interests to keep quiet.

He didn't anyway.

'W–where is it?' Thorne asked meekly.

It took a few seconds before Zaine managed to reply, through gritted teeth, 'it doesn't matter, let's just kill it!'

Thorne nodded, unsure in what other way he should respond to such a statement. He licked his lips nervously, preparing another question in his mind when he suddenly stopped and stood stone–still.

He hoped he was wrong but Thorne thought he'd felt something slide across his arms – something thin... cold...slimy.

Thorne gulped and slowly bent his head down, the sight before him confirming his fears. Curling and tightening onto his arms and legs were several long, red vines, their clammy touch causing him to shiver involuntarily.

'Oh, help–' Thorne began to shout, before he was unexpectedly thrust into the air, branches and leaves slapping and scratching him during his rapid ascent. He then came to a halt, his head snapping backwards and forwards with a crack.

In front of him was a large trunk of a tree and, to his dismay, the blissgiver. It lay on a branch, picking at its oddly pearl white teeth with a long talon.

The creature lifted its head, flicking something small from its fingertips and winked at him. 'Well, hello, Warlock,' it purred.

Thorne could not form words past a stutter.

The creature lifted a hand to its head, 'I'm sorry, what was that?'

Thorne growled and flailed helplessly under the grip of the vines in an attempt for freedom – it was no use.

'Help!' he yelled, 'Gods alive! Help me–'

The creature jabbed him in the stomach with its clenched fist, causing the remainder of air along with the rest of his sentence to rush out of his mouth in a pitiful wince.

The creature then clamped its chilling hands on his forehead, muttering, 'let's see…'

Thorne grunted in the effort to resist, realizing he was fighting a losing battle as he felt his body go cold and limp, a strong sense of nausea creeping into his stomach just as his vision blurred and then became completely obscured by darkness.

When he awoke, Thorne faced completely different surroundings – he was sat in an armchair that faced a fireplace for one. A smoking mug of what smelled like hot chocolate sat alongside a crystal–clear glass on the marble table beside him.

Above the fireplace, attached to the walls were silver boards displaying an odd variety of items – claws and animal heads, and rare treasures – sparkling jewels, pendants and ancient looking swords. In the middle, there was also a square clock, another antique by the look of it but still working nonetheless. The ticks seeming to echo around the quiet room.

Even his clothes had changed – the robes and pantaloons replaced by a leather waistcoat and a pair of tight–fitting trousers. His boots had also disappeared and instead he wore a pair of shoes that were looser but more comfortable.

This place, it was… tranquil but a bit weird. How had he got here? All he could remember was a cold feeling and then darkness. What the hell was going on?

Wham!

Thorne jumped, almost toppling his chair in the effort to quickly scramble out of it, while he pivoted his head frantically around the length and breadth of the room, searching for the source of the noise.

WHAM!

Thorne jumped again, a second later another sound accompanying the first – screaming, a woman's scream no doubt.

He lurched forward and tried to reach one of the swords hanging above on the wall. He couldn't reach it.

WHAM!

The source of the noise was getting closer, adding to his paranoia.

He leaped up against the wall, the tip of his fingers only grazing the bottom of the hilt this time. Thorne growled in frustration, then grabbed the table, the empty glass and the jug falling to the floor and smashing into jagged pieces which swam among the loose liquid. He held it up in front of him, the wooden legs facing the door opposite to him.

His heart pounded against his chest as he tried to conceive of who or what would come through the door. The door was then thrust open, and the person who stepped in was – to his complete surprise – a fellow Novice of the Spire, Mason.

His robes billowing behind him, he ran breathlessly towards Thorne and grabbed him by his waistcoat.

'Thorne!' he exclaimed, so short of breath he could only manage to utter a few words every moment, 'under attack... need... to leave...'

'What?' Thorne shot up from his seat with alarm, 'what's happening?'

'No time!' Mason said, dragging Thorne along with him, 'we need to leave!'

His legs, suddenly with a mind of their own, propelled Thorne through the open door, many twisting corridors with fancy rugs and walls lined seemingly endlessly with portraits, with faces that stared blankly at him, until finally he stopped at what looked like an entrance hall. Here a grand staircase occupied most of the area, its golden banisters reflecting the dazzling light from the chandeliers overhead around the expanse of the hall.

At the end of the room laid the wrecked remains of two large oak doors, their frames shattered, deep gashes scarring the surface. Towering triumphantly in front of them, stood the bandit.

The man was a clear foot taller than him with huge bulging arms covered in a wide assortment of crude tattoos and disfiguring scars. His hair was jet black and long, the lank locks falling around his hairy face like a veil. The bandit wore a torn leather chest pad, partly concealed by his tattered sleeveless tunic which fell to his knees.

Gripped tightly in the bandit's grimy hands was a large morning star, most of its spikes either bent or chipped.

Thorne gulped, feeling dwarfed by the bandit's size and hostility that seemed to burst out towards him.

The bandit gave him a toothless grin through the parting in his hair and yelled, 'I gonna gut ya lik'a pig!'

Without warning he then charged, bellowing out a horrid battle cry and swinging his weapon in wild arcs.

The first swing in his direction missed Thorne completely, the second time, a spike of the mace grazed the tip of his nose and the third ripped open his waistcoat and vest, revealing the bare – but fortunately unharmed – flesh.

The man giggled madly and heaved his weapon up again after spitting away the froth brimming his lips.

Mason then suddenly appeared in front of Thorne, his eyes aflame, shrieking, 'BURN! BURN HIM!'

Upon the novice's orders Thorne felt a vast amount of energy building up inside him, the raw power flowing through his veins and stimulating his senses.

He'd almost forgotten about the effects of Majik – the tingling fingers, the warmth and then the feeling of exhilaration when all this energy burst forward from his fingertips.

'Leave now!' Thorne roared, thrust his hands forward and let loose a stream of flames that turned the floor black as it shot towards the bandit. The bandit wailed and blundered around the hall as his body became enveloped in the flames.

'Yes! Yes! Burn him!' Mason clapped him on excitedly.

He'd heard his friend, but this time Thorne couldn't follow the order unconsciously. He'd depleted himself. He snapped his fingers in desperation. Nothing but sparks surfaced from his hands. Where had his energy gone?

He fell to his knees, brow sweating and panting heavily, forced to sit and watch as the bandit rushed towards him. The mace was held up above his head while screaming promises of revenge above the sound of the crackling flames.

Forced to watch the weapon fall upon him. Fortunately, darkness took him first.

Chapter 7

Was he dead?

But no, he couldn't be. How would he be able to think and feel otherwise?

Of course, that raised other questions in his mind as well – if he had, how had he died?

Honestly, he could not seem to remember.

However, if he was dead, perhaps the most important question of all was.... where the hell was he?

COME...

What?

He could have mistaken it for something else, but Thorne was quite sure he had heard a voice.

COME... COME...

He had definitely heard it this time – that voice, which was soon accompanied by a creaking noise, a gust of wind and then… light…

Strange, how its absence had not bothered him...

But wait. He could see. He was alive! He had to be.

But then why couldn't he move? It was like he was attached to the ground with his arms, legs, even the tip of his nose out of sight.

Even more importantly however, where was he? His surroundings didn't say much – all he could see was whiteness. An endless realm of white.

He blinked, and a second later something else appeared, although he couldn't tell what it was as it was shining so brightly and it was so far away it was merely a blur.

The light around him was starting to flicker and fade and Thorne could feel a chill creeping up his spine and a throbbing pain on the side of his head.

The last thing Thorne remembered before he plunged into darkness was a pair of gleaming eyes and what he thought was a hand that beckoned to him.

*

Thorne's eyes opened, darkness greeting him at first before they closed again soon after.

The second time they opened, his vision was less obscured but blurry nonetheless, and the disorientation made everything seem to move at a much slower pace.

He clenched a fist and caught a wad of grass – he'd fallen back on the ground. He tried to move the other hand, but it wouldn't budge. Was it broken?

He then saw something moving out of the corner of his eye – something green? White? What was it?

Thorne's eyes allowed him focus more, showing that the shape of the figure resembled a well–built man. The golden man?

The man fell to his knees beside him, grasped Thorne's robes and started to shake him.

Thorne's eyes then latched onto the man's hand and the gleam of silver that emanated from it.

'You...' Thorne mumbled.

Zaine opened his mouth, but Thorne couldn't hear what he was saying, even though he appeared to be bellowing the words at him.

'I – I can't...' he began.

Zaine twisted his head suddenly and turned back, grabbing Thorne by the hem of his robes and shouting out at him with visible urgency.

'–UP!' Thorne heard, as if through water. He shook his head.

'CAN YOU HEAR ME? GET UP! THE DEMON ISN'T DEAD!'

The dreaded words acting as a shock to his system, Thorne's vision began to clear drastically. He saw the trees, the vines and the shallow crevasse in the grass where he'd landed.

'My legs–' Thorne began weakly.

'Are fine,' Zaine said abruptly, 'now get up!'

Thorne didn't have the strength to argue and, with Zaine's help, was hauled to his feet. He staggered briefly before regaining his balance.

He gulped down the air greedily as he leaned on one of the trees, eyeing Zaine's sword with apprehension.

'Are you alright?' Zaine asked, snapping his head to the left and right to examine the surroundings.

'I'm fine,' Thorne replied, 'what happened to me?'

'You were entranced,' Zaine replied, 'the demon wrapped your mind up in fantasy.'

Thorne's hand drifted to the back of his head and he winced as his fingers brushed against the large bump that had formed under his hair.

'Did you... punch me?' Thorne groaned.

'Sorry,' the Swordsman shrugged.

'But – then how...' Thorne began, his confusion stripping him of the ability to form sentences.

'Look behind you,' the stranger said sharply.

Thorne did so and gasped in shock.

A large area in front of him, once abundant in plant life was now completely destroyed.

The long grass had been reduced to ashes which, along with a few leaves, littered the scorched ground. The trees had also become mere shadows of what they once were. Their immense bodies now shrunken and as dark as the ground they feebly stood on. Some were still alight at the top where a few branches and their leaves remained, the flames slowly devouring their colour.

He took a step forward, almost crumpling from exhaustion.

Had he really done all this?

Thorne then heard a crunch, which he'd initially assumed was the sound of his feet on the scorched ground but what were actually the burnt and tattered remains of some sort of clothing. He picked it up to inspect it more closely and he realized it was an overcoat.

Thorne paled and turned to Zaine who he now noticed, to his horror, was missing his own overcoat and his arms were dark and singed.

'By Ozin!' Thorne cried, 'I–I'm so sorry.'

'Just be on your guard' the Swordsman grunted in reply, 'the demon could be anywhere.'

Thorne gulped – he'd completely forgotten about the blissgiver!

He felt his hands tremble and his eyes darting around in his head. He was once again horribly aware of the danger they were still in and how inexplicably defenceless he was.

Before he could move, however, he heard the snapping of twigs and felt an icy breath blow around the back of his neck causing him to jump. He knew what was behind him without having to look.

'Blissgiver,' Thorne whispered.

A clawed hand extended on his shoulder spinning him round.

The demon's once vibrant eyes had lost their colour, their promise of boundless dreams replaced by the rampant flames of his worst nightmares. Screams. Soul-shattering screams, from children, women and men alike. In its eyes, Thorne saw his own reflected: two hellish, flaming orbs that sneered down upon him.

One voice began to stand out from the rest, bellowing above the cries, 'BURN! BURN IT ALL!' The image of the sadistic smile that went along with it was a still firmly implanted in his mind. It was a smile that promised no compassion, no mercy, only death and hate.

Thorne yelled, suddenly coming back to his senses, the familiar itch in his eyes arising as he felt adrenaline surge through his body.

He thrust his open palms against the creature. The Demon wailed as it flew across the burnt grass, offering a soft grunt as it smacked into a tree and crumpled to the floor.

'My Gods...' Thorne murmured.

Zaine arrived soon after, sword held in one hand and a vicious looking dagger in the other.

'What happened?' he demanded, 'did it...'

The Swordsman then saw the upturned tree and the supposedly unconscious blissgiver. 'How?' he mouthed.

'I...' Thorne stared at his hands in disbelief.

'How did you do that?'

'I... I don't know...' Thorne replied. It didn't make any sense, he had been powerless. And yet, at that moment when the blissgiver had touched him, he'd felt a burst of energy suddenly erupt inside of him... and then it was gone. He was back to being a powerless child... weak.

Zaine still hadn't averted his gaze. Thorne wished he could read the man's thoughts, as he wasn't sure whether the man was considering him as he would a potential threat or if he wasn't letting on something important to make sense of what had just occurred. He hoped it was the latter.

Zaine then unexpectedly pointed his dagger at him and for a split–second Thorne was worried that the stranger was going to use it against him, but instead he flipped the blade over in his hand and offered it, hilt first, to him.

'Just in case,' the man said.

Thorne wasn't sure what to do. He'd never been offered a blade before, let alone allowed to use one.

Before he could so much as thank the man, a soft moan emanated from the fallen tree beside them.

'Here!' the man said, thrusting the dagger towards him, 'take it.' His hand fell as he failed to anticipate its weight.

The Swordsman broke into a full sprint towards the awakening blissgiver. He hadn't even got close before it suddenly jumped back on to its feet, appearing before them apparently completely unharmed, giggling wildly.

It was staggering, the different conflicting emotions it brought out in Thorne. Part of him wanted to laugh with it, but the other half sorely wanted to punch it in its smug face.

'Enough of this sorcery!' The Swordsman bellowed.

When his blade landed, the Swordsman found that he'd hit nothing but thin air.

'Blast!' he growled.

A familiar giggle rang around the forest.

Thorne froze – the sound had come directly behind him... again.

'And now,' the creature began, with disturbing eagerness, 'you shall be my silent one forever.'

'NOOOOOO!' the Swordsman roared.

THWACK!

Blood. Lots of it. Not as much as Thorne had experienced with Rozenhall and the wolves but... enough.

It splattered on the ground like paint flicked from the brush of an overenthusiastic artist. At the time, Thorne believed he was drawing in his last breaths, until he noticed that the blood was not red, but purple. The stuff spurted out from the demon's chest, while the sword's pommel wavered. He had not moved away in time to avoid the blood from soaking the left sleeve of his robes and his hand.

'Ach–H–Hun–' the creature grunted between mouthfuls of its blood.

Thorne felt sick as he observed its wound and its feeble attempts to remove the sword from its chest with trembling hands.

The Swordsman's gloved hand gripped the sword, Thorne saw the creature's eyes widen and the colour change rapidly from red to black, then yellow.

'No... No,' the creature gurgled.

The Swordsman didn't spit, nor curse, nor offer form of words. He didn't even blink as he pulled the sword out from the demon, kicked it to the ground and plunged the blade into its navel.

The creature's body began to convulse. Froth began to build up at its mouth while its eyes rolled wildly in their sockets.

Then it screamed.

Thorne had never heard anything like it – it was so high-pitched, it could have shattered glass.

When it finally died down, Thorne continued to cling on to the sides of his head, fearful that his ears might burst.

'Is it dead?' he asked hopefully.

The stranger didn't reply, he just stood still, staring silently at his kill.

Thorne cautiously removed his hands from his ears and followed the man's gaze to the creature lying in a pool of its own blood. Its mouth was agape, and its eyes stared blankly at the green expanse above it.

He breathed a sigh of relief and began to turn away but stopped suddenly when something strange happened – he heard whispers. They were faint at first, just barely audible, but became increasingly louder and erratic as he approached the corpse.

'What are you doing?' Zaine inquired.

'I… don't know,' Thorne mumbled in response. He couldn't possibly explain. There was something that obligated him to move towards it.

He was now just a footstep away from the body and the whispers began to reach their deafening climax.

'No! Stop!' the stranger shouted, suddenly alarmed, but he could not reach Thorne in time.

Thorne's feet now rested a mere inch from the creature's head and a second later 'the corpse' latched its hands onto his ankle, refusing to let go.

The creature regarded him with its cold black eyes, which then flared violently and his surroundings started to melt all around him.

'Oh no…' Thorne groaned.

It was Dalmarra that appeared to him this time, but the scene that had unfolded before his eyes was one of complete and utter chaos.

The stalls that lined the streets, where merchants would sell their rare and peculiar goods, lay smashed and broken on the cobblestones.

People ran screaming and yelling amongst the roar of flames that licked across the streets, setting both buildings and people alike on fire.

He felt a hand on his shoulder and he whipped round, hands raised. Naught but shadow greeted him. A mass of the purest darkness that drew the light of the feeble embers flickering by Thorne's feet into its cold embrace. The darkness that stood before him was shaped like a man, but a man it was not.

When the shadow spoke, Thorne could not help but collapse to his knees. Not because this thing had taken his energy but because it had drained all hope from within him. It was like experiencing the utter destruction of everything he cared about in one instant. In its presence, he could not hope to have anything to live for, let alone fight for. This shadow was the very antithesis of light. Of hope.

'You cannot stop us!' it told him. 'We will return'.

Chapter 8

It was a quiet night at the Skrunai camp. The tranquillity disturbed only rarely by the occasional cry of a slave, who was swiftly silenced with the snap of a whip.

The Baron was especially pleased with the progress that had been made. Although, one would not know it from his cold exterior. He stood impassively on the hilltop beside his cabin, observing the on–goings of the camp. Dozens of men and women, chained together in orderly lines, were being guided to their crude metal cages. Not a second would pass where a whip didn't snap mercilessly across a back, or curses spat out at their cowering forms.

He looked on impassively. Their suffering didn't bother him in the slightest, as long as they were all in acceptable condition and there was coin to be made. Really, it was the smell that bothered him. Fortunately, he was safe from such unpleasantness in his aromatic cabin. He closed his eyes and breathed in the air, he could almost smell the gold on the breeze.

How could the Warlocks, the Brotherhood, and all the other petty organizations criticize his magnificent work? The fools, the Baron thought.

Satisfied with what he had seen, the Baron turned back and strode into his cabin, slamming the door shut behind him.

What the cabin lacked in size, it made up for in grandeur. The side walls both had large leather couches, adorned with golden laced pillows and cushions, tucked against them. The floor was made of smooth tiles of marble and at the end of the room was an ornate fireplace holding a crackling fire that embraced the room with its light and warmth.

Above, on a shelf, was a row of golden candle holders, precious pearls and rubies that the Baron had 'acquired' over the years. Directly in front of the Baron was a large ebony table, where piles of gold coins lay scattered across the wood, gleaming under the glow of the fire, along with yellowed scrolls of parchment and blotting paper.

He made his way to the couch on the left, whisking out a bottle of wine and a glass from the cupboard behind him, before slumping onto the lavish leather and emitting a long blissful groan. He poured himself a drink but paused before the glass touched his lips.

He could have been mistaken, but he was certain he'd felt a cold breeze across his skin, inciting the hairs on his arms to stand on end. His eyes darted to the door, which now stood ajar, waving back and forth on its hinges by the influence of the wind. He was sure he'd closed it.

Growling venomously, the Baron stood up with his glass and slammed it shut again for a second time. When he'd turned back around however, he came face to face with another man. The Baron gasped and dropped his glass, the smash echoing around the cabin.

The man himself was dressed in simple peasant clothes – a belted tunic tucked into a pair of travelling trousers and boots. His hands were covered by thin black gloves and he had a mysterious looking ring on his right–hand index finger bearing an insignia of a knife embedded in a skull.

His face was also mostly concealed, hidden by a hood that covered his eyes and shadowed the bottom half of his face.

Recovering from the initial shock, the Baron reached for the dagger by his belt and ripped it free.

The man stood stock still.

The Baron hesitated for a second, then madly started swiping and thrusting the dagger at the man whilst roaring vile insults. The man dodged every single one, moving gracefully out of the way without appearing to break so much as a drop of sweat.

'Damn trickster,' the Baron growled.

As the Baron thrust his dagger forwards, the man suddenly whipped out his hands and grabbed the Baron's wrists, placing pressure with his thumbs, causing the Baron to yelp and drop the dagger. Before it touched the floor, the man kicked it up and caught it with his left hand, using his right to throw the Baron onto the table, scattering coins around the surface and floor, and held the dagger an inch from his exposed neck.

'Finish it,' the Baron spat at the man.

The man laughed, and then spoke, with a surprisingly smooth voice, 'believe me, I'm tempted.'

The Baron gulped but refused to show any further signs of fear.

'Fortunately for you, The Shadow stresses 'collective effort,' so I merely have a message for you.'

The man then stabbed the dagger into the table, inches away from the Baron's left hand and released him.

The Baron got up muttering curse words under his breath, while taking a long look at the dagger. After much deliberation, he decided against pulling it out of the table, for the sake of his life.

'Very well then, how did you get in?' the Baron inquired.

'By the door, obviously,' the man said sarcastically.

'Into my camp, you scoundrel!' the Baron growled.

'Well by the front gate if you must know. Unfortunately, I wasn't in the mood to chat and exchange pleasantries with your guards, so naturally they're all dead now,' the man said simply.

'WHAT!' the Baron roared, 'HOW DARE YOU! THE SHADOW WILL HEAR OF THIS!'

'Of course,' the man said, leaning on the table beside him, 'I'm sure The Shadow will be delighted to hear about the incredibly poor state of your security.'

Again, the Baron's eyes flitted to the dagger just a few inches away from him, and again thought better of it.

'Fine then, just give me the damn message, assassin!' he spat.

The man chuckled, 'so, you are aware of my profession?'

'You claim to have killed several of my men and made it here without raising the alarm, and you're wearing that stupid ring!'

The assassin grinned, rubbing his ring thoughtfully before replying, 'beautiful, isn't it? Your... operation, however, trading slaves? How crude.'

'My business is none of your concern,' the Baron growled, 'I'll admit though, I'm curious as to how The Shadow managed to get the assassins into his pocket.'

The man's lips twitched at the corner, 'my colleagues and I have our own agendas. Our relationship with The Shadow is conducive to achieving both our aims.'

'Then you underestimate him and it will be your undoing assassin.'

'Or yours, Baron, but I didn't come here to exchange idle chit–chat. The Shadow's message is simple – the Warlock has made it out of the forest and is now coming your way.'

'Already? But why should I care?'

'Because he is not alone, slave–master, he was helped by a rogue Divine Son.'

'A Hunter…' the Baron said turning around to pull the dagger from his table.

'Precisely.'

'And what the hell am I supposed to do about–' the Baron began, whipping round to face thin air. The assassin had disappeared.

The Baron shook his head and threw the dagger back on the table. If the assassin was to be believed and the Warlock was finally out of the forest… Well, it would only be a matter of days before he and his companion were back on the main roads. The clock was ticking.

'TOOOOOOOOOMMMMM!' the Baron bellowed at the top of his voice.

A few seconds later a large, bald, burly man with squinting eyes and a prominent forehead appeared.

'Mr Baron, sir,' Tom said.

'Get me my maps now, its urgent!' the Baron said.

'Maps? What's maps?' Tom asked with a vacant expression on his face.

'What's maps?' the Baron repeated. 'You blithering idiot! Get me your brother now!'

The burly man sprinted off in the opposite direction, leaving the Baron fuming by his desk. Tom returned seconds later with a smaller, wiry man holding in both arms several rolled up scrolls.

The Baron picked one and rolled it out on the table – it displayed the land of Horizon, from the city of Dalmarra to the Black Mountains.

The wiry man looked at it with admiration, his brother, however, stared at it with a quizzical and confused expression on his face.

The Baron beckoned the wiry man, Tim, and pointed out different locations on the map to him.

'We need carts and men sent out here, here, and here,' the Baron explained, 'got it?'

'Yes, Mr Baron, sir.'

'I want it done quickly and cleanly. Do you understand me, Tim? Quick and clean, otherwise there'll be hell to pay.'

'Yes, Mr Baron, sir. Right away, sir.'

'Oh yes, and Tom…' the Baron began.

'Yes, Mr Baron, sir?' Tom replied.

'Fetch me another bloody glass, I need a drink.'

108

Chapter 9

Thorne awoke to the smell of berries and vanilla, so comforting and calming, it almost lured him back into a deep sleep.

He scraped the ground around him with his hands but his fingers could not grasp a single blade of grass. He opened his eyes. The leafy ceiling that had once shielded him from downpours of rain had disappeared. It had been replaced by what seemed like a hundred candles bobbing up and down in the air above him under a ceiling of plastered planks.

The thick, imposing trees of the forest had gone. Walls adorned with tapestries and shelves, containing an assortment of jars, pots and herbs, had taken their place.

Was he still in the forest?

Dread pooled in his stomach, as he remembered the blissgiver's vice–like grip and the vision it had imposed upon him. He had thought nothing would shake the core of him as much as the sight of seeing his home city drowning in blood and flames. He shook away thoughts of flame–licked cobble streets and pushed himself to his feet, staggering and wincing in the process. He hadn't realised how much the Silent Forests had worn his body.

He half–walked, half–limped to the door at the end of room but paused in moving his hand towards the handle when he heard voices on the other side. One of them belonged to Zaine and the other... a woman?

'...what did you expect... growing tired of it...' Zaine's voice rang in the other room.

The woman's voice followed more shrilly, '...out of your mind... could have died...'

'...going to anyway... Warlock got in the way...'

As he leant an ear closer to the door he heard the voices pause.

'...think he's up...'

Thorne barely had time to jump back, as the door swung open, revealing the Swordsman, arms covered in fresh bandages, and his companion.

Zaine was sat on the floor, running a blood-stained cloth covered with a pungent green solvent across the breadth of his blade.

The woman standing beside him wore a gorgeous floor–length dress of shimmering maroon, which appeared to flow over her. Her nails were long and painstakingly well-polished, glinting under the light. She also wore a veil, which, combined with her dress covered her from head to toe, revealing naught but her dazzling smile. Yet there was something different about her. He got the feeling he was only scratching the surface with her appearance.

'Ahh, our guest is awake,' the woman beamed, 'please, join us.'

Thorne had to bite his tongue to prevent an outburst when he stepped inside the room. He'd felt a sudden spike in Majik, all which emanated entirely from the woman. It was a feeling he'd not come even close to since his departure from the Spire. But this was something entirely different. While it comforted him to be near another Majik user, he felt somewhat overwhelmed by the force that probed him.

110

'I trust you are recovered?' the woman asked.

Thorne nodded, 'yes... but, where am I?'

'This is Zakariyanna's place,' the Swordsman said, nudging the woman beside him, 'you'll be safe here.' He then proceeded to tugging at the bandage on his arms with apparent discomfort.

'Stop that, they'll fester,' the woman tutted.

Albeit with a grimace, Zaine nonetheless accepted the scolding, to Thorne's bemusement.

He wondered how long they had known each other, and secondly, what was it with everyone he'd met outside the Spire and the need to conceal their faces?

'You know each other?' Thorne asked, deciding he was not brave enough to ask the second question.

The Swordsman offered a rare chuckle. 'Do we?'

'For forever it seems,' she smiled, and turned to Thorne, 'but we have all the time in the world to discuss that, for now I am concerned about you.'

'Me?'

'Remember the blissgiver, Warlock?'

A horned head and that annoying giggle surfaced in Thorne's mind. He shook it away, 'what do you mean?'

'The fogspawn established a connection with you, did it not?' Zakariyanna asked.

'I... what?' Thorne gulped.

'Wouldn't stop yelling in your sleep for days,' Zaine muttered.

Thorne's head was spinning. Days? He'd been here for days? How ill had he been?

'If you will excuse me,' Zakariyanna interrupted Thorne's thoughts, 'I should probably get you a few herbs, you're looking a bit peaky.'

With that the woman drifted past him into the room he'd awoken in.

'Peaky?' Thorne said, putting his hands up to his cheeks.

'Threw up everywhere,' the Swordsman muttered as he passed Thorne, 'filled a whole bucket...'

'Zaine!'

'Coming,' Zaine said, sheathing his sword.

'Hey wait!' Thorne rushed to the door. He'd been sick as well? What had they meant about the blissgiver establishing a connection? And who was this woman?

'Won't be long,' Zaine said, closing the door behind him.

Thorne stood staring at the door for what must have been a minute before giving up to pace around the new room.

He wasn't quite sure what to make of all this. First his guide had been viciously killed in the forest. He'd then bumped into this moody mercenary and had his own dance with death, and now he was here! In some enchanted house in the presence of some... sorceress? It all seemed a dream. He almost expected Death and his scythe to pop out from behind one of the bookshelves, bearing some more cheery news.

112

He then strode towards the wall to have a closer look at the tapestries he'd noticed earlier. Thorne had to admit that they were really quite incredible and had clearly been hand-woven with great patience and skill.

He paced around the room, his arms folded against his chest, eyeing each tapestry for a short while before moving on to the next. His eyes eventually stopped and held on the one in the darkest corner of the room.

At the far left of the tapestry, kneeling, Thorne assumed from exhaustion rather than awe, was a knight. His golden armour and the sword he held high were both spattered with blood.

At the other side, towering over the comparatively fragile-looking knight was an imposing beast. It was gigantic with huge flaming wings and spikes the size of a grown man erupting out of its spine. A torrent of flame spiralled from its gaping maw, encircling the lone soldier.

Thorne could not tear his eyes form the tapestry, he was captivated by it. Strangely, he could have sworn he'd seen this knight somewhere before...

'I wove that one myself,' Zakariyyana said, causing Thorne to jump.

'It's... it's amazing,' he said, suddenly conscious of how disconcerting it was to not be able to see the woman's eyes.

She smiled and Thorne blushed, stupidly concerned that she could somehow hear his thoughts.

'It is kind of you to say,' she beamed, 'the fable of Hrokomar has always interested me.'

'Hrokomar?' Thorne said, 'as in 'the Vales of Hrokomar'?'

'The very same,' Zakariyanna said, 'you have heard the stories?'

The Masters of the Spire frowned on the idea of anything other than tomes focusing strictly on matters of Majik essential to the function of a Warlock. So, the few fables that reached students of the Spire were always passed on by word of mouth from traders that came by.

'A few, I think,' Thorne replied.

Zakariyanna caressed the tapestry with the back of her hand and extended a finger at the golden knight. 'Do you know who this is?'

Thorne shook his head. He knew he recognised the knight from somewhere. Perhaps he'd just heard a description once, which matched the depiction of the tapestry.

'The knight was known as Fierslaken,' the woman explained, 'former King of Horizon, prior to the cities' claim to autonomy, and lord of the decimated city of Räne. Legend says he was the fiercest warrior to walk this land and fought with the strength of dragons.'

'Dragons?' Thorne's interest peaked, mystified by Zakariyanna's words.

'Yes, tis' quite a tale if you would care to hear it?' Zakariyanna offered.

'Please,' Thorne answered eagerly.

The woman laughed and then launched into her tale.

Twas hundreds of years ago when great beasts of legend such as this walked the earth, inhabiting the islands known as the Fire Isles. They were known as dragons. They were fearsome creatures who

114

often warred amongst themselves, never settling for a moment. Despite their violent nature, however, it was said that man revered them and worshipped the beasts like Gods. They built magnificent shrines and monuments in their honour, some which still stand today.

But not all were content with their destructive rule, hundreds who had lost their homes, family and cattle to these dragons were furious and wanted blood.

It is said that they were led by a legendary warrior called 'Fierslaken'.

After numerous brutal battles over a great many, bloody years, the dragons were slaughtered to the point of extinction and most of their great monuments burnt down.

The last dragon left was Hrokomar, the most majestic of all. Fierslaken managed to goad the beast into a duel to which many starry nights bore witness. There are still parts of the Vales of Hrokomar to this day where neither grass nor flower dare rise from the ashes of dragon-fire.

And yet, to the surprise of many, the great dragon Hrokomar was slain by the warrior and his name forever sealed in glory by dragon blood.

Some say that after the battle he decided to bury the beast as a mark of respect. Others say that he, instead, drunk the beast's blood, till its body was dry, and hung its head in the great hall of Räne.

Of course, the truth of events that occurred all those years ago has been distorted by time. Still to this day do scholars discuss at length the great battle.

It was said that the All-Father, God of all Gods, Ozin, gifted the warrior and all those of his bloodline with Godly power, to look after the common people for eternity. Others, however, believe that Ozin was furious with the warrior for destroying such a magnificent race of beasts. They say that his rage blackened the sky as he lay a curse upon the warrior that would consume him and all his line for eternity.

'So, the end–'

'A myth,' Zaine interjected, appearing suddenly, 'nothing more.'

'You have never been one for such tales have you, my dear Zaine?' Zakariyanna laughed.

'No, I have not,' Zaine replied, in a tone that seemed to bring finality to the topic of conversation.

The woman maintained her smile, albeit a little thinly Thorne observed for a moment, before it vanished entirely. He briefly considered probing Zakariyanna further but decided otherwise. He could always ask Zaine later.

'Now,' she turned to Thorne, 'before we attend to the blissgiver, I understand that there is a rather unusual artefact, which is currently in your possession. Would you like to see some light shed on this little mystery?'

Thorne frowned and looked down at his robes. He could feel it under the garments, but it was well out of sight. The woman couldn't have possibly seen it, and he certainly hadn't shown it to Zaine.

He raised his eyebrows at the Swordsman in confusion.

His companion simply shrugged.

'I'm a seer, darling,' Zakariyanna chuckled lightly, 'I'm afraid you're going to have to get used to this.'

'A seer?'

'I can see into the past, present, the future, when given an opportunity to do so.'

'So... you're like a palm reader then?'

The woman laughed raucously. 'Not at all, no! I merely can establish a connection with a variety of objects and people I feel drawn to. Of course, I can force a connection with someone if I need to.'

'How?' Thorne inquired, keeping a firm grip on the rod by his belt.

'How else? What connects us all, dear Thorne, if not blood?'

Thorne then slowly pulled aside his robes and unhooked the rod. He turned to Zaine, who nodded, and then reluctantly handed it over.

'You'll get it back soon,' Zakariyanna smiled reassuringly. She then turned her attention to the rod, tracing the long nail of her index finger along its grooves. The usual dazzling smile had been replaced by a frown; an expression that her face seemed unaccustomed to.

'Well? What do you see?' Zaine demanded.

The seer remained silent for a moment, continuing to trace her fingers over the metal. She eventually broke contact to reply in an intrigued tone, 'this is no ordinary object...'

Thorne frowned. Perhaps his earlier suspicions hadn't been far off after all.

He became slightly concerned when he spotted a blue light radiating from the seer's hand, but he chose not to say anything. She played the light across the surface of the rod, murmuring softly to herself.

117

Zakariyanna paused, running a forefinger over the irregular, raised runes that formed a ring around the base of the rod. 'I wonder...'

Suddenly, the rod began to vibrate. Thorne was startled by another sudden spike in Majik, as the rod's engravings started to furiously flash green. It then soared away from Zakariyanna's open hand, into the centre of the room, rotating slowly around its axis; every candle it illuminated was immediately extinguished.

Thorne watched in incredulity as one of the ends of the rod became incredibly bright; so much so that Thorne had to shield his eyes with his hand. Then, without warning, the light emanating from the rod too was smothered. The room barely illuminated by the few flickering candles that remained alight.

'Wh–What was that about?' Thorne stuttered, staring at the slowly rotating rod.

'Wait,' Zakariyanna whispered, raising a hand.

As if in response to her motion, the rod hummed back into life and released a single green ball of light, which orbited the rod, following its slow rotation. Gradually, the rod increased its pace. Matching its speed, the ball crackled and hummed, moving further from the rod, as if through centrifugal force.

Suddenly, the rod fell silent and stopped rotating. Without warning, the ball flew at Thorne and, before he could raise his hands, plunged into his chest.

He staggered backwards, gasping and pulling at his clothes frantically. Zaine made to move towards Thorne but Zakariyanna grabbed his arm. 'No, we must wait.'

Thorne glanced up at Zakariyanna. 'Get... it out...of me!' he whispered imploringly.

In truth, it hadn't hurt at all, he just felt strangely numb around his arms and face. The green light had now begun to glow through his skin. He felt a strangely familiar itch, as his eyes flared.

Zakariyanna, much like Zaine, was transfixed. 'I'd read tales but this,' she breathed, 'this is quite... extraordinary.'

There was a brief silence, broken only by the hum of the rod, as it started spinning again.

'Extraordinary?' said a familiar voice, *'I am far more than that.'*

Chapter 10

'Can you see one,' asked Varg.

'Smell, not see,' Vince replied curtly.

'Same difference,' Varg grumbled, holding the reins of the horse in one hand, so he could use his free hand to scratch an itch on his backside.

It was raining in Féy. It always seemed to be raining in Féy, Varg realised, as the cart rattled and jerked along the uneven, cobbled pathway.

It was still busy though, choc–a–bloc full of people about the place. The men walked briskly to and from shops, using the large newspapers they'd bought earlier in the day to cover their balding heads from the incessant rain. The women stood idly by the buildings, under the overhanging roofs, holding elaborate yet silly looking, frilly umbrellas over their heads, despite the fact that they appeared too flimsy to survive even the lightest of breezes.

It was said that Féy was a city of great culture, to Varg however, it looked like a city full of idiots, a big city full of idiots. How were they ever going to find one kid in the middle of all this?

'Smell anythin' now?' he asked Vince, poking his absurdly hooked nose.

'Oi!' Vince exclaimed, 'don't do that!'

'I swear to the Gods, Vince, if we don't find that little sod soon I'm going,' Varg growled, adding with malice, 'and I'm leavin' you here.'

Vince glared at the bearded man, regarding his spot-covered face with dislike, 'yeah? Just try it, and then see how good *you* are at finding that little sod?'

Varg snarled and spat on the road beside the cart, 'just hurry up a bit would ya then, I'm bloody freezin'. I swear this 'aint worth an 'undred gold pieces.'

'two 'undred, stupid,' Vince reminded him, 'and that's just up front, the Cloaks are promisin' a thousand *each* for when we find the sod.'

'Humph,' muttered Varg.

The gold was certainly tempting, but he would've given all the gold in the world for a warm bed right about now.

'The cloaks had better pay up, or they'll be gettin' more than just words from me,' Varg promised, running his hand across the smooth blade by his hip.

That was just for show of course. He needed Vince to know that it was he who was in control. He kept the truth to himself, and the truth was that the Cloaks and their masters scared the living daylights out of him.

He could remember vividly the time, two weeks ago, when he'd visited one of the local pubs in Dalmarra, 'The Grey Grit'. The 'r' had fallen off a month before, leaving the sign to display 'The Grey Git', which was both amusing and decidedly apt, given the innkeeper's demeanour. So, Varg decided it had earned five silvers for a jug of beer.

He should have known something was amiss when the aforementioned, mean–spirited innkeeper, an obese man with a heavily waxed, curly moustache, took his coin with a smile too wide for his face, and told him to 'have a nice day.'

No-one ever told him to 'have a nice day,' the kindest thing someone had told him the last time he'd handed over his gold was to shove his 'zitty little head down a barrel and bug off.' Politeness didn't really go hand in hand with innkeepers, particularly this one, and especially when it was Varg on the opposite end of the bar.

Unfortunately, he realized that the drink was drugged when it was too late – when he was on the back of a horse snoring against a cloaked figure in front of him. That was when he had met Vince, the hooked nose man who, like himself, had been sitting behind his cloaked captor with his hands tied behind his back and his legs strapped to the horse's body.

'They drug you up as well?' he remembered Vince ask him, 'I swear that's the last time I go to a pub.'

Of course, he was only half awake at that point and he merely grunted in response before succumbing to sleep again, the hooked-nosed man's words not registering clearly in his head.

Once their captors had arrived at their intended destination, he and Vince had been untied and thrown into the mud.

'What the 'ell?' Varg had growled at the Cloak, spitting out a mouthful of muck, reaching for the dagger at his side that, of course, was no longer' there.

The man had then grabbed him and pulled him close to his face. Under the cloak, his captor wore a black metallic mask which completely obscured his face.

'Utter one more word and, by Athrana, I'll kill you here and now,' his captor said. He hadn't doubted the cold sincerity of the man's words for a second and just managed to gulp in reply.

122

'Do you understand me, filth?' the Cloak had asked, pressing his own dagger against Varg's exposed neck to let a trickle of blood flow onto the ground.

Varg nodded quietly.

Satisfied, the cloaked man had wiped the dagger on Varg's tattered shirt and then dragged him by the scruff of his neck.

Vince had followed in behind with his own captor, whistling a song completely out of tune.

'It's alright,' he'd said, 'if they wanted to kill us we'd be dead already!'

'You think I don't know that?' Varg had growled back, 'just shut the 'ell up would ya.'

Vince shrugged and continued with his tuneless whistling.

Inside the cave the Cloaks lit torches illuminating the many tunnels before them.

'This is for you, scum,' his captor had snarled, placing a thick strip of leather over his eyes.

Varg closed his mouth, recalling his captor's previous promise before he could retort in some way.

He remembered as he was guided through a tunnel, completely blind and helpless, that he'd never felt so cold in his life, or quite so bloody afraid for that matter.

Where was he? He'd thought, and what the hell had he done to deserve this?

Okay, when he did look back, he was a bit of a thief... and a con... and a murderer... but a man has to make a living right?

They stopped suddenly and that was when Varg heard a cold, chilling cackle of a laugh that sent chills down his spine. He'd felt so exposed, very conscious of his bare neck, and he'd tried to tuck his chin into his chest only to have it pulled sharply back up by the Cloak.

'*You've done well,*' a deep, husky sort of voice had said.

He felt his body lurch forward, as the Cloak bowed graciously to the hidden speaker.

'Forever your servants we are, my lords,' the Cloak replied courteously.

Lords? He thought. How many of these freaks were there?

He tried to raise the leather strap on his face by shaking his head and furrowing his brow. The Cloak instantly caught on to what he was attempting and struck him hard across the face.

'You are not permitted to look upon your betters,' his captor had hissed.

'*Let him be,*' another voice commanded, more guttural.

'*Yes,*' the husky voice agreed, '*we don't wish to harm a potentially valuable resource.*'

'*Then let us ask of him what we seek and send him on his way,*' the third voice said, smooth as you like but about as comfortable as the edge of a blade.

'*Yeeeessssss,*' they all agreed simultaneously.

Who were these men he'd thought, they were bloody strange, that much had been for certain, but what were they on about? What 'potentially valuable thingamijig?'

124

'W-Who are you?' Varg stammered.

The Cloak struck him again.

'*Let him be!*' the guttural voice said more sharply.

His captor hissed in response.

'*You ask a valid question, cutthroat,*' the husky voice said.

'*We imagine you must be quite confused and we do apologise for the manner of your arrival,*' the silky voice had said.

That was when he had made a stupid mistake, believing himself to be in control of the situation.

'Damn right you should be, you buggers,' he had said boldly, 'now let me go before I- AGH!'

The husky voiced 'Lord' had growled and he'd felt as if his head was being stabbed with thousands of tiny needles.

'ARGHH! PLEASE!' Varg screamed, and then it stopped. He could not recall feeling as relieved as he had when the pain had gone.

'*Consider that a reminder of who has the power here,*' boomed the guttural voice.

'*You are here because we demand it,*' said another.

'*And you will die if we command it,*' added the last.

'What do you want?' Varg cried.

'*Oh, many things, but from you? Just one small task shall suffice for now,*' said the silky voice.

'This should be interesting,' Vince muttered.

The Lords ignored him. *'We wish for you to roam the land of Féy,'* the silky voice said.

'Why?' Varg moaned.

He then felt another sharp pain, this time in his chest.

'Because we demand it!' boomed the husky voice.

'My friend is correct,' the silky voice purred, *'but my fellow Lords, how can he do what we need without knowing our wishes?'*

'Hm. Very well...'

'Agreed.'

'Cutthroat,' rasped the husky voice, *'we want you to find a particular child gifted in the arcane.'*

'Gifted in the what?'

'The arcane, you fool! Majik!'

'But how in the blazes am I gonna' do that?'

'You humans are useless by yourselves, we understand this. Fortunately, however, you are not alone here. Bring the re-ject forward!'

There was a shuffling of feet and he twisted his head and heard the other captive, 'oi!'

'Silence!'

Vince fell quiet.

'Are you aware of the reason you are here, re-ject?' asked the silky voice.

'Is it because I'm incredibly good lookin'?'

126

The husky voice snarled and the other man screamed, 'Ow! OW! SORRY!'

'You're not here to joke with us, re-ject, you're here because we demand it! And you will do what we say because we command it!' the guttural voice growled.

'Okay, okay,' Vince muttered dejectedly.

'Cutthroat! The re-ject will help you find this gifted child, and once you have found him you will bring him to us!'

'Why should I work with him?' Varg asked.

'If you don't, you will fail. Your sense of smell is blinded by your commonness. The re-ject, on the other hand, was once an applicant for the Warlocks but they thought him unworthy to even attempt their tests. However, he has been touched by Majik and will recognise its unique presence wherever it may be,' said the silky voice.

'Fine then,' Varg spat, 'anything else, your *lordships* want?'

'No, that will suffice, but we also understand your human needs and we will provide you with payment.'

That rang a bell in Varg's head and his attitude instantly changed.

'How much?' he asked, adding quickly, 'my lords.'

'200 gold pieces should meet your requirements for the meantime, and you'll receive a thousand more when the task is completed,' said the silky voice.

'And only when it is completed,' added the husky voice.

And that had been the end of it. They were taken back out, their blindfolds removed to see the horse and cart waiting for

127

them along with Varg's prized dagger and the promised 200 gold pieces sealed in two leather purses.

They'd spent weeks hunting for this 'arcane kid' and they'd not seen a damn sign of him.

It was to be expected of course, Féy was vast and huge; while they were in the lower markets of the capital, the kid could be on the higher or on the other side of the city. If they failed to find the child in Féy they would then have to move their search to the surrounding cities or, worse still, the dreaded mountains.

He buried his head in his hands. It was hopeless; they were never going to find this child.

'Is everything alright?' Vince asked.

'Please for the love of 'ell, tell me you smell somethin'?' Varg begged.

'Nope,' Vince replied.

'Nothing? Well what can ya smell now?'

'What? Right now?'

'Duh.'

'Pies and piss if I'm being honest.'

'No, you dolt! Can you bloody sniff some Majik?'

'I told you, if I find someone I'll tell you, besides I'm too hungry to find anyone,' Vince replied, wrinkling his nose. 'This weather doesn't help either mind.'

'We've got a job to do,' Varg said.

'You need me to get the kid, and I'm telling you I'm starvin',' Vince replied.

He then pointed to the right side of the street. 'Look, there's a butcher's right there,' he said eagerly, 'I say we go in and share a bite of somethin'.'

'Fine,' Varg muttered wrenching the reins to bring the cart to a halt.

He then paid the carriage man, who'd stepped forward to meet them, a few silvers and told him to keep the cart where it was.

'Share a bite,' Varg grumbled under his breath as he kicked open the butcher's door, 'I'll have my own bloody bite.'

*

Vince lobbed the remains of the pork in his mouth and patted his belly appreciatively. Féynians certainly knew how to cure their meat, that's for sure, he thought, as he lounged on his chair inside the butcher's store.

He and the bearded man, Varg, had been looking for Majik potentials for almost a week now with no luck. He really couldn't understand how the Warlocks put up with the boredom, considering it generally took them several weeks to find recruits, and that's if they were extremely lucky and had more men to do it.

How would two men, only one of them able to sense Majik, be capable of finding one child in a city? It was impossible;

he knew it, Varg knew it, and so did the Cloaks and their masters.

It was probably all a joke.

He sighed, realizing in disappointment that it was time to go. He looked over at Varg who had already finished his two sausages and was now gambling away the rest of his gold with two other burly men in some stupid card game.

Vince shook his head sadly and prepared to get off his seat. He should get the cart back off the carriage man and then–

He froze and reached out to the air in front of him, waving a hand to and fro as if to clear away smoke.

He had suddenly felt… he had sensed Majik. He could feel it in air like tiny vibrations that reverberated through his senses. He couldn't quite describe the smell, or the sensation of feeling the presence of Majik. It was like taking a hit of Whiteye, his drug of choice. It made him feel almost delirious. He wanted more. He needed it.

It was then that a boy walked past him, only past the first ten years of his life at most. He wore a pair of torn shorts, a dusty shirt, and a cap covering his coal–smudged face. He was also shoeless.

He was munching on a sliver of horsemeat, completely unaware of the fact that he was being stared at in amazement by the thin, hooked-nose man to his right.

Vince licked his lips. It was now or never he realized.

He then jogged to the end of the room, attracting a few glances from the shop's occupants and stopped at the front door blocking the boy's path.

The boy looked up and frowned at him, or at least he thought he did.

'Scuse' mista,' the boy said.

He didn't answer, he just stared ahead at his companion willing him to take a glance. Just one glance, that was all that was needed.

'Scuse!' the boy said, louder this time. Now, everyone was beginning to notice. Varg had looked up this time to see what all the commotion was about but so had the two burly men and they were blocking his view.

He weighed up the options in his head, he could grab the boy and make a run for it and hope Varg would be behind him. That would risk inciting the shop and all the people in it, or just let him go and try to find him afterwards.

There was really only one option for him to take.

Vince cursed his fortunes and stepped out of the child's way, grumbling 'sorry.'

The boy grunted and then left the butchers. Varg came to him soon after, moody with his losses, 'what was all that about?' he demanded, 'and why are ya so pale?'

'Th–the boy,' Vince stammered.

'Boy? What boy?' Varg spat.

'Th–the one th–that just left,' Vince stuttered, 'it was him. He's the one, the one we're looking for.'

Varg then went pale too.

'You let him go?' he hissed. 'You idiot, we've been tracking this bugger fer days and you let him go?'

131

Varg stormed out of the butchers, Vince having to jog after him to keep up. They both mounted the cart waiting outside, elbowing the carriage man onto the ground.

'Wait a minu–,' began the carriage man.

'Go!' Varg growled, whipping the reins.

The horse neighed and the cart wildly lurched forward and rolled ahead.

'Which way,' Varg roared over the torrent of rain.

Vince closed his eyes and followed the scent. It was weaker now, but he could still just, barely make out the smell of the kid and see the trail he'd left, like smoke from a fire.

'Over there,' Vince shouted back, pointing at an upcoming street, 'through there.'

The cart made a sharp turn and they rolled down another street, houses and shops flying by.

'There!' said Vince.

They saw the kid walking up the street, passing a bunch of the umbrella ladies on the way, and then he turned around the corner and disappeared from view into an alleyway.

'We've got him!' Varg barked with delight, 'cornered like a bloody rat!'

*

The boy woke up and groaned, his head still sore from the punch he'd received.

He'd always been told that the alleys were safe, nobody but the 'rabble' like himself and the other coal workers went there. Why did that have to change now? Why had the two older men been after him?

'Boy's awake,' a man said.

He tried his sit, but he realized to his dismay that his arms and legs had been tied down to the cart.

He struggled against his bonds, his body thrashing against the wood of the cart. It was no use.

'You're a live one,' the hooked-nose man said staring down at him.

The boy spat at his face in response. 'Argh,' the man growled in disgust.

'What?' asked the other man.

'Twit spat at me,' the hooked–nose man moaned, wiping his face with a dirty sleeve.

'What did you expect?' the man chuckled, 'with a face like yours...'

The man scowled, 'you're one to talk.'

The bearded man laughed again.

'Let me go,' the boy demanded.

'Fraid' we can't do that, kid,' the bearded man said.

The boy swore at the man, shouting at him with all the venom he could muster.

'Take these,' the bearded man said, handing the other the reins.

The hooked–nose man grunted sourly.

The bearded man then came into view his arms resting on the top of the cart, his face just a few inches from the boy's. The man was ugly as hell, with a smell to match, his breath heavy with mead and meat. He was also covered with spots and small scars across his sagging cheeks, evidencing a strong battle with acne, which made him appear far older than his years.

'Alright, boy,' the man smiled, revealing a set of yellowed teeth and shrivelled gums.

The boy swore at him in response.

'You got a mouth on ye, boy,' the man said, drawing a heavily notched dagger from his belt, 'maybe I'll enjoy cutting it off of ye.'

The boy pursed his lips, his eyes fixed on the blade.

'I thought so,' the bearded man said, pocketing his blade and returning to the front of the cart with a laugh.

The boy closed his eyes, fighting back tears. Why was this happening to him? Why?

Suddenly the cart slowed down to a halt and he heard the two men dismount, one tended to the horse and the other came for him. He was cut loose of his bonds and chucked carelessly to the rough ground.

He cried out, but despite his pain he tried to make a run for it. However, his legs were sore and gave his intentions away and he was knocked to the floor again.

'Get up!' the bearded man ordered, thrusting him to his feet.

He grimaced as he felt the man mercilessly clench a hand over his bruised arm.

The strange men with the cloaks that he'd overheard his captors discuss in the cart, were waiting for them by the entrance to a cave nearby; torches held in one hand and leather strips in the other.

When the strips were finally placed over his eyes and he was directed into the cold of the cave, the boy did something he thought he'd never have to do.

He prayed.

*

'Masters, the men you sent out have returned with a boy,' spoke a Cloak.

The child heard nothing but silence in response, and then a second later a soft voice, vibrating within the cavern greeted them. *'So, you have returned...'* the voice said.

'You are late,' another said, once with a voice like steel, *'do you wish to test our patience?'*

'Be calm my brother,' the soft voice said, *'It is good that they have returned successful, rather than not at all, wouldn't you agree?'*

'Let us hope they have been more successful than the others,' the voice growled in response.

The boy frowned. Who were these strange men?

'Others? What others?' the boy heard one of the men ask.

'Let us see this child, for ourselves,' another said, its voice seemingly rasping from its throat.

'Nah, nah, nah,' he heard the bearded man say disapprovingly. 'We did your job, now 'and over the gold.'

'You dare?' said the steeled voice, *'you dar-'*

'Wait! Brother this human is correct, he has done us a service and is now due his payment,' said the soft voice.

'Our payment,' the hooked–nose added. He was ignored.

The steeled voice paused, chuckled and replied with what seemed like a hint of glee *'but of course, my brother is correct. You are deserving of payment... human.'*

The moment the voice had finished its sentence, he heard a sizzling sound off in the distance, or close by, which made him jump. He couldn't really tell how far away it was as the sound just echoed all around the cave.

He realized it sounded a lot like they were heating and cooling metal.

'Good,' the bearded man said, 'now give it over!'

The voices weren't angry with him anymore, instead they seemed to be chuckling quietly amongst themselves, and this alarmed him more than anything else.

'Bring the cutthroat and the re-ject forward,' the voices instructed, *'leave the boy where he is.'*

He then heard a shuffling of feet and the Cloak's grip on his shoulder tightened, stopping him from making any sudden moves.

'Open their mouths,' the steeled voice commanded.

136

'Wait, wha–?'

The men grunted in pain and he heard multiple thuds as they fell to their knees.

'Oh Gods no! No! PLEASE! 'AVE MERCY!' the boy heard one of the men beg.

He then heard an odd sloshing sound, and the screams soared into the highest crescendos the boy had ever heard. And then it was all silent, and he was left, shivering madly at the thought of how his kidnappers had been horrifically murdered.

He may have been young but he'd seen and heard enough to know that they had died in one of the most horrible ways possible. The boy remembered the sizzling sound of metal from working in the factories and coal mines and the smoke that clogged his airways was from molten gold. Even he would not have wished such an awful death upon them.

And now I'm left with them, the boy thought, the sudden terrifying reality striking him.

The voices cackled, their laughter sending cold ripples across his body.

'*Bring the boy,*' one of the voices said.

The Cloak behind him propelled him forwards, his hands digging into his shoulder.

He was all alone now. No one could help him. He closed his eyes and submitted himself to the darkness. He prayed, but the Gods were silent.

Chapter 11

The light intensified as the hummimg voice echoed around the room, illuminating the shock Thorne dimly knew his face must be showing at this moment.

For years this object had remained that, just an object; yet twice now, in the space of a few weeks, it had decided to break its silence. Decided... Thorne shook himself mentally. Mere objects could not speak, and yet, this was a strange world he lived in. So few things seemed impossible here. The line between reality and fantasy was so blurred it was miraculous that chaos and madness didn't greet him at every corner.

'Thorne?'

Snapping out of his delirium, Thorne raised his head to see the seer and swordsman gazing at him.

'Did you hear that?' Thorne asked.

'Hear what?' Zaine replied.

'The... the voice...' Thorne said.

The bandages that covered Zaine's face scrunched together into a frown. He shrugged his shoulders and turned to Zakariyanna, who crossed her hands together and remained eerily silent.

Thorne ran a hand through his hair. The absurdity of his words only now just striking him. Hearing voices now? Ozin's Throne! Had the whole experience finally broken his mind?

'Thorne...' Zaine reached out towards the Warlock, only to have his hand pushed away.

'I'm fine!' Thorne snapped, 'It was just a mistake...'

He tried to convince himself otherwise, though he was truly concerned with what the pair of them must have thought of him then. But he was certain he had heard that voice. That same voice that had accused him of being a 'thief' just a few weeks ago, just before his encounter with Death. Gods alive... he really was going mad.

The silence seemed to last an eternity before the seer finally broke it with seemingly uncharacteristic hesitancy.

'Perhaps... whatever you may have heard, Thorne, was meant just for you?'

'It was a mistake,' Thorne mumbled, reaching for the rod.

The seer - with what Thorne thought to be some reluctance on her part - held it out for him to take. Thorne mumbled his thanks and hooked the rod back onto his belt.

The seer's mouth had formed a noticeably hard line under her veil, as distinctly apparent as her sudden loss for words. A trend Thorne found somewhat alarming. Did she know something he didn't? What was she withholding from him?

'What was that light?' Zaine said.

'I cannot say,' Zakariyanna replied, 'I am sure it is harmless but perhaps the young Warlock should be wary of this artefact.'

'Seems like a cheap parlour trick to me, dwarf manufactured maybe,' Zaine muttered, crossing his arms, 'you can't seriously believe it could be dangerous?'

139

'There are things in this world that are so ancient their true purpose is hidden, even to me,' the seer said, 'I would treat this artefact with an open – but wary – mind.'

Thorne felt an involuntary shiver creep down his spine when the seer turned to face him. It was uncanny how uneasy she made him feel, even with her eyes hidden behind a veil.

He turned to the door but not before Zaine laid a heavy hand on his shoulder.

'Where are you going?' he said.

'I thought I'd go out, I need some air,' Thorne stuttered.

'What's wrong with you? Don't you want to find out about what the blissgiver did to you?' Zaine countered.

'I–' Thorne paused. He had not come to see his master die. He had not wished to travel to the City of Light with a strange man. He wanted to go home and forget all thoughts of monsters, visions and talking rods. Everyone had seen the rod light up like a firework but only he had heard its voice. Or at least, he thought he had.

He was sure the Seer knew more than she cared to tell him but the idea of pressing this powerful being for information made him anxious, as did the thought of reliving those last moments with the blissgiver. But he supposed it couldn't hurt to have some forewarning of what was to come. 'I guess...' Thorne said hesitantly, 'what do I need to do?'

Zakariyanna stood in the centre of the room, beckoning him closer. Reluctantly, Thorne edged forwards. She gently lifted his hands from his sides and held them in her own. Even this close to her, he could barely see past the opaque veil. Zaine aside, he'd never been more curious and yet apprehensive to

140

see what lay hidden beneath. Was she blind? Perhaps her and Zaine had disfiguring scars, too horrific to be touched by the light of day.

The seer chuckled, and Thorne found himself blushing. He was almost certain she read his mind. He shook himself free of the ridiculous notion and cleared his throat.

'What's going to happen?' he asked.

'Nothing particularly painful,' she said, 'but I'm going to need something from you first.'

I'll bet it's blood, Thorne thought dispiritedly, remembering their earlier discussion.

'Oh yes.' Zakariyanna continued, as if replying to Thorne's thoughts. 'My majik cannot be precise without first witnessing your past, I must take into account everything you've done and everything that you are.' Zakariyanna explained, 'For that, I must take something that is part of your very being,' She said, reaching her hand deep inside the many folds of her dress.

Thorne suddenly pictured Rozenhall's body in the enclosure – all the blood soaking into the grass and sloshing down the throats of the alpha wolves – and staggered backwards, expecting a huge knife.

Zakariyanna produced a pin. 'I only require a few drops,' the seer said kindly. Thorne blushed and held out his hand.

The seer gripped his hand.

'Is this really necessary, boy?' a familiar voice tickled his ear, *'you humans never learn.'*

141

Thorne hoped the seer missed his grimace, as she gently pricked the end of his thumb.

She then turned his palm upside down, holding her hand underneath, and squeezed his thumb. A drop formed at the end but, to his surprise, it did not fall into the seer's hand; instead, it hovered above, forming a small crimson sphere. Further droplets fell from his thumb and, once the sphere had swollen to the size of an eye, she relaxed her grip and ran her index finger over the end of Thorne's thumb. When her hand had moved away the stinging had ceased and the cut had disappeared completely.

The sphere of blood lowered agonizingly slowly towards Zakariyanna's palm, pausing just above her skin.

She lifted her head towards Thorne, 'no matter what happens, do not fear or worry. I am perfectly safe. If I appear to be in great pain do not attempt to interfere, lest you wish to suffer great torment.'

Thorne gulped and nodded in return.

The seer leant forward, sighing as the blood vanished into her skin.

Thorne felt his eyes widen but held his tongue, not wishing to interrupt the seer, considering the vast effort she appeared to be making just to concentrate on whatever she was doing. He felt his skin bristle and the hairs on the back of his neck stand on end as the Majik levels in the room suddenly spiked again. If Zaine was at all affected, he was very careful in hiding it.

The seer's hands began to tremble as her body – much to Thorne's alarm – rose from the ground. The glow of the candles in the room began to slowly diminish at the rate at which the seer's utterances gathered in pace and volume. Her hands drifted in the air in front of her, stroking things that only she could see.

'So many possibilities... So many outcomes... So much... Pain...Fire,' they heard her whisper, 'shadows... shadows in the dark.'

Then, without warning, her hands shot back down by her sides, her head snapped up towards the ceiling and she screamed.

Thorne made a move towards the seer but was held back by Zaine's iron grip around his arm.

'She's your friend, Zaine!' Thorne shouted.

For a moment, Zaine's grip loosened, and when he looked up at the Swordsman he thought he saw the man's jaw sagging ever so slightly.

'She knows what she's doing,' Zaine replied calmly, his grip solidifying again, although Thorne was certain that even the Swordsman had never seen her like this before. How powerful was this woman, whose Majik sent shockwaves through his senses, threatening to tear them both apart at any moment?

'The long night is nigh!' the seer gasped. Although it was not in her voice that the words had come forth. Or perhaps it had been, but one of many all desperately attempting to claw above the others to the fore; the words entering the room contorted.

As abruptly as it had ensued, the screaming ceased and the seer plunged towards the ground. Zaine barrelled past Thorne and caught her just before she smacked against the floor.

'Yanna,' the swordsman whispered, gently releasing the seer to her feet, 'what did you see?'

'I...' the seer lifted a hand to her head, 'that was... unusual.'

'You screamed,' Thorne said, and then felt his skin pale as he realised what this could mean for him. She'd seen something bad in his future, something really bad. He fought against the shudder, which caused his knees to quiver and tried to gather his composure. 'What did you see?' Thorne asked warily, instantly regretting the words as soon as they departed from his lips.

The seer was distinctly hesitant before offering a reply.

'The future is by no means a certain thing, Thorne,' the seer began, 'so many things can alter the path one can take, not just your own choices, there are so many things to consider–'

'But what did you see?' Thorne repeated.

'Yanna,' Zaine urged her, 'the boy needs to know.'

She removed her hand from her head, exhaled, and then in a voice that barely rose above a whisper, 'my dear, if you reach the City of Light, all that awaits you is... all I could see... I saw flames... I saw you being consumed by flames.'

Chapter 12

The wind blew around the mansion, causing the trees to swing about. Their few remaining leaves that flew from them and swirled in the air, like a swarm of bees, parted as the cloaked man strode through. The wind seemed to shriek as he neared the house, rattling against the windows as it tried to escape him.

His cloak billowed about his ankles as he stopped in front of the grand double doors that towered over him, daring to block his path.

The corner of the man's mouth curled and he snapped his fingers. The doors creaked open, releasing a wind that rushed out of the house with a groan, desperate to be free.

The cloaked stranger marched forward into a corridor, the doors slamming shut behind him immersing the interior in darkness. The man waved his hands and the braziers on the walls came alight with fire as he passed.

A tiny man waited for him in the middle of the foyer. The man had stubble on his cheeks and an uneven mop of hair that hung lankly around his ears. He wore a dusty grey tailcoat, pinstriped trousers, and tattered shoes.

The man was hunched over, his eyes squinting past the flames of the candle he held on a plate.

'M–m'lord–' he stuttered, cowering before the man.

'Put that out,' the hooded man ordered, not even paying the other man a glance as he walked past him.

The hunched man laughed nervously and quenched the flame with his fingers, stowing the plate and candle in the volumous pockets inside his tailcoat, and followed behind.

The man came to a sudden halt beside an oak door.

'Are they all inside?' he asked.

'Yes m'lord,' the cowering man replied meekly, 'all with the exception of Mr Baron, m'lord.'

'Of course, and I understand that he has a message for me, Sontiris,' the hooded man said, holding out an open hand expectantly.

Sontiris fumbled in his pockets and drew out a folded envelope.

The man took it and ripped out the letter inside. He took a brief look at the content, before throwing it into a nearby brazier to burn.

'It will have to do,' the cloaked man said, grasping the door's handle. 'Follow me,' he instructed.

'Yes, m'lord,' Sontiris mumbled, tagging along in his master's wake, as he passed through the now open door into the huge hall.

The room had a cavernous ceiling like those found in worship halls. The mustard walls were bare and losing their colour, the corners turned black from mould and mildew.

In the middle of the room was a long table where several men sat, candles illuminating their anxious faces.

'Gentlemen,' the man purred.

The men flashed their heads in the direction of the cloaked man, expressions of unease displayed on their grim faces, which they tried, unsuccessfully, to hide by hanging their heads.

'Shadow,' the men murmured.

He chuckled softly and slowly sat himself at the front of the table overlooking all its occupants, and then adjusted his hood for effect.

The hunched man limped behind, laughing timidly along the way, and stopped by The Shadow's side.

The Shadow peered from face to face but found no-one with the courage to return his gaze.

He also noticed to his satisfaction that none of his colleagues had even touched their wine, and kept their hands as far away from the glass as possible. Clearly their previous meeting hadn't quite faded from memory.

'I trust you are all well?' The Shadow asked with mock care.

'Yes, my lord,' some of the men mumbled.

'I assume some of you have reports to make?' The Shadow inquired.

The men whispered amongst themselves and then all heads turned to one of the men closest to The Shadow; a large man with a bright red Mohawk.

The large man, who The Shadow recognised as Evren, a bodyguard to the Council, stood from his chair and cleared his throat onto his clenched fist.

'My lord...' Evren said uncomfortably, 'I... have news.'

'I am listening,' The Shadow said, folding his hands together calmly.

The man licked his lips, glancing anxiously at his colleagues before explaining, with difficulty, 'one of the Regal councillors, Raël has been found... dead, in his chambers... my lord.'

'Oh? And how did his lordship end up as such?' The Shadow asked.

'He was murdered my lord, by the assassins.'

There were angry murmurs among the men.

'Quiet,' The Shadow hissed, and they fell silent.

'Go on,' he instructed the man with an inclination of his hands.

He shuffled his feet and stared at the table, 'officially the Regals blame the Brotherhood of Wolves.'

The Shadow sighed, 'I'm afraid it seems that not all the assassins are a part of our cause.'

'Yes, my lord.'

The Shadow looked up and shook his head slowly, 'he was under your protection, was he not Evren?'

Evren could not meet The Shadow's gaze. He instead mumbled something incoherently and nervously picked at his nails.

'I beg your pardon?' The Shadow asked.

Evren exhaled deeply and, with clear reluctance, 'that is not the only... regrettable information we have to offer...'

'Really? What else do you have to share?' asked The Shadow.

'We found information on the child, my lord,' said Thomas, a balding man with a goatee, slowly got to his feet, 'we believe to be the heir of Fierslaken.'

The Shadow leaned forward and took a sip of his wine, 'and what *information* is this?'

'My lord, we're dreadfully sorry to tell you this... but the child... the boy was captured by the Necromancers.'

A hush fell over the room, and the men glanced fearfully at The Shadow who seemed to have become frozen in place at the end of the table. One hand was clenched on the table's surface and the other was curled tightly around his drink.

CRACK

The Shadow crushed his empty glass in his hand and let the pieces tinkle individually onto the floor.

The men closest to The Shadow flinched and sat rigidly on their chairs, hands clamped to their thighs.

They were all in trouble. They had never seen The Shadow show any sign of anger, but now, they feared, they were about to.

'He was instrumental to my plans,' The Shadow said in a soft but lethal voice, 'I am... most displeased.'

Evren sat back down on his seat and unconsciously rubbed his neck.

One simple task, The Shadow thought, one simple matter to trust them with and he had again misplaced his trust.

He pointed at the loose glass on the floor, 'Sontiris.'

149

The hunched man bowed and gathered the pieces with a cloth, stowing them in another pocket inside his tailcoat.

The Shadow ignored Sortiris as he worked, and glared at his colleagues.

'While you have made a disastrous mess of things, gentlemen, it is, thankfully, not one that is completely irreparable,' The Shadow growled.

There were murmurs of assent, silenced when The Shadow raised his hand.

'We must resolve the issue between the Regals and the Brotherhood before a faction war ensues,' The Shadow continued. 'They will both be needed in what is to come...'

'Indeed, they will,' said another voice, strikingly female.

A woman walked forward, her bare feet making soft taps on the floor.

The men may not have felt it, The Shadow didn't expect it from them, but he could feel something strange about this woman. It was not just the aura of supreme confidence that oozed from her, no, but the Majik. So much Majik. It seemed to burst from every pore in her body.

The woman, despite her brimming confidence, hid everything but her smile, with her maroon dress and veil.

She sauntered past The Shadow, warmly touching his shoulder, and took the empty seat nearest to him, all to the surprise of The Shadow's men.

They watched open mouthed as she gazed at them all with a broad grin.

'I quite like it here!' she exclaimed, breaking the silence, 'it has a certain... feel to it.'

'Who is this woman?' Thomas demanded.

She turned towards the bald man, who frowned at her.

'Ah, Thomas,' she greeted him, 'looking as unsightly as ever.'

The strange woman's comments lightened the mood in the room and several of the men laughed.

'You dare woman?' Thomas snarled, his face turning a blotchy red. He then drew his dagger and pointed it at the woman, 'maybe I should teach you your place.'

'Maybe you should try,' she smiled.

The man's frown deepened and then he yelled out in shock and pain, as the dagger's blade melted into his hand until he was left holding the hilt.

'But not today,' she added.

Thomas swore.

'Silence,' The Shadow commanded.

The man glared at the woman, as he nursed his scalded hand, whimpering softly as a strong burning smell drifted across the room. The group wrinkled and rubbed their noses in disgust, but The Shadow could not help but smile.

'I have missed you,' he told the woman admirably.

'And I you,' she beamed, 'but I came to discuss the matter of Thorne; what does the Baron intend to do with the Warlock?'

'My lord, she has no right–'

151

The Shadow lifted his hand in the air again, and then leaned back on his chair and tilted his head around to examine the room.

'She is quite right,' he said out loud, 'it's quite a lovely house isn't it.'

The men around the table murmured in approval and shifted uncomfortably in their chairs, wary of how The Shadow would end his statement.

'Do any of you know who owns this house?'

'You, my lord?' the men answered, glancing at each other confusedly.

The Shadow smiled, 'I do now of course, however, it was not always so. I think you all know exactly who owned it before, because I acquired it shortly after Vervanis left my service...'

He could see now, with satisfaction, that many of the men had gone pale. The woman, on the other hand seemed bemused by the tension The Shadow had brought.

It was then that he added maliciously, 'enjoying your drinks my friends?'

Half of the men froze in their seats, while the other half pushed away their glasses in unison, as though fearful that it might suddenly explode in their faces.

'Curious how quickly men's hearts shrink,' the woman murmured, 'are they really worth saving?'

The men didn't hear her, or, as The Shadow liked to think, were contemplating deeply how he planned to kill them.

'So, you wanted to know about the Warlock?' The Shadow inquired, 'do not worry, I have no quarrel with him, but I cannot allow the Hunter to interfere.'

'Zaine, as far as I know, is headed for the Hunters' Camp,' the woman said sternly.

'That may be so, but he may wish to accompany him after his visit and, quite frankly, it would suit me better if the Warlock went alone,' The Shadow replied.

'I will give you one warning, Shadow, if Zaine is hurt, If I find out–'

'You will not,' The Shadow promised, 'I intend to do no harm to him, but I must take precautions. You are a seer, do I tell a lie?'

There were a few quiet gasps around the room, and several of the men near the strange woman shuffled away in their seats, drawing as much distance away from her as possible.

The Shadow had many odd friends the men understood, but bringing a seer... in Horizon, it was thought to be bad luck to share a room with a seer.

'No,' she replied, 'but you know what will happen if I find out otherwise...'

'Like I said my lady: you will not, but why do you care so much for this man, especially considering the fact that he is, I've been told, a traitor and murderer?'

'You surround yourself with such,' she replied, waving her hand at his men.

'Good company I suppose,' The Shadow smiled wryly.

153

'Too right,' Thomas chuckled, albeit louder than he thought, falling silent as soon as The Shadow turned an ear to him.

The Shadow then bent over to the side to whisper something to Sontiris, who giggled nervously in response and then limped back in the direction of the door.

'Now, allow me to show you how I keep the rabble under control,' he whispered joyfully to the seer.

The Shadow then turned to the group in front of him and clapped his hands to address them. 'My friends! I thank you for coming to meet me here, but before this meeting is adjourned, there are a few... other things that must be dealt with. Our plans will come to fruition and we shall have what we strive for!'

The men nodded silently in approval.

'However, although I am not pleased with many of you, I am willing to overlook most of your failures.'

The men looked up worriedly. The Shadow's statement had felt more threatening than reassuring.

'Thomas! Evren! Both of you are no longer needed in my service, you may now both leave in peace,' The Shadow said.

The men stood up and frowned at him. 'M–my lord?' Evren stammered.

'You failed to protect the Regal councillor and, as such, you are accountable for the trouble brooding between the Regals and Brotherhood.'

Evren hung his head shamefully.

154

'And you, Thomas,' The Shadow rounded on you were responsible for the intelligence on the boy. Because of you, the child is now in the hands of our worst enemies.'

Thomas's voice trembled as he spoke, 'I- I have given everything-'

'No!' The Shadow growled, standing up suddenly, encouraging the men to sink further into their seats, 'I have promised you the world and you have returned with nothing.'

Thomas visibly shook with The Shadow's words and Evren had sunk into his chair.

'As you wish, my lord,' Thomas bowed.

The Shadow waved them off, and the pair strode towards the door, through which Sontiris had left.

At first there was quiet, as the remaining men glanced anxiously at each other, wondering what was to follow.

Then, as soon as the door had slammed shut, they heard the screams. They were such terrible screams that human ears should never have to hear, and yet The Shadow smiled.

The seer bowed her head and closed her eyes, appearing discomforted.

Then as the screams began to subside, The Shadow turned to face those still seated at the table and asked grimly, 'who else would like to disappoint me?'

Chapter 13

Thorne had not slept well for days since the seer's prophecy, and when he did succumb to the night, he found no solace in his dreams. He dreamt of a long, winding stone staircase which seemed to go on forever. Although, he could never bring himself past the first few steps, for fear of what lay in wait for him. At the top of the stairs, by the middle of the tower, in front of a vast set of oaken doors, stood some evil. Or rather it did not stand, nor did it take shape or falter in the wind. It rippled in the air, leering over him, a mass of shadows that had greedily drank both the light from his dream and all sense of hope. It threatened to take him too.

'Thoooorrnnneeee!'

The voice had come from behind him. What new evil would his dreams present to him tonight?

He could only bring himself to slowly twist his head and observe the demon from the corner of his eye.

Amidst the darkness he saw nothing. But before he thought to turn back, he saw two plumes of smoke burst out, like foggy breath from a horse's snout on a winter's day. What manner of monster would crawl out from the darkness Thorne wondered. Despite his expectations, neither claw nor fang emerged. In amongst the hot smoke, a pair of green eyes blinked open before him. No, green was too simple, an almost offensive description. These eyes shone like emeralds in the darkness, glistened like diamonds in sunlight. Their fierceness brought him little comfort but, strangely, neither did they fill him with fear. He simply stared back, blinking in synchronization with the emeralds before him, fixed with pure wonder.

*

'Enough!' Thorne gasped, dropping the staff Zakariyanna had gifted him, his sweat–drenched body collapsing to the ground with it.

Zaine had insisted on gruelling combat drills a couple of days after they had left Zakariyanna's home.

It had been, seemingly, never-ending hours of learning how to hit Zaine accurately and with speed. The swordsman must surely have known his plan was doomed to fail. Without Majik, Thorne felt useless. He couldn't manage to land a single blow on Zaine, without hurting himself in the process, or unless Zaine allowed him.

The worst injury he'd given the tall warrior was a tiny burn on his arm. He'd received about twenty nicks himself (self–inflicted mostly) on his hands, in addition to a horde of welts and bruises.

'I thought we agreed you would *not* use Majik,' Zaine said, grimacing as he patted the burn on his arm.

'What else could I have done?' Thorne demanded, wiping his forehead with the back of his hand. 'They gave us books, not swords in the Spire. Even if I had been training with a blade, you move too quick. I have never seen a man do... what you do. Look at you! You have barely a bruise to show for it!'

Zaine sighed and sat down beside him, cleaning his sword with a cloth. 'You were better,' he said, 'a lot quicker and you did manage to hit me.'

'Once,' Thorne scoffed, 'and you let me do it.'

Zaine shrugged, his focus remaining on the blade before him.

Thorne shook his head in incredulity. He'd been travelling with this man for several weeks now and, in that time, he'd learnt nothing about him but his name and his inhuman abilities. He could not quite put a finger on the relationship they shared. He couldn't call it a friendship. But while Thorne could not say he ever felt at ease in Zaine's presence, he held a quiet admiration for the Swordsman.

'What are you?' Thorne blurted out the question, blushing momentarily after when he realised his blunder.

An eerie silence broke over the pair, as Zaine paused the ritualistic cleaning of his blade. When he spoke, Thorne felt he was weighing his words carefully.

'A man without a home,' the swordsman replied simply, then turned his attention back to the sword.

Thorne stood, frustratedly, before his companion for a moment, debating whether to press him further but thought better of it. What was so terrible about this man's past that he could not bear to answer his questions with anything other than cryptic remarks? Yet all the time Thorne had an uncanny feeling that the answers were right under his nose.

'Have you ever considered forgetting about Majik altogether?' the Swordsman inquired.

'What do you mean?' Thorne frowned.

158

'Have you ever thought that Majik is perhaps not what it once was? Like it is slowly departing this world?'

The thought had never crossed Thorne's mind, but the question unsettled him. Majik was a powerful thing, he felt privileged to be one of the few learning how to wield it. It was not a choice he could just make. He couldn't just 'turn off' the Majik within him. How could he? Even if he was given the choice? He had the power to mould his dreams into reality. Fire in the palm of his hands. Moving things with the blink of an eye. What else could one wish for?

'I'm a Warlock... or, at least, I hope to be. What else is there to do for me in this world, if I lost Majik?' Thorne returned, looking the swordsman for what seemed like the first time, right in his silver eyes.

A silence descended, broken by the squeak of Zaine's sword, as he ran the cloth down the other half of the blade. 'Have you ever considered that perhaps this world is no longer deserving of Majik?' he said. 'Sorcerers of old would cross continents to help others in need. Nowadays your people huddle together in your blasted tower, indifferent to the world outside, as you desperately fan the dying embers of Majik. Crime has taken control of Horizon, corruption, greed and war has seized the factions, and foreign nations live in fear of the shackles of slavery. Is it any wonder that Majik has chosen to depart such a world? You Warlocks were once capable of moving mountains, now you struggle to lift mere rocks.'

Thorne frowned, staring at Zaine, while trying to take in what he had said. In truth, he was struggling to remember seeing the masters exhibit the *great power* Warlocks were meant to possess. Thorne shouted in frustration, 'Majik or not, what hope do I have! You heard what the seer said!'

159

He remembered the words vividly. The room had gone awfully silent after Zakariyanna's prediction. There Zaine had stood, holding up his friend whose face had turned almost translucent. He, probably equally pale as the seer, stuck in a moment that seemed to drag for hours.

The Warlock in him tried to insist that this was all nonsense. This palm reader was a mere illusionist, nothing more. But her sincerity, and Zaine's sheer trust in her, seemed incompatible with his thoughts. Furthermore, if his recent experiences meant anything, there was more to fear in this world than had been taught in the safety of the Spire. Nothing, it seemed, was impossible outside. Demons, death, so why not prophecies?

He shook himself. What was the point of all this? If he was to die, what could he possibly do to stop it?

'So, you've given up?' Zaine asked.

Thorne shot the swordsman a sour look but could not bring himself to disagree.

'Hmm,' Zaine grunted, 'well, let me tell you what I believe: I believe no future is unchangeable. I'd trust Yanna with my life, and I trust her visions. But nothing is set in stone. Do you understand? Your fate is your own. Anyone who believes that their lives are decided by the roll of the Three's dice are deluded or foolish, or... both.'

'Sounded pretty set in stone to me,' Thorne muttered sullenly.

The swordsman sheathed his sword and let out a great sigh. 'Yanna's visions are not to be taken lightly, but they do not always tell the truth of the future ahead. It is more guidance than prophecy!'

160

'Well, it's guiding me to my death, at the moment,' Thorne retorted sulkily. He jumped to his feet, brushed off the grass that had collected in the creases of his robes and walked off.

'Where are you going now?' Zaine asked quietly.

'To lie down,' Thorne replied curtly, 'I think I've had enough for one day.'

'It's still early,' Zaine said, 'we could do with another hour or so...'

Thorne glared at him and turned to the structure in front of him. They had found the ruin whilst travelling the plains. A cracked stone statuette of a beast's snout, filled with dagger like teeth, all but confirmed this was one of the old dragon shrines. Time had not been kind to the statue, however the structure of the ruin was more or less intact and had provided welcome cover from the elements for the two travellers. Vegetation had claimed the shrine, with roots and leaves forming a vaguely comfortable bedding above the rock. Flowers of whites and yellows had bloomed in the corners of the ruin, lapping up the light that shone through the cracks in the ceiling.

When Thorne reached his bedroll, he found a number of crows nipping at the bag that contained his provisions.

'Shoo!' Thorne shouted, waving his arms. The crows squawked madly and, in a flurry of wings, they disappeared into the sky.

With a weak smile, he threw himself on the bedroll and buried his hand inside his satchel.

'Do you intend to spend the rest of the day like that?'

Thorne jumped.

What? He thought, withdrawing the rod from his belt.

The object showed no sign of activity.

He peered outside the ruin and found Zaine still a fair distance away, running his cloth carefully over his blade. He ducked his head back in and held the rod in front of his eyes.

'Can you actually talk or am I going mad?' he whispered desperately.

The rod did not answer.

Turning his head quickly in wide arcs to make sure he was alone, Thorne pressed the rod again.

'Please. Help me, I fear... I fear– I don't want to die!'

Again, his questions were unanswered. With a cry of exasperation he tossed the rod inside his satchel.

What was he to do? He could not return to the Spire without completing the mission bestowed upon his former master. The Binding had seen to that. But if he attempted to complete the mission... well, his fate was sealed, according to the seer.

Thorne buried his face in his hands. What had he done to deserve this? How had he upset the Gods for them to leave him with this choice?

He faced life as an outcast, a mere wanderer. Or death.

In the depth of his mind, the Swordman's words returned to him... 'a man without a home.'

Before he could ponder this further, a rustling noise awoke his senses. He lifted his head and almost jumped.

162

At the entrance of the shrine a girl stood. She could have been no more than 10 years of age, covered in rags for clothes. She did not look like anyone Thorne had seen. Her skin was not pale like his or Zaine's, but dark as the night. When she spoke her accent was considerably harsher than anything he had heard in Dalmarra. He had heard of her people before, from the Scorched Isles. A supposedly desolate place where only the strong survived.

'Hello, I'm Thorne. Who are you?' Thorne asked.

The girl drew closer repeating the same sounds she had before with increased fervour.

'I'm sorry, I don't understand,' Thorne said, shaking his head.

The girl was becoming increasingly distressed, as she persisted with her cries.

'Perhaps my friend can understand you...' Thorne said calmly, while moving slowly towards the entrance to the ruin, trying not to alarm the girl. 'Zaine!' Thorne said in as loud a voice he dared.

Suddenly alarmed, the girl bolted from the shrine, only to run headfirst into the swordsman. She screamed at Zaine and pounded her tiny fists on his torso. Zaine crouched down in front of the girl, held her fists in his hands and muttered something back to her, in what, Thorne thought, was the same language.

The girl immediately stopped bawling and looked into the swordsman's eyes with wonder. She ran a hand down his bandages and muttered something quietly back.

Thorne was taken aback. He had hoped Zaine would have some understanding but how did his companion know how to speak the tongue of the Scorched Isles? Had he met this girl before?

He watched the pair exchange a few more words, then his companion turned to him. 'She needs help, her family is in danger.'

'What do you mean? Who is she?' Thorne said, pointing at the girl.

'A girl who needs her family, she says her settlement was attacked,' Zaine replied.

Thorne paused. 'Attacked by what?' he enquired nervously.

'Nothing you need to worry about. You're not due to be barbequed until we reach the City of Light, remember?' Zaine retorted with a grin. Zaine prodded the girl forward and marched along with her.

'Oh, very funny,' said Thorne, scooping up his satchel and jogging after the two.

*

Thorne scowled and looked ahead, past where the girl stood pointing.

The land was utterly barren. The grass ended in a circle around the settlement, then there was just dry soil and sand, which whirled about in the air with the cool breeze.

Inside the desolate circle were several meagre huts. Thorne thought that they seemed to be constructed poorly – just bundles of grass and straw tied together in a knot at the top.

164

The covering was kept in shape by thin planks of rotting wood exposed within the foliage.

There were nine huts which all circled around the centre, where loose clothes, more wood, and a few other random objects were strewn about carelessly on the ground.

But his gaze was drawn to the huge, hulking great trees beyond the camp that towered over everything. Although he realized that this forest couldn't be the same one he'd been to previously, it was still rather unsettling to be around.

'I don't like this,' Zaine murmured behind him, 'there's something... amiss.'

Thorne scowled. 'Oh, now it's a bad idea?' he said, following the girl into the camp. They went with her into the closest cabin where they saw a small table with its legs snapped and frame cut in several places. There were also more loose clothes and half–eaten food - bread and deer meat - strewn across the floor. They even found a cracked dagger among the mess of wood and clothes, stained with dry blood.

'Ajfr! Ajfr!' the girl called out.

They followed the girl past the table where she stopped and pointed at the mess of planks and wicker baskets on the floor.

Zaine lifted them up with both his arms and threw them effortlessly aside.

'A hole,' Thorne observed.

'She must have hidden here,' Zaine said.

The girl then tugged at Thorne's pantaloons and pointed at the entrance.

Zaine asked her something, or at least Thorne gathered he had, in the girl's language, to which she duly nodded.

'Ain,' she agreed.

The girl then led them to the centre of the camp where there was a pile of blackened, smoking logs that met altogether in the middle.

The wood still emanated a strong burning smell.

'A hearth?' Thorne asked.

Zaine crouched down to examine it closer. 'A hearth,' he confirmed, 'still warm... they were taken recently.'

'Who could have done this?' Thorne asked.

'Not much sign of fight, little left in tracks, these people are professionals,' Zaine said. 'My money's on slavers.'

Thorne scratched his head. There was little evidence bar the clothes and objects to suggest anyone had lived here at all.

'Dokram,' she told him, pointing at the hearth.

'Sorry?' he replied.

'Dokram,' she reiterated.

'What do you want me to do?'

'Dokram!'

He glanced at Zaine, who shrugged his shoulders but she continued to repeat the same word over and over again while indicating the set of burnt logs.

'Dokram! Dokram!'

166

Thorne rubbed his chin thoughtfully. 'Maybe... her friend's stuck under it.'

'She does seem quite distressed about it,' Zaine pointed out, 'but still...'

'Well, we're going to have to have a look then,' Thorne said.

He then stepped forward and raised his leg.

'Wait... something's... amiss,' Zaine muttered, sniffing peculiarly at the air.

Unfortunately, Thorne hadn't heard him. So intent on doing what he thought was right, he kicked the logs away and with a resounding *CRACK,* the ground gave way beneath them.

'What the–' Zaine growled, the rest of his sentence disappearing along with the ground.

Thorne yelled out in shock and the girl began to wail. Then there was silence.

Chapter 14

'**WAKE UP...**'

Thorne groaned, and through the fog of his eyes he saw something glinting.

He felt hands softly lift him to his feet, bracing him when he staggered.

'**HELLO AGAIN.**'

'Who?' Thorne mumbled.

'**GREETINGS,**' said a smooth voice.

Thorne squinted and his eyes began to pick up on his mysterious surroundings.

He was back in the white room again, everything was maddeningly the same colour except for the wooden door with the silver handle at the end of the small room.

Directly in front of him, his arms curled behind his back was the golden man. Now that his sight had been given time to focus, he could properly see the strange man.

He wore a white tunic which fell to his ankles and covered his arms up to his wrists. He had a slightly darker shade of gold than his skin for hair. The man had a perfectly set nose, downward sloping eyebrows giving him a mischievous look, gleaming white eyes with no pupils or iris and he wore a broad smile.

'You again,' Thorne pointed at him.

'**YES, IT IS I,**' the man smiled, '**HOW ARE YOU FEELING?**'

'I–' Thorne began, then his eyes widened as he suddenly remembered what had happened to him; screaming as he was falling... falling. 'I'm dead, aren't I?' he asked the golden man, dreading the answer.

'**WHY DO YOU THINK THAT WAY?**' he replied.

'I–I fell...' Thorne muttered absent-mindedly, recalling the sickening sensation he'd felt in the pit of his stomach.

'**YES YOU DID, FALL INTO THE TRAP THAT IS,**' the man said, shaking his head sadly.

'So I'm– I'm dead then?'

'**WE SHALL SEE...**'

Thorne frowned. *What kind of an answer is that?* He was either dead or he wasn't, so which of the two was it?

Unfortunately, his efforts of repeating and rephrasing the question were in vain. He began to worry that the golden man's reluctance to tell him about his current state was because he only had bad news available to give.

'What of the others?' Thorne asked, 'Zaine and the girl?'

'**IT IS BEST I DO NOT SAY,**' the gold man replied.

'What do you mean?' Thorne demanded.

'**YOU WILL FIND OUT, I PROMISE,**' he assured Thorne.

Thorne opened his mouth to speak, but he couldn't think of anything to say.

'**IT IS REGRETTABLE, YES, BUT FORTUNATE, AS NOW I — THROUGH THE WILL OF MY MASTER — MAY SPEAK TO YOU.**'

169

'About what? And who is this *master* you speak of?'

The golden man smiled and guided him towards the door where he slipped in a glowing gold key into the silver keyhole.

'**AFTER YOU,**' he said, inclining his hand towards the door.

Thorne raised his eyebrows sceptically at the door. 'Where does this lead?' Thorne inquired, 'to your master?'

'**SOMEWHERE... DIFFERENT,**' the golden man replied.

Thorne sighed. He had no choice but to follow this odd... spirit.

He looked the door up and down. What wonders lied beyond he thought, as he grasped the handle and pulled open the door.

'Gahhhh,' Thorne gasped, shielding his eyes from the blinding light that issued from within.

'**YOU CAN LOOK NOW,**' the man told him after a minute, pulling Thorne's hands away from his face.

Unwillingly, he obeyed and was awestruck by what he saw. Hundreds of shining stars that surrounded him and comets that flashed past him, leaving trails of colour in their wake.

'Where are we?'

'**NOWHERE IN PARTICULAR, AT THE MOMENT.**'

Thorne rolled his eyes and tried to discern for himself what was happening, which was when he realized that he wasn't actually standing but flying. He was surrounded by the starlit sky everywhere he looked.

This was certainly the oddest yet most exhilarating dream of all.

Before he could comment on this peculiarity, however, the dark starry sky suddenly vanished with a blink of an eye and a new scene unfolded before Thorne's eyes.

'What the–?' Thorne began, completely stunned.

They'd arrived at the back of a large hall, which stretched on for several hundred yards.

Dining tables and chairs were stacked neatly against the torch–lit walls, to allow for the huge crowds that had gathered inside. The tightly packed bodies were separated by a thick red carpet and lines of heavily armoured soldiers with pointed helmets obscuring the top half of their faces, their swords held out in front of them, points on the floor.

Clunk!

Clunk!

Clunk!

Thorne looked past the soldiers to see a remarkable spectacle.

A man at the end of the room wearing dazzling, scaled gold armour – almost rivalling the shine of the golden man beside Thorne – clunked his way up the fragile, small stone steps, warmly grasping the hands of the soldiers. The crowd roared in delight with his every step.

Just beyond the sparkling knight was an imposing, but spectacularly shaped stone throne.

The throne consisted of two man-sized, snarling dragons, whose L–shaped inner wings met together to form the seat. Behind, the wings, the creature's tails intertwined together to form the back of the throne. Shooting out of the dragon's

171

open jaws were stone flames, which formed the magnificent throne's armrests.

The golden knight had short dark hair, but when he turned to sit, receiving a chorus of appraising roars from those gathered, Thorne saw he also had a gold mask covering his face.

Thorne noticed, to his surprise, that the man had a familiar looking rod attached to his side, which gave off an equally familiar green glow.

So, there were more of these?

He placed his hand on his shoulder but didn't find the strap of his satchel. Thorne sighed, it was to be expected. This was a dream after all... he hoped.

At the front of the throng of commoners, a priest garbed in purple robes, with a bushy snow–white beard that curled around his neck like a scarf, stepped forward.

He placed his hands together, as though in prayer, and bowed his head to the golden knight, who inclined his head politely in return.

He saw the priest's head bob slightly and Thorne assumed he was talking to the masked man, however, he was inaudible over the cheers of the gathered crowd.

'I SWEAR!' the golden knight boomed suddenly, his tremendously powerful voice causing Thorne to tremble, and the crowd to applaud and pump their fists ecstatically into the air.

Satisfied, the purple garbed priest bowed to the golden knight and then received a large wooden chest from a member of his entourage.

Thorne stood on the balls of his feet to try to get a better view. He saw the priest open the chest and heard the awed murmurs from the crowd. The priest drew out a gleaming gold crown, to match the masked man's golden armour, with amber flames spiralling across the sides and a sparkling red ruby set in the middle.

Thorne could make out the movements of the priest's mouth, as he whispered something to the awaiting warrior, and then slowly lowered the crown on the golden knight's head.

A hush fell over the audience, as the ruby began to glow brightly consequently after being placed on the man's head.

'I NOW PROCLAIM YOU, FIERSLAKEN, HIGH KING OF HORIZON!' the priest bellowed.

'ALL HAIL!' the people yelled in unison, clapping their hands and stamping their feet so loudly that Thorne had to clamp his hands tightly on top of his ears.

It was then, as he looked away he noticed something strange: a hooded man at the back of the group who stood apart from the people, quietly observing the scene.

What really scared him, however, was the long-handled scythe the stranger held by his side, which was shaped like a spine, and then the blade with the writhing faces, silently screaming.

Thorne paled as the hooded stranger turned around to face him and then with its hand, the skin missing from the yellowed bone, pulled down its hood to reveal the flame–eyed

173

skull. Death gave a brief look of exaggerated surprise and then waved at him.

The blood drained from Thorne's face, he blinked and the hall and all its occupants disappeared. Thorne and the golden man had returned to the white room.

For a moment he was speechless, staring open–mouthed at the door they'd passed through. He wasn't sure how it had happened or even *if* it had happened. Perhaps it was a figment of his imagination. But somehow, Thorne thought that they'd actually travelled back in time.

It was impossible! There was no Majik, no matter how powerful, that could do that. But how could this be a dream when it was so realistic, when he actually seemed to exist there.

'**QUITE AMAZING, WAS IT NOT?**' The golden man asked, laying a hand on his shoulder.

Thorne jumped at the touch of the spirit's hand. 'What did I just see?' he asked.

'**THE CROWNING OF THE FIRST HIGH KING OF HORIZON,**' the golden man replied.

'Yes, I heard that!' Thorne retorted, 'but why was Death there? And the king had my rod, and–and–'

'**SLEEEEP,**' the golden man sang, placing a finger on the middle of his forehead.

'But–'

Before he could finish, Thorne felt himself begin to slip away.

Falling...

Falling...

Falling forever...

*

'Where now?'

'Up the hill right there, the boss would like to have a word with him.'

'I thought 'e wanted us to gut the pig.'

'Why are you carrying him then?'

'Because you told me to.'

'Exactly, now shut up!'

Thorne eyes opened but he was greeted only by darkness. He worried briefly that he'd lost his sight but was relieved to realise he'd been blindfolded with a piece of dark cloth folded tightly around his head and mouth.

He also began to be aware of a pair of hands at his back and at his calves, roughly gripping his robes.

Thorne could feel, he could breathe, and hear. He had somehow survived the fall. But what of Zaine and the girl?

'e's movin',' said a voice.

'Bugger's waking up, come one Tom, we're nearly there,' said the other.

Thorne could hear the man's ragged breath as he carried him but worse was the putrid smell.

Thorne heard the slamming of a door and he grunted as he was dropped roughly onto a hard surface. At least it was better here, he could feel the warmth of a nearby fire. The aroma of the room was kinder to his nose, he could smell a pleasant mix of flowers and the sweet perfume of what he presumed was fruit.

'Now, now gentleman, is that a pleasant way to treat our most esteemed guest?' tutted a third man disapprovingly.

'So sorry sir, but Tom isn't exactly the brightest–'

'Oi!'

'What? It's true.'

'Quiet! I will see our guest myse– What the devil? Who in Ozin's name did you bring?'

'Exactly the one you wanted, sir!'

'This is the Warlock you fool!' growled the third voice, 'I told you to bring the other.'

'You said the one with the glowing eyes!'

'One job I gave you morons! One bloody job! And you got me the wrong one! You got me the one I said specifically to bloody leave!'

'I–'

'Silver eyes I told you! Everyone knows they have silver eyes!'

'But–'

'Just shut up you idiot! Leave us be, now!

Thorne heard the sound of footsteps, the creaking sound of the door as it opened and shut and then the frustrated growls of the third man.

He then felt himself being picked up to his feet and guided to a soft chair, where the bonds holding his arms together and covering his mouth were cut and removed. Thorne thought it best not to speak, bearing in mind how angry the man seemed.

'Quiet, hmm?' the man commented dryly, 'calmer than I expected.'

He remained tight–lipped as the man then removed the blindfold. Thorne groaned as his eyes, blinded for some time by darkness, were abruptly introduced to the light once more. His sight was hazy, with multicoloured lights dancing in front of his eyes, as they adjusted to the sudden change.

The man then came into focus and Thorne gasped.

He had black hair, greased back over behind his head, which shined in the light. He had harsh, cold brown eyes, almost black, and an angular cruel looking face, which wore a mocking, seditious sort of smile revealing a perfect set of pearl white teeth.

'Hello, Warlock,' said the Baron with a grin, 'I don't think we've had the pleasure.'

177

Chapter 15

'Wanya!'

'Wanya straga!'

Zaine eyes flashed open and he saw the little girl thumping her tiny fists on his chest, stopping when she saw his eyes open. He jumped to his feet, cricked his neck side to side, and stretched his arms. He checked for his sword and breathed a sigh of relief when his fingers found the pommel.

Zaine looked down and saw the large hole he'd been dragged from and the scrape marks on the sides of the hole, presumably made by their unconscious bodies. That would explain the piles of ropes lying near his feet.

It had been a trap.

Luckily, he hadn't broken any bones, and nothing had been stolen, the little girl was staring up at him… Zaine looked around frantically. The Warlock was nowhere to be seen.

'Zaine…'

Zaine whipped round, his hand on his sword, but found no-one.

'Zaine…'

He looked at the girl who stared back at him silently. Could she hear the voice as well, he wondered?

'Down here…'

Zaine leaned over the side of the hole and looked among the rubble and spotted the glow of the rod.

'Thorne!' Zaine shouted but received no reply.

'Is it safe?'

'Yes, come up, quickly!'

Zaine stared open–mouthed as the rod detached itself from the rubble and floated upwards towards the bandaged man.

Putting aside countless questions, Zaine asked, 'Where's Thorne?'

'Not here,' the rod replied, *'he has been taken I am afraid.'*

'Taken?'

'Yes, by two men in fact. They came after a few minutes to check you both and then they pulled you out with the ropes. One was rather big and burly, and the other was a thin fellow. They argued over which of you to take for a considerable time and eventually they settled on Thorne.'

'Who were these men? Did they have a recognisable uniform, accent, anything?'

'I spotted an odd tattoo on the bigger man's hand – a muscled arm holding a dagger impaling a gold coin.'

'Skrunai,' Zaine growled.

'Indeed.'

'Why didn't you do anything?' Zaine demanded.

'What was I supposed to do?' the rod retorted.

'Fight them! You could have saved Thorne!'

'As you are aware, I am in no position to fight. No one must know I am sentient AND I have to be wielded by one with Magik, to focus my powers.'

'And now Thorne could pay the price…'

179

The girl stood against the frame of one of the huts, her head hanging.

'You led us into a trap,' Zaine growled in her language, advancing towards the girl.

'I–I didn't m-mean to,' she whimpered back to the man who menacingly towered above her.

She fell on her backside as he approached and cried, shielding her face with her arms.

He then crouched down onto his haunches and asked in a kinder, gentler tone, 'are you hurt?'

She shook her head.

'Did the Skruna– the bad men force you to find us and take us here?'

She nodded this time, looking on the verge of bawling. 'Have my momma and papa,' she whispered.

'So, her story was mostly true.'

'They'll have most likely taken him to the same camp where this child's parents are held,' Zaine thought out loud.

'Indeed, perhaps the child could-'

'No! She's gone through enough; I can find the tracks and get there myself.'

'Very well...'

The rod stopped glowing and then attached itself to Zaine's belt.

'I'll find my friend and your parents,' Zaine promised her, 'but I want you to hide here and wait till my return, I'll be back soon...'

*

Thorne pushed forward the white knight on his side of the board and muttered 'Check...'

The Baron did not keep a clock, and he had no idea how much time had passed.

The Baron had left the cabin to deal with *important matters*, or so he had been told. Thorne had yet to say a word to the Baron, so he doubted he made good company.

The Baron had left him an ornate chessboard, before giving him another creepy grin and disappearing through the door of his cabin. The Baron had, at least, told him where he was. A Skrunai slave camp. Admittedly, the shrieks coming from outside the cabin had given him a fair indication that it was somewhere unpleasant. The Baron had warned him, in no uncertain circumstances, that he was a prisoner as much as them, albeit currently afforded better circumstances.

Thorne heard the tap of footsteps along wood and looked up to see the Baron stride through the doorway towards him, with a confident, mocking smile, one of his servants trailing meekly behind him. He took the seat opposite to Thorne, with seemingly exaggerated slowness, and then silently observed Thorne's game.

Thorne ignored him and continued to play with his head down, his face flushing in anger. Now no longer giving himself a verbal commentary of the game but slamming taken pieces down on the adjacent table with more force than necessary. The Baron merely smiled, and folded his hands together as he watched, taking casual swigs from the wine glass handed to him by his burly servant.

When the game had finished the Baron clapped his hands together. 'Oh, bravo Thorne, bravo!' he said, 'however, I've never really seen the point of such a game…'

'Then why are you watching?' asked Thorne, 'why did you even bother getting a board and a set of crystal pieces?'

The Baron shrugged, replying nonchalantly 'why not? It seemed like a good idea at the time. But enough about me, why do you play?'

Thorne paused, reminding himself that he wasn't talking to this man, and folded his arms.

The Baron barked out a mirthless laugh and regarded the board silently for a while, stroking his chin.

'Then I suppose you won't mind if I join you?' he inquired.

'Why should I?' Thorne couldn't stop himself.

'Well… this is *my* board… and being here is so much more comfortable than being out there,' the Baron said, with a particularly malicious grin.

The servant chuckled sycophantically. Thorne blushed angrily.

Thorne pushed the chessboard to the middle, offering him the white pieces, which he took with a mock bow, and began placing on their required positions.

'So…' Thorne began, 'do I need to show you the rules?'

'No need,' the Baron replied pleasantly, 'I may not agree with you about the importance of chess, but I am quite the player nonetheless.'

'Hmph,' Thorne muttered.

The Baron grinned, and with the tip of a finger, pushed a white pawn forward. He then looked straight into Thorne's eyes, ignoring the contempt held strongly by his opponent and said in an amused tone: 'let the game begin…'

*

'I ain't seen you before,' the red–faced man said, doing the best he could to reduce the distance from his head to that of the man who towered above him.

Zaine folded his arms and regarded the man through the holes of his mask with extreme dislike, growling, 'and I have not seen you either. Am I to assume you are, perhaps, an impostor?'

'I ain't sayin–'

'I know who is who in this camp, and I also know what the policies are for dealing with masquerading brigands,' Zaine said.

'Masqa– what?' the guard blustered. 'What policy?'

Zaine stroked the large scabbard by his waist and in a dark voice he growled, 'perhaps my sword can better tell you.' He grinned triumphantly behind his mask as he observed his chosen words strike home with the dim guard, causing the man to go quite pale, astonishingly so considering his usual colour.

The guard glanced at his own sword, seemingly coming to the conclusion, Zaine could tell from his uneasy expression that he was outmatched, both physically and mentally. He nervously scratched at the tuft of hair residing on his cheeks and muttered disjointedly, 'g–go on in. I'll let the boys know you're comin'.'

The man then shuffled anxiously towards the gate, wiping the sweat off his brow with the back of his tattooed arm, before banging twice in succession on the wood of the large gate.

From the top of the lofty, sharpened wooden stakes another guard emerged examining the pair below with a bored expression.

'Alright, who's coming?'

'Another one of ours!' the guard bellowed back.

'Checked him through?'

The man looked anxiously back at Zaine and gulped. The swordsman quietly growled and tapped the pommel of his sword.

'All checked!'

The other guard nodded and then disappeared from the top of the battlements, and a second later Zaine heard a horn being blown. The sound seeming to vibrate the tall stakes

184

surrounding the Skrunai camp. Then with a metallic whir of gears and the sound of the un–oiled hinges, the gates slowly opened inwards, revealing the horror within. Zaine grimaced and walked into the slave camp.

In lines of twenty, men, women, and children were pulled by ropes, binding their wrists and feet, across the camp. Some were thrown into spiked metal cages and were whipped bloody until they were compliant. Others were directed to heaps of wood, where they were forced to hack through the seemingly endless piles.

Everywhere he walked, the air smelt strongly of sweat, excrement and blood.

'Move it!'

Zaine whipped his head round, automatically adjusting his stolen uniform. He growled, when he saw the guard dragging the leader of the line of slaves by the scruff of his neck, his knees bloody as they scraped across the uneven, muddy ground.

'Please sir,' the man begged in his nomadic language, tears darkening his dirt covered face.

'Shut up with yer mumbo jumbo!' the guard spat in response, giving the slave a sharp dig in the stomach with his knee.

Zaine strode defiantly towards the guard and grabbed him by the shoulder, whirling him round to face him. 'I'm taking over,' Zaine growled, his fingers digging as hard as they could into the man's skin.

'Who the 'ell are ya?' the guard demanded, pushing off Zaine's hand.

The warrior clenched his fist, his knuckles cracking in the process so loudly that the guard and several of the slaves jumped. 'I'm... taking... over...' Zaine said, stressing each word individually.

The guard screwed up his face and grumbled, 'fine... take the buggers,' and threw him the rope, stomping away in the opposite direction.

Zaine watched him go, his fingers playing across his sword's scabbard. He decided to ignore the temptation. He then regarded the group before him. Many of the slaves would not look at him, and others stared at Zaine with wide desperate eyes. All of them, he noticed particularly the men had multiple, long, pencil thin, white scars stretching in straight lines over their chests, backs, arms, and legs. Several of the scars intersected and others he saw had clearly not been given time to heal and had formed as bumpy weals. The children, most notably so, were almost skeletal, their skin stretched so thinly over their protruding bones they looked a fall away from shattering.

What madness had brought about this? Zaine thought disgustedly.

One of the children tugged at a man's arm and whispered something to him, receiving a sharp 'shhh!' in return.

Zaine turned to the man with scraped knees, 'where were you supposed to be taken?'

The man reluctantly pointed ahead of them at the row of cages lying at the end of the camp in a semicircle. The children began to bawl, and the others turned pale, their gaunt bodies trembling.

'Tell them that they will not be going in the cages,' Zaine told the front man in the nomadic language.

The man frowned at him, 'what?' he asked confusedly, and then became more composed, and leaned forward inconspicuously and whispered in the same tongue, 'you speak like us?'

Zaine nodded and then, noticing that his group was beginning to attract attention from some of the other guards, he hissed urgently, 'follow me.'

The man gulped and hesitantly turned to the others in the line, whispering something unintelligible to them.

He saw the uneasy looks on the groups' faces. This would be harder than anticipated, Zaine thought. He strode on ahead, giving the rope a slight tug. The man at the front nervously looked back at his companions.

The man was silent, for the walk across the camp, only moving his head to glance fearfully at the towering warrior beside him.

The man cleared his throat and then muttered something towards his muddy feet.

'What?' Zaine asked.

'My– my name is Emir… sir,' the man stuttered.

'Zaine,' the warrior replied.

The man nodded, not meeting his gaze. .

'You have no need to be afraid,' Zaine said.

'I'm sorry, sir. But we do.'

'Who do you think I am?'

'I don't know,' the man replied after a pause.

Zaine smiled and then whispered, 'get on the floor.'

'I'm sorry?'

'Get on the floor!' Zaine yelled at the man, raising his fist above him.

The man gasped, tripped over his own feet and landed on his side in the dirt. The others struggled for breath, anticipating yet another horrendous beating.

Zaine crouched beside the man and grabbed the front of his tunic, pulling him an inch away from his face, his other hand grabbing the knot by his hands.

'Don't ever do that again, you hear me?'

'Y–ye–yes s–sir,' the man stammered, his eyes following the movements of his hand.

Zaine released Emir, who slowly pulled himself up to his feet, the hatred evident in his eyes.

'You are just like the rest...' the man said.

Zaine pulled the rope causing the man to lurch forward, and come to a halt in front of him.

'Really? Then how can you move your wrists?' Zaine grinned.

Emir looked at Zaine questionably, and then turned to his hands, he twisted his arms and with an expression of complete shock, his arms twisted inside the knot.

'How?' Emir asked, speechless.

188

'It was the best I could do; if I moved on to your ankles people might get suspicious,' Zaine replied.

The man shook his head, 'I don't know what to say...'

Zaine smiled and then discretely lifted the mask up so it only covered his bandaged forehead.

The man gasped as he gazed into the warrior's eyes, muttering incredulously, 'Hunter...'

Zaine dropped the mask down, and gave the rope a slight tug again, letting the group trail slowly behind him as they walked.

The man gazed at Zaine open–mouthed in astonishment.

'How– you–'

'Tell me Emir: how soon do you want to be out of here?'

'Right now, sir.'

The warrior smiled, and then tilted his head to his right and whispered something quietly to the man beside him. Emir listened intently, nodding to show he understood, and visibly shaking with excitement.

'This... if this works...'

'It will work.'

The man then whispered to the woman following in line behind the pair and turned nervously back to Zaine. 'What word shall we listen for sir?'

Zaine thought for a moment, and then murmured back, 'rebel.'

*

'So, why have you brought me here?' Thorne asked, capturing one of the Baron's bishops with his only remaining knight.

The Baron looked back at Thorne with his customary mocking smile, 'I so rarely get such pleasant company.'

He then took the knight with a pawn, chucking the captured piece carelessly into his pile.

'I would have thought the reasons for that were obvious,' Thorne replied scornfully.

Annoyance flickered briefly over the Baron's face before the familiar sneer returned. 'My master wants you alive and well... currently. Perhaps you should bear that in mind,' the Baron snapped, adjusting the cuff of his sleeve.

They continued their game silently, the fire crackling soothingly behind Thorne as he played, encouraging thoughts to emerge from his mind.

Where is Zaine? How can I get away from here?

Thorne reluctantly faced the Baron and muttered, 'so, your master wants me to be kept here for how long?'

The Baron smiled, tossing another captured piece into his pile, and replied 'oh, just until we find your companion.'

Thorne felt his heart skip a beat, and hope flourished within him, 'he's alive?' he blurted out.

'Maybe, maybe not, we'll see,' the Baron said.

Thorne felt suddenly uplifted. The Baron must have noticed it too, as he added snidely, 'why are you so pleased? I wouldn't expect a rescue from such a man.'

'What do you mean?' Thorne frowned.

The Baron laughed, regarding Thorne with delighted surprise, 'you don't even know the *truth* about him? Ha!'

The truth? Thorne thought, biting down on his tongue in an effort to resist a tempting retort, what did the Baron mean? Was he playing with him?

'The truth,' continued the Baron joyfully, 'is that your 'friend' has been rejected by his own people.'

'What people and why should it matter?' Thorne said defensively.

'Dear me, you really don't know what he is, do you? You don't have a clue what you've been travelling with all this time,' The Baron laughed, 'have your people kept you so in the dark?'

The Baron leant back in his chair and stared at Thorne in mock incredulity. 'What ever does The Shadow see in you?' he muttered, then suddenly paled at his blunder.

'The Shadow?' Thorne frowned, 'is that your master?'

The Baron quickly composed himself and returned to the game.

'You misheard me,' he said, pushing a piece forward.

'I heard you perfectly,' Thorne retorted, 'are you scared of him?'

The Baron abruptly rose, swung his arm across the table, scattering pieces across the floor, and slammed his cane on the table.

In a tone that belied his rage, the Baron murmured, 'excuse me?'

Thorne withdrew his hands, conscious of how close they were to the wolf shaped head of the Baron's cane.

'I fear no–one,' the Baron hissed, thrusting the cane towards Thorne's chest. 'And as for The Shadow,' he said, prodding Thorne's chest twice with the cane for emphasis, 'you will forget I made any mention of him.'

Before Thorne could muster a reply, the door of the cabin slammed open against the wall and a wiry man stepped inside, the shins and ankles of his trousers besmirched in mud.

'My lord,' the man said breathlessly, staggering in the Baron's direction, 'the camp– they–they all–'

'What about the camp? Speak up man!' The Baron commanded, withdrawing his cane from Thorne's chest.

The wiry man breathed and exhaled deeply, 'they're loose, the slaves, all of them, one of the guards–'

'WHAT!' the Baron exploded, his face turning beetroot red, and his cheeks puffing out.

The wiry man flinched, and took an involuntary step back. The Baron looked back at Thorne, then at the shaking wiry man, and back at Thorne again, his eyes narrowing. He licked his lips, grabbed the wiry man by the scruff of his neck, dragging him along to the entrance where he chucked him outside.

The Baron then departed the cabin, hissing venomously, 'and you will stay exactly where you are!' and nodded to the burly servant.

Chapter 16

Zaine parried the blood-spattered guard's rusted sword with a casual flick of his own and plunged it through the man's chainmail armour effortlessly, as though it were made of paper. The guard let out a brief groan, as he dropped his sword into the mud, his body, swiftly draining of life, sank to the ground.

Emir, the man he had freed first, stood behind him, hacking his way through the guards with surprising speed and ferocity considering his emaciated state.

His stolen sword ripped through the guards with precise lethality, only pausing when he himself incurred a deep gash from one of the slavers' knives. The slave uttered a startled gasp, clutched his bleeding side and fell on his knees in the mud with a splash. Zaine pulled the guard back before he could finish the job, and with one hand, he decapitated the man. Zaine checked his surroundings and then ran towards the slave, rain spattering across his bandaged face.

'Are you alright?' he asked Emir.

The slave laughed, keeping his hand clamped firmly on top of his leaking wound, barking back with delight, 'they fall like fleas!'

Zaine pulled the man up to his feet, leant down and ripped a piece of cloth from a dead guard's shirt and the belt from the guard's trousers and placed them in the slave's hand.

'What is this for?' Emir demanded.

'You have an open wound,' Zaine replied, 'protect it.'

The man grinned and strapped the cloth to his waist.

Zaine lobbed a knife behind him without looking, the blade striking a guard a few feet away in the head.

'Ha!' Emir exclaimed, 'but I can't go on with you right now,' he said adopting a dejected expression as he looked at his injury.

Zaine glanced hurriedly behind him. The slaves were getting backed into a corner by the better armoured guards. If he went over to help, Emir would probably be killed, but if he stayed...

'Go on,' Emir sighed, 'before they get to my kinsmen.'

'Are you sure?' Zaine said.

'I'm dead anyway,' the slave murmured.

Zaine observed the man's wound with a grimace, noticing the blood leaking through the cloth.

He could stay...

'Go!' Emir bellowed hoarsely, wincing as his grip tightened on his side.

The screams at the other end of the camp were becoming more intense. It was now or never. Zaine growled in exasperation, kicked a sword across the mud to the slave, turned and sprinted off in the opposite direction.

'Keep yourself alive!' Zaine shouted back to him. He received no reply.

There were about a hundred slaves left, the rest of their brethren surrounding them in circles as bedraggled corpses.

195

The guards had them against the walls and were one by one executing them.

'Why do they not fight?' Zaine wondered.

'Fear,' the rod offered.

'But they can be free!'

'Some of them appear to have known oppression their entire lives. Their fear of resistance is natural and sadly infectious.'

Zaine watched the fight with disgust, the children were at the back crouched into little balls in the mud, only a few men fought back, but were soon surrounded by slavers who viciously cut them down.

'Wait, what of Thorne?'

'He isn't around the camp, so he'll be holed up somewhere else.'

'And what if he is in trouble?'

Zaine stopped running, only a few metres from the slaughter, his sword raised above his head.

'You could not have thought of this earlier?'

'I'm surprised you did not.'

Zaine sighed and shook his head. 'He will be fine,' he thought back.

'Really? How aware are you of his power?'

'I know enough.'

The voice fell silent, and Zaine returned to the screams of the dying slaves. He was only a few metres away from the fight he could still help them.

196

'You'd better stay alive Thorne,' Zaine growled and, with silent determination, the warrior sprinted into the fray, sword held high.

*

Thorne grimaced as chains were wrapped tightly around his arms, scowling at the burly man before him.

'Is this – ungh – really necessary?' Thorne asked.

The burly man glanced at him quietly, his grin revealing a number of yellowed, cracked teeth, some with golden caps. He pushed the Warlock down roughly onto a chair beside the Baron's table, wrapped another set of chains around the chair and Thorne. He then turned his back and started rummaging through a large sack he'd brought with him. Thorne watched the man's back for a few seconds and, as quietly as he could, wriggled his arms and legs. They would not budge. Thorne sighed, and tilted his back on his chair in defeat.

Admittedly, even if he was able to freely walk around; the door was locked and there were no windows, no obvious means of escape. So why did the Baron order this?

There was a jingling sound, like that you'd hear from a set of keys and the man began to laugh hysterically. It was a gruff manic sort of laugh and Thorne wasn't comforted by it in the slightest.

'Hey! Why did you tie me up?' Thorne said, 'it's not like I'm going anywhere with you here.'

'Can't blame the Baron for being careful,' the burly man laughed. He recognised the man's voice.

'Wait… I know you, didn't you carry me here?'

'Shut up, Warlock,' the burly man spat, pointing a knife in his direction, 'or I'll make sure you do, if you catch my drift.'

Thorne frowned at the sight of the blade but thought it best to do as the man instructed. While he knew the threat was hollow, given the Baron (not to mention the mysterious *Shadow*) wanted him alive, he was very conscious of how completely at the burly man's mercy he was. The man dropped the knife on the table and returned to rummaging through his sack.

Thorne closed his eyes and groaned quietly. There had to be something he could do! Zaine was out there, he had to be. What if he was in trouble? He quickly shook the thought aside and turned his focus towards the manacles on his arms. There must be a way in which he could remove them, even one of them. He couldn't think of any majik he had been taught that would work in this situation. Certainly not something that was powerful enough to break metal.

His eyes fell on the burly guard. Perhaps he could incapacitate him somehow? Like he did with the blissgiver back in the Silent Forests. Again, unlikely. He had no idea how he'd done it the first time and he'd been within touching distance of the creature.

Thorne struggled against the chains binding him to the chair, an ultimately futile effort, which left him sweating and the burly man chuckling.

There had to be a way!

He lifted his head and looked at the door, then at the burly man and finally at his chair, and grinned. There was a way. Sort of. He hoped.

Thorne coughed.

The burly man ignored him.

He coughed again, more dramatically.

'What did I tell you about talking?' the burly man barked, snatching the knife from the table.

'I was just thinking, I mean wondering, but if you were told – I–I mean trusted! – with bringing me here, you must be pretty important to the Baron?' Thorne trembled.

The burly man lowered the knife and scratched his head with his free hand. 'I guess... what's it to you?' The man pushed his face in front of Thorne's, spittle flying from his lips.

'Well... If you're that important – obviously! – aren't you, I don't know, his right–hand man or something?'

'Well, yeah... I guess,' the man agreed, narrowing his eyes.

'Well... if you're his right–hand man, why are you here? Shouldn't you be out there with him? Protecting him?'

'He wants me here, I stay here!' the burly man pointed at the ground with his knife.

'Yeah, I get that completely, but then who's looking after him?' Thorne inquired.

'I dunno,' the man shrugged his shoulders, 'Devan, I guess.'

'Well, okay, so is Devan the right–hand guy as well?'

'Nah, Devan's an idiot,' The burly man chuckled.

'Then why would the Baron choose him, instead of you?'

The burly man fell silent and turned his gaze to the floor.

'Think about it,' Thorne pressed him, 'if you're his right–hand man, why should Devan be beside him? Look at me, I'm not going anywhere with these chains'

The burly man nodded, 'I… don't know.'

Thorne held back the urge to grin.

'Look, I don't want to presume anything, but If I were you, I would be out there. Think about it, him and Devan alone. what if he thinks Devan should be his right–hand man?'

'He wouldn't!' the burly man cried, striking the table with the handle of his knife, 'he needs Boris, I'm his right–hand man!'

'Yes! Yes, you are!' Thorne said.

Boris paused for a moment, turned to Thorne and crouched beside him, the edge of his knife dangerously close to one of the Warlock's fingers.

'You know what I'm gonna do?' Boris whispered.

Thorne tried his best to look innocently curious. Boris held his gaze for a moment and Thorne began to worry for a second that he was searching his eyes for deception. Fortunately, Boris' mouth formed an uncomfortable grin and he shot to his feet, marched towards the door and thrust it open. An array of noises from metal clangs to screams pierced the Cabin's walls, enticing a sour expression on Boris' part.

'Eurgh,' Boris grimaced, 'not good.'

It couldn't be a coincidence that a fight had broken out. Zaine must have found him! Thorne had to remind himself again to

200

stay calm. Boris looked at Thorne and then back out of the door, chewing on the bottom half of his lip.

'Boris, you're his right–hand man, aren't you?' Thorne said.

The burly man nodded, albeit unconvincingly.

'Show him. If you let Devan stay out there, he'll get all the credit, and all the credit you'll get is for child minding!'

'I don't childmind,' Boris murmured.

'That's not what Devan will say,' Thorne said.

After what seemed to drag on for several minutes, the burly man slapped the frame of the door and clambered outside, yelling at the top of his lungs, 'Boris is coming!'

The door snapped to a close behind him.

Thorne laughed.

He couldn't believe that had worked.

All that was left now of his, albeit considerably makeshift, plan was the chair. There was no chance of him breaking free of the chain binding him to the chair but what if he broke the chair instead? Theoretically, this should be the easier option. But there was so much potential for this to go wrong. He could try and rock the chair hard enough for it to fall onto its side, hopefully breaking it and causing the chain to loosen. But that would be putting a lot of faith into the fragility of the chair and, given the wealth of the baron, something told Thorne that the quality of these chairs would be assured. Keep that in mind for later perhaps. He shot a glance towards the door, wondering how much time he had before someone replaced Boris.

So, the chair probably wouldn't break on impact of it falling... but perhaps he could weaken it first? He looked down at his chains and smiled. Of course, he was being stupid! Melting the shackles would be next to impossible. But setting the chair on fire, however... There was a slight risk, what with him being chained to it. But if he set it alight, well, that would weaken the wood enough, so if he fell onto his side the chair would surely smash!

Or, he would be chained tightly to a burning chair.

All that remained was for him to act on his plan.

Chapter 17

Tap. Tap. Tap.

The man drummed his fingers impatiently on the wood of the desk, his eyes fixed on the small crystal globe before him. The man was no ordinary man. He was a Regal. In fact, he wasn't an ordinary Regal either; he was the Szar, Warlord of the Regals, granted the second most honourable position that one of his kind could ever achieve. Although, in his opinion, it was *the* most important position in all the Regal Empire.

He was responsible for the Regal Armada; he was responsible for defending the homes of thousands of his kin, and he would be responsible for wiping out the Lycans of Horizon. He leaned back in his fur chair, relishing the thought of such an accomplishment.

The Lycans, what a filthy race of savages, he thought. His eyes caught the silver handle of a draw of the desk, intricate symbols etched in the surface of metal.

He sat up and pulled the draw open. Inside was a stack of yellowed parchment, old trinkets and, lying on top – the centre of attention – were three large claws.

The Szar delicately picked up the Lycan claws, running a finger along their metallic–like texture. He then turned to the small globe before him and waved a hand over it. The crystal reflected back a man with an angular, long-chinned face, bearing a curved nose and wide eyes. He was a young man still; only eight hundred years old, but his scars told a different story. With the claws, he traced the shape of the scars that ran in jagged, deep lines diagonally down across his face from his left eyebrow to the right side of his jaw.

He glared at his reflection. He had once been handsome but now… that had all been ruined.

If he closed his eyes, the Szar could picture the battle in which he'd gained those scars.

Wounded, bloody and panting, he hefted up his sword, grunting from the pains of his bleeding chest. The dying Lycan looked up at him hatefully and growled. The Regal spat on it and buried his sword in its body, stabbing it over and over again, until finally its spasms ceased, and its arms fell limply by its sides.

Another roar, he turned around and screamed in pain, as a clawed hand slashed across his face. He clutched at his head, blood leaking between the fingers of his gloves.

The Lycan lashed at him again with a deafening roar, but the Regal was ready, and he countered with a back slash of his long–sword. The beast howled as it clutched the bleeding stump of its arm and then lashed out with its remaining clawed hand.

He ducked under the arm and drove his sword up into the Lycan's muscled chest.

It winced and slumped to the ground. Dead.

A knock at the door brought him back in the present. His eyes flashed open and darted to the door in front of him.

'Come in,' he said, hastily dropping the claws in their draw and slamming it shut.

The door opened slowly and a head popped around. It was a woman, her blond hair falling sleekly down the side of her face, greatly emphasizing her beauty.

'Sister!' the man smiled, 'please. Come in.'

The woman smiled in return and closed the door behind her, before crossing the room to meet him, her footsteps echoing around the oval room. In her arms, she held folds of white velvet, a blue glow resonating from within.

She stopped before the desk and bowed her head before him, 'Ismäera preserve thee, my lord,' she said politely.

'Ismäera preserve all,' he replied, and then paused before adding 'you know, sister, there is no need for formalities when we are in each other's company.'

'Of course... Draeden,' the woman said.

'Ilumina,' Draeden whispered back.

Illumina then carefully laid the velvet bundle in her hands onto the desk.

'You brought the blood, excellent!' Draeden smiled.

'Of course,' Illumina nodded, unravelling the bundle to reveal three vials of gleaming blue.

Draeden smiled, examining each tube individually with a monocle.

'Have the Elders granted us permission to use the Heaven's Star?' the woman asked gesturing towards the crystal globe.

'Naturally,' the Szar replied, placing the monocle carefully on his desk. 'Shall we proceed? I imagine you must be quite eager to find the Phoenix.'

Draeden thought he saw his sister's features soften briefly.

'No,' she said, 'I mean, it won't be him, will it?'

'Human life is considerably short,' Draeden conceded, 'but there is no telling the impact of his power.'

The woman nodded and took a vial from the open bundle, uncorking it with a long nail, her brother copying her actions. They then poured the liquid onto the globe; it dripped onto the surface, like crystallised tears that sparkled under the glow of light from the ceiling window. The blood disappeared into the pores of the globe and swirled around inside the artefact to form a dark blue cloud.

The woman leant forward, the tip of her nose a centimetre from the cloudy globe. She gasped suddenly and then her face dropped as the cloud lightened and turned a light turquoise behind an illustrative scene that had begun to form.

'It isn't him,' she said morosely.

'This isn't the Phoenix?' Draeden asked, tapping the globe.

'No, not at least the one I remember,' Illumina remarked.

His eyes turned away from the globe and he buried his hand in a draw, in search for a quill and parchment.

'Wait... who is that?'

Draeden's eyes followed the hand of his sister, which pointed at another man in the distance, hacking his way through combatant after combatant.

His eyes squinted at the globe, scrutinizing the figure.

'I know that man...' the Szar whispered.

He turned to his sister, who gazed quizzically at him, a look of utmost contempt on his face, 'a Hunter... Zaine,' Draeden snarled.

206

*

It was utter chaos outside, slavers fought slaves, as rain pounded them from above. Everyone seemed to be covered from head to toe in mud, which made it all the more difficult for Thorne to spot Zaine.

'Zaine!' he yelled at the top of his lungs, as he descended down the hill.

No one could hear him above fighting, let alone answer his call.

He passed multiple bodies on the way, both slavers and slaves. Blood oozing out of fresh cuts and stumps. He fought hard to push back the thoughts of his old mentor Rozenhall, savaged by alpha wolves.

By good fortune, he finally noticed his companion. His uncovered torso was covered with blood, frankly it was miracle his bandages had survived. The man stood in line with what remained of the slaves. But he was holding his side with one hand and fighting off the slavers with the other. Thorne had never seen him this tired before and the slaves were completely outnumbered.

Thorne didn't know quite why he did it, but he found himself sprinting into the fray, lobbing fireball after fireball in a line at the crowd of slavers. The rain limited the damage considerably, but it caught their attention and cleared enough of path through towards the slaves.

'Zaine!' Thorne cried, diving through the mud towards the swordsman.

His companion looked down in bewilderment, 'Thorne?'

'Hey,' Thorne said spitting out of a mouthful of mud, 'sorry I'm late.'

'Late?' Zaine laughed, 'this is my rescue mission– LOOK OUT!'

The warning came too late or perhaps Zaine's hand had slipped on Thorne's mud soaked robes, either way fortune against him. As soon as the sword plunged through Thorne's stomach, time seemed to slow.

A dull ringing filled his ears over the background fighting. Was this what it was like to die? His eyes lifted slowly to meet Zaine's, whose mouth was open in an anguished cry. Something warm began to dribble down the sides of his mouth. He coughed, and droplets of blood spurted over his boots.

'You fool!' one of the slaver's shouted, 'that's the Warlock!'

In all fairness, Thorne thought this would hurt a lot more. Not to say the initial plunge hadn't. He looked at his surroundings again and noticed to his surprise that everyone had backed away, even the slaves. Only Zaine had remained, crouched in front of him, his own sword plunged into the mud, and his free hand holding what remained of the pommel of a sword.

In that moment, the dull ringing in his ears began to dissipate and he began to become conscious again of the rain pounding his back... and aware of an odd burning smell.

Thorne looked back down and gasped. Below him, what he assumed to be the remains of the sword, sizzled and bubbled among the mud and his chest.... Well.. His wound had disappeared to be replaced by a searing, bright amber glow that highlighted the veins in his chest, rapidly spreading warmth across his arms and down his legs.

It was difficult to describe how he felt. The ringing had disappeared, time appeared to have returned to normality and he felt... good. Really good in fact. It was like he was punching the blissgiver into the tree all over again. The slaves had dropped their weapons and in almost perfect unison fell to their knees, bowing their heads towards him. Zaine stood before them, still hanging tightly onto the half-burnt pommel.

*

The Baron swigged down the remains of the bottle of wine and threw it down furiously onto the stone floor.

He winced as a shard caught him by the leg and he staggered and fell, howling as his hands were cut by the sharp, shattered remains of the bottle on the floor.

He groaned as he looked around the ruins of his cabin. The walls had turned black with fire and there was a massive hole where the door should have been, the wind scattering loose pages and coins on the floor.

He was ruined. The Warlock and his pet Hunter had destroyed everything. All those months of hard work ruined in a day.

'Well, well, well, what do we have here?'

The Baron stumbled to his feet and whipped his head round to face the intruder, who leant by the doorway of the cabin.

'You! You came,' the Baron gasped at the Assassin.

The man smiled under the shadow of his hood and pulled his hand out behind his back drawing a dagger, blood dried over the surface of the metal. 'You called,' the man said calmly, handing the Baron the dagger.

'Yes... I bloody well did!' the Baron growled, thinking through his words, 'I have a proposition.'

'Oh?' the Assassin said, folding his arms together against his belted tunic, 'and what is it that you propose?'

The Baron licked his lips nervously and then strode towards a cabinet at the other side of the room. One of the few pieces of furniture that had survived the Warlock, or rather that...monster he'd become. He dug his hands into a pile of parchment, throwing each useless one carelessly over his shoulder with a curse. The Assassin hummed a tune quietly to himself, his feet tapping an annoying rhythm on the floor. The Baron grinned wickedly when he found the parchment required, walked over to the waiting Assassin and handed it to him.

'A target?' the Assassin asked.

'I'll get to that soon,' the Baron replied curtly, 'just look at the damn thing, will you?'

The Assassin chuckled and slowly unravelled the knot around the parchment and then opened it up.

'You know who it is?' the Baron demanded.

210

'Yes,' the Assassin replied, studying the parchment with an intrigued expression, 'I don't suppose it's the same fellow who did this is it?' the man asked, pointing at the scorched walls.

The Baron resisted the temptation to lash out at the Assassin and said through gritted teeth, 'of course.'

'Huh,' the Assassin said.

'What?' the Baron snarled, 'worried that it'll affect your stupid Balance! What?'

The man paused and then quietly folded the parchment and placed it in the Baron's hands.

'What?' the Baron demanded.

The Assassin ignored him, placed his hands inside his pockets and began to walk away. The Baron growled into his hands, ripped the parchment in half and chased after the Assassin.

'Don't you walk away from me! Don't you bloody dare!' The Baron barked, 'I am the Baron!'

The man looked back, examined the ruined cabin behind him and muttered, 'a Baron no longer I think,' and then strode down the hill.

The Baron clawed at his own face in exasperation and then ran at the end of the hill and screamed, 'I'll pay you gold!'

The Assassin stopped in his tracks. 'How much?'

'As much as you need!'

'Two thousand Skys.'

'A thousand!'

'A thousand and seven hundred.'

'A thousand and five hundred!'

The Assassin stroked his chin for a second and then nodded in agreement 'very well, we have a deal.' He waved and continued on down the hill, whistling a tune.

'I want him dead Assassin!' the Baron bellowed hoarsely, 'and the Hunter too! I don't care how you do it, just kill them both! You hear me? Kill them!'

Chapter 18

Thorne felt the familiar, soothing touch of rain, the water rolling down his cheeks.

His eyes, now able to focus, observed the rhythmic pace of Zaine's metal greaves, as they bounded across the stone path in a series of *clunks*.

Thorne's head rested against the stranger's bare back and he felt the warrior's gloved hand held firmly on his back, keeping him in place.

'Zaine...' Thorne muttered, 'Zaine...'

The warrior halted suddenly, 'you are awake?'

'Yes, let me down will you?' Thorne replied.

The man sighed and then carefully lowered the Warlock onto the ground, steadying him when he stumbled on his feet.

'Are you alright?' Zaine asked.

Thorne groaned in response, shaking off the man's arm from his shoulder. The Warlock leaned over, letting his back take the full brunt of the rain, wiping away the droplets from his eyelids. He groaned again, his closed eyes bringing about a number of unpleasant recollections; he could hear the roar of flames and picture an endless pile of bodies. He could see glimpses of carnage all around him and then... darkness.

'What... what happened?' Thorne asked weakly.

'I found you unconscious, I carried you out from the camp,' the warrior replied, eyeing him warily.

Thorne pinched the bridge of his nose and closed his eyes once more, inviting the return of the vivid memories. He sat crouched on the ground for a minute in silent contemplation and then growled in frustration. It was hopeless; he didn't have a clue about what it all meant. He felt a droplet of water hit his chest and shivered. Thorne's eyes sprung open and he snapped his head down to observe a slit in his robes, rimmed with blood.

'Zaine,' Thorne pleaded, 'what happened to me?'

The warrior crossed his arms and held Thorne's gaze silently.

'Zaine,' Thorne began irritably, feeling heat suddenly surging through his body, 'I need to know.'

'Let's move on… we'll be at the city soon,' Zaine turned his back on Thorne.

Thorne growled in frustration and leapt at the man, aided by some sudden strength that allowed him to lift the warrior up by his waist.

'Thorne,' Zaine began, with surprising calm, 'you're boiling–'

'Tell me!' Thorne demanded, shaking his companion furiously. He could feel the heat surging inside of him, but he refused to notice the stinging sweat that rolled into his eyes and down his arms and chest.

Zaine placed his hands gently on Thorne's shoulders. 'Thorne, this isn't the right time,' Zaine said.

'Gods damn you Zaine! It's never the right bloody time!' Thorne snarled.

'Listen to... yourself... look at what... you're doing,' Zaine said quietly.

Thorne felt his ragged breaths spread out slowly until it smoothed out entirely, and he was left clinging on to the Hunter's waist.

What was he doing?

CRACK!

Chapter 19

Thorne whipped around. His amber eyes again furious, he pulled the dart from behind his back and tossed it aside.

'Who did that?' Thorne demanded.

Silence and then another *Crack!*

But he was prepared this time. The dart whizzed towards Thorne's hand and then disappeared in a handful of flames.

Thorne's ears perked up and he could hear voices. Somewhere close, whispering and hiding like rats.

'What manner of man is this?'

'Our orders were for a Warlock.'

'This can't be a Warlock... that dart should have paralysed him.'

The voices appeared to be coming from behind a large boulder close to the path he stood on.

'Found you,' Thorne said, launching a torrent of flames down both sides of the boulder, setting the dry grass alight.

The two assassins, startled by this Majik, leaped from behind their hiding place and let loose a torrent of darts.

Crack! Crack! Crack! Crack! Crack!

Most missed, but a few managed to find their mark, causing the Warlock to stagger. Thorne grunted through gritted teeth, as he pulled the darts out one by one from his torso.

Thorne looked up, finding one of the assassin's standing before him; a thick beard poking out underneath his hood.

'Where's your friend gone?' Thorne demanded, tossing the darts aside.

The remaining assassin held his silence but began a rapid rhythm of movements with his hand; clench, hold up two fingers, clench, release – *Crack!*

Several things happened at once. The second assassin dropped silently to the ground a few metres behind Thorne and pulled a long, thin knife from the inner folds of his robe, and threw it. Zaine, who had been watching this rapid sequence of events from his prone position, largely with his mouth agape, cried out in warning as the assassin landed, 'LOOK–!' But barely had the first sound left Zaine's mouth before Thorne twisted. He plucked the knife from the air, much to the surprise of the second assassin and, in a continuous fluid movement, hurled it straight back at his attacker, the knife burying itself into the assassin's shoulder.

'–out?' finished Zaine, quietly.

'Grimm!' the bearded assassin bellowed, as his companion collapsed onto the floor.

But as Thorne advanced, the assassin whipped his hand into a pocket and drew out two small, stone–like objects. He barked a curse and threw them in Thorne's direction. they exploded a metre away from him and instantaneously began to release thick clouds of smoke obscuring his vision.

Thorne could hear paced footsteps that seemed to come from everywhere, as though the smoke was reflecting sounds all around him.

Crack! Crack!

The first dart missed him completely but the second caught his ankle, distracting him briefly. It was enough. He heard a cry, and then saw a flash of silver that arced down from above, slashing across his arm, biting hungrily into his skin.

Thorne cried out, collapsing in a heap on the ground. The wound burned. What poisons had the assassin coated his blade with? He could feel his blood pounding down his arm, a pain like tiny daggers pushing out from within his skin spreading like fire down to his hand.

The smoke around Thorne began to clear. And from its depths he saw another flash of silver arcing towards him as another cloud of darkness ushered itself from the corner of his eyes.

'It's over,' Thorne thought briefly before succumbing to unconsciousness.

Zaine's parrying blow met the blade of the assassin, as he had leapt in for the kill, throwing the assassin briefly off balance. Recovering quickly, the assassin rolled into a crouched position and–

Crack.

Zaine shielded his chest with his glove, the dart rebounding off a metal knuckle.

The bearded assassin leapt to his feet snarling and began to release a torrent of darts. Zaine sprinted on, expertly avoiding the path of each dart, sliding under the assassin's blade, and slicing his own across the man's hip. The bearded assassin cried out in pain this time and collapsed onto one knee.

Zaine drew out his sword and placed the tip at the man's throat, lifting the Assassin's chin so he could look directly into the man's eyes.

'Yield,' he said.

'How?' the Assassin demanded, 'how?'

Zaine pulled off his mask and tossed it aside, revealing bright silver eyes.

The assassin let out a mirthless laugh. 'Ha! Thorin neglected to mention we were hunting a Divine Son,' he said.

'I hear your masters neglect to mention much to you these days,' Zaine replied.

The assassin merely shrugged, 'are they so different from yours?'

'No,' Zaine admitted, holding his cracked pendant before the assassin, 'but at least I tried to do something about it.'

He then brought his sword down and across in one clean, fluid motion. The assassin's body slumped lifelessly to the floor, head rolling open–mouthed across the stones.

Zaine stood wordlessly for a few seconds and then sheathed his sword, bowing his head towards the body.

Crack.

Zaine caught the dart in his glove, dropped it and crushed it under his boot.

'You never give up do you, Grimm?' Zaine sighed.

Grimm stared silently at the Hunter and then dropped his arm.

'You killed him...' he muttered.

'One of us was going to die.'

'Wait,' Grimm said, before Zaine could turn away, 'you said my masters neglect to tell us much. What do you mean?'

Zaine looked into the boy's eyes, matching his piercing gaze.

'You know exactly what I mean,' Zaine sighed, the boy was young. Too young for this. 'I think you and I know both know already there is much wrongdoing within your order.'

The boy fell silent, staring at the ground, and then without warning, darted off into the distance.

'I'm sorry, boy,' Zaine said, turning away towards Thorne. It was as he was walking away that he suddenly felt a burning sensation around his neck.

He paled. It was nothing surely? Fate would not dare to cut him down now? He looked down at his chest and gasped. The veins of his chest were illuminated and writhed under his skin.

'Not now,' Zaine muttered, 'Please, not now.'

*

Thorne woke to a throbbing pain in his arm, groaning as he pushed himself off the floor and looked around. Naught but the grassy vales and the stone path surrounded him. How had he got here?

Thorne pinched his eyes and thought back: it had been raining, and then he was being carried by Zaine...

Zaine... Zaine...

Thorne looked around frantically then his eyes widened suddenly and he paled. 'Zaine!'.

220

He jumped to his feet and sprinted to the fallen swordsman, dropping to the floor by his body. The stones by the stranger were marked with specks of blood and the man's skin was covered with pulsing red veins.

'How?' Thorne muttered. He then leant over and put his ear on the man's chest. He heard nothing.

'Zaine please wake up... please,' Thorne begged, receiving nothing in reply but the howl of the wind, which carried his cries beyond.

Thorne banged his fists on the ground and screamed in the air. He laid there a few minutes, or maybe hours; he couldn't remember how long. He stood up sparing a final glance to his fallen friend, and then he ran, and ran, and ran.

*

She approached the body and kneeled, lifting her veil, so she could see into his eyes unimpeded.

'Oh Zaine,' she said caressing a bandaged cheek. He felt so cold.

She closed her eyes and quietly wept. A gold tear running from each eye, down her cheeks and falling onto the warrior's chest, disappearing in his skin.

The red in his veins receded up to his shoulders, forming two writhing circles of red by his neck.

She kissed his forehead. 'It is time,' she murmured 'Daruvai–Huntarum.'

221

The woman then gently lowered Zaine's head to the ground staring at him quietly for a short while before dropping her veil and then leaving.

She turned back to face the warrior and smiled under her veil. 'Be at peace,' she whispered.

Chapter 20

The man hugged his overcoat tight to his body, as he observed the view before him. A landscape shrouded by darkening cloud, with only the snow–capped mountains rising up through the dense mist and the fog.

He was almost on top of the world.

If he slipped now he would be falling for hours. He closed his eyes, trying to imagine the thrill of the fall – the whistle of the wind in his ears, his coat flapping as it fought against the air. The exhilaration, the sheer ecstasy.

A strange rustle behind him, the man whipped round, sword held before him. There was nothing but a few bushes and other scarce spots of vegetation.

Curious... He swore he could have heard something...

The man sheathed his sword and returned to his view.

Something stepped out into the snow.

He turned again and jumped. There was something shining brightly behind one of the bushes... a translucent shade of blue...

It padded slowly to him and then stopped an inch away looking up innocently into his bright silver eyes.

The ghostly image of a beast with a lion's body from head to midsection, the other half was that of a bear. It had a tail like a serpent, with a club shaped head that had numerous large spikes attached to it. In its midsection were two magnificent wings that were folded to its sides.

The man crouched down and looked into its eyes.

The beast regarded him coolly and then opened its jaw, revealing a set of large fangs, and roared. The words that reached the man's ears, however, were resoundingly human.

'Daruvai-Huntarum!'

A series of images burst into the man's mind, clawing their way through his mental barriers and rooting themselves deep into his memory.

He could see a man lying on blood–spattered ground, a woman kneeling beside him, her head lying on his chest. She was wearing a beautiful maroon dress with overlapping layers of silk at the bottom. He did not know her... but the other, he did.

The man took an involuntary step backwards, almost slipping on the ice behind him.

'Zaine,' he whispered.

The beast closed its mouth, shaking its fur once before fading into the white background.

The man stood stock–still, shocked by what he'd seen. 'Zaine,' he repeated to himself in surprise, 'Zaine.'

His face hardened, 'I'm going to kill the fool.'

*

Thorne burst into the tavern, the slam of the door behind him causing him to jump and attract the attention of the people inside. He blushed and hung his head, as he walked up to the counter.

'Evenin' friend,' said the bartender. A middle-aged man with a grimy face, thick facial hair and an eye-patch, 'what can I getcha'?'

'A room,' said Thorne, rummaged into his robes and drawing out five silver coins, which he placed in the man's outstretched hand.

The innkeeper grinned and dropped them into the front pocket of his apron with a metallic *clink*.

'Which one?' the man scratched his head.

'Whatever you have.'

The man frowned at Thorne, shrugged and then pointed to the right of the counter to a rather battered staircase, one of the banisters completely ripped off and lying beside.

'Thank you,' Thorne said, trudging off.

'Stay as long as you like, friend!' the eye-patched bartender barked to him up the stairs.

Thorne nodded but didn't turn around. Guilt-ridden thoughts plagued his mind as he walked up the staircase. Zaine…

It was all his fault…

He reached the top of the stairs coming to small corridor with three doors, each covered with notches in the wood. The middle door was slightly ajar, so he grasped the crude handle and pushed. As soon as he stepped inside, a hand came seemingly out of nowhere, grabbing him by the shoulder and hauling him further in.

Thorne went flying and landed with a grunt on a bed. 'What the–'

'Shh,' the man said and closed the door behind him and locked it with a key.

The man turned back to him and smiled pleasantly, 'I mean you no harm,' He wore a hooded black travelling cloak and matching black trousers, and Thorne noticed that the man wore no shoes.

The stranger had a large moustache that curled across the top of his lip and fell down the sides of his chin. He had long mangy hair that reached his shoulders, a heavily wrinkled brow and hard, weary eyes. But what shocked Thorne was the man's wolfish grin which revealed a prominent set of sparkling white, deadly sharp teeth; the incisors, in particular, were far larger than they ought to be.

'Hello, Thorne,' the man bowed, 'My name is MakVarn and I'd like just a few minutes of your time. I believe I have an interesting proposition for you.'

Thorne edged back on the bed his breathing rate increasing. This couldn't be happening…

'Lycan!' Thorne gasped.

*

'Just think about it,' MakVarn said opening the door, 'You're not obliged to do it; it's entirely your choice.'

Thorne gaped at the man. He couldn't believe what he'd just been told, it was pure insanity.

'Still think you're dreaming eh?' the man chuckled.

Thorne nodded.

'Well… we'll meet again I imagine and perhaps you'll have an answer for me then?'

Thorne didn't answer. The man shrugged and walked out of the room without another word or glance at the Warlock.

Thorne listened to the sound of the man's footsteps as they receded on the staircase then dashed to lock the door. Thorne groaned and then threw himself onto the bed, face first. It was all madness. A Lycan, an actual Lycan, or so he had inferred from the man's wolfish appearance. Certainly, his *offer* had all but confirmed it. What was he going to do? It seemed completely and utterly ridiculous, what the man had asked him. There was no way in hell he was going to–

There was a gentle tap at the door, which interrupted Thorne's thoughts. Wearily, Thorne unlocked the door and opened it a few centimetres; enough to be able to peer down the corridor.

In the shadows, Thorne could see the outline of a hulking man, with shining eyes. 'Well, isn't this a pleasant surprise,' said an all too familiar voice.

*

'You were a fool to believe I would never find out,' the Shadow said, with barely suppressed rage, as he paced around the cabin.

The Baron lay, stapled to the table in his cabin by two daggers through his shoulders.

'My lord, I–'

'I gave you one task, Baron. One task,' the Shadow boomed. Each word resonating around the cabin, causing the remaining coins on the floor to rattle. 'A task so gloriously simple and yet you still failed in it.'

'My lord, but…' he groaned.

'Even after you had so miserably failed, you did not report to me.' The Shadow's voices descended to a deathly whisper, 'no. Instead you then decided to go completely against my plans and arrange the Warlock's death.'

'I'm sorry, my lord!' the Baron whimpered.

'Oh, I'm sure you are. Now.'

He looked up to see the Shadow standing over him, tall, dominant and oppressive.

'Just kill me then,' the Baron spat.

The Shadow chuckled and then clapped his hands. A second later the Baron's two servants, the wiry Tim and burly Tom appeared. They both sported a number of bruises and cuts but had large grins on their faces.

'Mr.Shadow, sir,' Tim and Tom bowed.

The Shadow handed them an open scroll without paying a glance at the pair and then folded his hands behind his back.

228

Tim scan-read the scroll and winced, 'ouch. That's going to hurt quite a bit!'

'Oooooh!' Tom chipped in brutishly.

'What? What's going on?' the Baron demanded, his head moving frantically between the Shadow, his two former servants, and the scroll, 'what's going to hurt?'

The Shadow ignored the Baron and then turned to the two servants, handing each a bulging bag. 'Don't worry about leaving a mess, this place is ruined anyway...'

'Shadow! I've been a faithful servant,' the Baron shouted desperately.

'Indeed. Thank you for your service,' said the Shadow, as he placed his gloves back on his hands and walked out of the ruined cabin. Away from the ascending screams of agony and into the night.

Chapter 21

'Did you miss me?' Zaine asked, smiling weakly.

'It's not possible...' Thorne muttered, stepping back, 'It can't be you...'

'Why can't it be me?'

'The man was right – I *am* dreaming.'

Zaine chuckled, took a step forward and flicked Thorne on the forehead.

'Ow!' Thorne growled, rubbing his head furiously.

He looked up into the man's eyes. Zaine... Thorne rushed forward and hugged his friend.

'Zaine!' Thorne said, into his chest.

'The very same,' Zaine chuckled, but then with a startled gasp he dropped to a knee and grasped his shoulders, his fingers rubbing against the odd red circles.

'What's happening?' Thorne said, trying to drag and half carry the Swordsman into the room. The feeling of enormous relief replaced instantly by worry.

'It's alright,' Zaine grunted, pulling himself up with the door frame and, with Thorne's help, staggering to the bed. 'I'll be fine.'

'You're clearly not,' Thorne retorted, 'and what are those?' He pointed at the odd marks on Zaine's shoulders.

Zaine closed his eyes, and through gritted teeth replied, 'don't worry about it, I've had worse.'

'Don't worry about it?' Thorne cried, 'are you out of your mind?'

Zaine shrugged, painfully.

'But… I don't understand… you're alive…'

'To be honest I thought you'd be happy with that little fact.'

'No! I am, I just…' Thorne gulped guiltily, 'I thought I killed you.'

'Well you obviously didn't.'

'Zaine… I lifted you off the ground… and then…' Thorne's voice faded, 'I don't remember.'

'I dealt with the assassins, and then…. This happened.'

'Assassins?' Thorne blurted in disbelief.

'Yes… Sent by the Baron I think,' Zaine grunted, and then threw himself to the side of the bed and retched violently.

He grabbed Thorne's hand and pulled him forward, the Warlock's body suddenly jolting forward. 'They… they are coming,' he said. the Swordsman's voice coming out as a rasp from his throat.

'Who are coming?' Thorne whispered.

'My kind,' Zaine replied, closing his eyes, his fingers loosening around Thorne's arm as he slipped from consciousness. The man's hand dropped and fell beside his heavily sweating body, just as one last word slipped from his lips.

'Hunter.'

What in Ozin's name is a Hunter?

Thorne edged back towards the chair in the corner of the room and dropped onto it, exhausted, and fell asleep.

Less than an hour later, Thorne awoke with a start, and jumped up immediately. Zaine was still asleep. So, Thorne collapsed back into the chair.

Zaine said they would be coming... His own kind. His last word kept running through his head. 'Hunter.' What did he mean by that?

*

Thorne awoke suddenly and jumped to his feet. He could hear raised voices coming from downstairs in the tavern. What was going on? Thorne rushed to the door and eased it open as quietly as possible, glancing nervously behind at the Hunter. Seeing that he was still asleep, Thorne tiptoed to the stairs, pausing at the top of the staircase to view the scene below.

Surrounded by a ring of spectators, which parted at the till where the bartender stood trembling was a man with bright silver eyes, a sleeveless overcoat and a shock of blond hair. Thorne gasped. It had to be another Hunter, and Thorne could have sworn he'd seen him before.

'I was summoned here,' the Hunter said, his voice was smooth like Zaine's but more... boyish, bearing a sort of cheeky, playful tone but still commanding like Zaine.

'You got no summons from me, demon,' the bartender gulped.

Demon? Thorne frowned. He looked no less a man than Zaine did.

The Hunter took a step forward, his face coming under the light, so Thorne could see his face. The man's youth much belied the sheer confidence that resonated from his voice. But unlike Zaine, he had no bandages...

'I am not a fool, I received a summons for help and I know it's for one of my kind,' the man growled, 'now where is he?'

The innkeeper gulped again but did not answer and then suddenly one of the crowd of men around the Hunter leapt forward with a yell and threw a fist. Without looking, the Hunter caught the man's fist in his hand, twisted it, causing the brawler to scream, and then threw the man over his shoulder and against the bar. With an almost simultaneous series of metallic scrapes, the men drew out their battered daggers, thrusting them out in front of them, encircling the lone Hunter in a ring of steel and iron.

The Hunter laughed and drew out his long sword, twirling it skilfully in his hands, so it became merely a blur in the air. 'Really, there are only ten of you?' he said.

Several of the men dropped their daggers and ran out of the door. The others quickly backed away from the reach of the sword, sheathed their daggers, and held their hands up. When the Hunter was satisfied, he sheathed his sword, giving it an appreciative pat.

Suddenly, his eyes snapped to the top of the stairs and Thorne.

The Warlock froze and before he could move the Hunter had leapt up the stairs and grab him by the scruff of his neck.

233

'Well hello, Warlock,' the man greeted him, 'you're rather young to be so far from home, aren't you?'

'I have to go,' Thorne replied, but the Hunter would not release him.

'Not so fast, Warlock,' the blonde Hunter said. 'You see, Zaine was not the only person I saw in my vision, I also saw a young Warlock and... another, a rather strange woman.'

Thorne paled. What had the man seen?

'I know he's here, so you might as well tell me.'

'Why? What do you plan to do to him?' Thorne said, pulling himself free from the Hunter and backing along the corridor.

'An interesting question. What do you think I'll do to him?'

'I think I'd rather not take the risk.'

The man chuckled and unsheathed his sword, pointing the tip at Thorne's throat. It needed to move only a few inches to sever his head.

'Zaine, Warlock, has been branded a traitor of my people, he was banished several years ago, commanded to never return or summon another Hunter's help.'

Thorne's eyes widened.

'A traitor?'

'Yes, he was branded so by our *great* leader, Zolft,' the man said, emphasizing the word *great* with what seemed like sarcasm.

Thorne gulped, 'so... you're here to...'

234

'He was banished, and the price for breaking his sentence is death,' the blonde Hunter replied.

Death. The word rung around Thorne's ears. The man was going to kill Zaine!

'You can't!' Thorne said, immediately regretting his sudden bravery.

The man sighed and removed the blade from Thorne's throat, placing his sword back in its sheathe.

'Do not worry,' he smiled grimly, 'fortunately for Zaine, I am a friend. So, tell me, where is my kinsman?'

*

The Hunter traced his fingers across the red circles on Zaine's shoulders which had begun to increase in size since Thorne had last seen them.

'Zaine,' the Hunter whispered, 'It's me, Dez.'

Dez... Thorne frowned and then looked in surprise at the man, suddenly realizing where he'd seen the Hunter before. It was when he and Zaine were fighting the Blissgiver and it changed form. How odd now that he was seeing the real thing.

Zaine stirred, muttering incoherently, but his eyes did not open.

The man sighed and turned to Thorne. 'It is as I thought – the banishing is close to reaching its final stage…'

Zaine grunted, his body convulsing briefly on the bed, causing Thorne to jump and then he was silent.

'The banishing?' Thorne said.

Dez looked at Thorne incredulously. 'He never told you?'

Thorne shook his head.

'Zaine... He's dying. Or at least, his health has been deteriorating for over a year now.'

'Because of this?' Thorne pointed at the marks on Zaine's shoulders.

'Yes, exactly so, a banishing is the worst punishment we can dish out to our own people. It's... controversial to say the least. It... changes you.'

'What do you mean, 'changes'?'

The man shook his head, 'never mind that now, we need to get him out of here.'

Thorne looked at Zaine. His skin had turned deathly pale and his veins had become more pronounced under his skin.

'There's only one place we can take him,' Dez said, 'and quite frankly, it's as much an unhealthy choice for him as it would be to just leave him here.'

'Where?' Thorne frowned.

'Home,' the Hunter sighed.

*

The Hunter trudged on ahead through the marsh, humming an odd song under his breath, Zaine's body stirring on his shoulder.

'We're nearly home my friend,' Dez whispered, giving him a soft pat on the back before resuming his strange humming.

Thorne trudged along behind, jumping, and skipping over the various puddles and deeper mud pits that threatened to swallow him up. The stench was also so terrible that he had to hold his nose, the air so strongly pungent, it made him feel light–headed just breathing it in.

'You alright there?' the Hunter shouted back.

'Yes,' Thorne lied, 'when will we actually *get* there?'

'Soon,' Dez chuckled, continuing his humming.

'What is that?' Thorne frowned at the man.

'What?'

'Your singing.'

The Hunter chuckled, 'I'm allowing us to pass through the wards safely, so they don't rip us to shreds as we go through.'

Thorne paled. Wards? Out here in these marshes?

'Wards?' Thorne said.

'Oh yes,' the man replied, 'by the way, they take only a few seconds to reactivate, so perhaps you might want to keep that in mind.'

Thorne looked up from his feet, gasping when he realized the distance separating the two of them, and he sprinted ahead to meet the Hunter. His boots thick with mud by the time he did.

The man laughed. 'Well, you can be quick, can't you?' he said, grinning.

'Wards?' Thorne demanded, 'what wards?'

'Of course,' the man replied, 'how else would we remain where we are without being discovered?'

'But–'

'They were made by Warlocks several centuries ago. Surely you must have heard of this?'

Thorne shook his head, frowning deeply. Warlocks and Hunters? How had the Masters neglected to tell him? Or anyone else for that matter?

'Did we do anything else?' Thorne inquired.

'Yes, I believe your kind played a part in forging the Fountain, now that you mention it,' the Hunter replied.

'The Fountain?'

Dez glanced behind him, 'Not one for history lessons your people, eh?'

The man's hand then whipped out and stopped Thorne before he could take another step.

'Wait,' he whispered urgently.

Ahead of the three men the marsh ended leading into an empty plain. It was eerily similar to the one in which Zaine and Thorne had found themselves, after leaving the Silent Forests. The man became silent, then began a faster, up-tempo song which heavily emphasized the vowels in his odd words. He placed his hands around his neck and took off a thin chain, at the bottom of which hung a bright green pendant, and threw

238

it out in front of him. The pendant hovered in front of the man's face in mid–air and then began to glow brightly, making Thorne shield his eyes. Thorne recognised the pendant, he'd seen it before... Of course, he had! Back in the Silent Forests! But his pendant was a lot darker and cracked through the middle. When the pendant's glow diminished, Thorne stared ahead in disbelief.

'Welcome to our home, Warlock, Dez said, seizing his hovering pendant and, with his free hand, making a sweeping gesture.

Thorne was standing beneath a large stone archway. The sole entrance to the Hunter's camp, as a two-metre-high wall spread seemingly for kilometres, from the archway to the left and right of the camp. Before them, hundreds of huts were spread out into the distance, seemingly arranged in concentric circles from some distant central point. Many of the huts illuminated by fires flickering outside.

'By Ozin...' Thorne muttered.

Seeing he was beginning to fall behind again, Thorne shook himself vigorously and ran to the Hunter, who was deep in conversation with another man at the arch.

'–I can't,' Thorne heard him say.

'He's dying, for all the Gods' sakes, Amar let us through,' Dez growled.

'You know the rules, Dezavin,' the guard hissed, 'letting in a banished one means death for you, and as far as Zolft is concerned, anyone associated with you.'

'That's if he finds out and surely you wouldn't be stupid enough to tell him?' Dez glared at him.

239

The man's jaw clenched. He glanced anxiously behind him before whispering back urgently 'I don't like the situation we find ourselves in as much as the next Hunter, but–'

'But what? He didn't just coincidently come here for no reason, he's here to challenge him!'

'Not in this state.'

'And this is the only place with the appropriate cures to help him! Every minute we waste debating here brings Zaine closer to his last breath.'

The man blew out of his nose in annoyance, sighed and then stood out of the way. 'Go on in,' he said, 'if you're fortunate enough, you might make it to Charmer's without being seen.'

'My thanks, my friend.'

But before Thorne could take another step forward he was halted by the tip of the man's spear.

'You brought a Warlock child, as well?'

Thorne frowned. 'I'm not a child,' he grumbled under his breath.

Dez looked back and sighed, 'Amar.'

The man rolled his eyes and lowered his spear, 'fine, I guess if we're letting in a banished one, we can let in this mighty Warlock too, eh?'

Thorne smiled in thanks and then caught up with the blonde Hunter.

'What was that all about?' Thorne asked.

'Zaine can tell you later,' Dez replied, shifting the man's body slightly on his shoulder.

240

'Will he make it?'

'He will – he's a tough one,' the man replied, but even he sounded unsure.

They went past a number of huts, fortunately no–one challenged them. Thorne's head swivelled around nervously as they passed by each hut, expecting danger at every corner. However hard he tried, he couldn't drown out the thoughts that plagued his mind. Who was this Zolft that everyone seemed to hold in such contempt?

'We're here,' Dez whispered, relief heavy in his voice.

His thoughts quickly dissipating, Thorne followed the man's gaze to a hut, light leaking through small cracks in the door. He was also sure he could hear hushed voices from inside but couldn't make out what was being said.

'Open the door, will you?' Dez grunted, 'quickly now.'

'Are you sure?' Thorne asked. 'there are some people in here.'

'Its fine, trust me,' the man hissed, 'just open the damn door.'

Thorne bit his lip and reluctantly grasped the notched handle of the door and pulled.

'–too risky, we could do it only if we had–'

The room fell silent and the pair of men inside turned to face the door. Frowns etched upon their faces. However, before Thorne could say anything, Dez barged past into the room.

'Talk of the devil,' one man laughed, tall, bald and burly, with a clean–shaven face and an earring that made a circle in his earlobe. 'Wait... what the hell?'

'My gods, the banishing!' another man gasped, slightly shorter than the other, darker skinned with a strip of hair running down the middle of his head. Though, what was more distinctive about him, Thorne observed, was the fact that he was missing the middle finger of both his hands.

'Be quiet!' Dez hissed, 'do you all want the entire guard on us? No? Then shut the hell up.'

Thorne followed in behind, closing the door quietly behind him. The room was fairly small, although this would have been emphasised less without the presence of so many Hunters. The room had a stone floor and several wicker chairs. The walls were lined with cloth and, back by the wood burning stove, there was a stone plinth on which lay a large bow and a long sword, similar to that of Zaine's.

To the right side of the room, Dez had laid Zaine down on a straw bed.

'Will he be alright?' Thorne asked.

'He'll be right as rain,' the bald man growled, he then glanced down at Thorne, and jumped, 'Chimera's eye, Dez! Who's this little child?'

'I'm not a child… and I'm not *that* little,' Thorne grumbled, under his breath.

Dez winked at the bald man and placed a hand on his shoulder. 'This young Warlock is Thorne. Friend and brave defender of Zaine, Boulder.'

Thorne blushed.

The man raised an eyebrow at Dez, shrugged and then proffered his hand to Thorne. Thorne took it, feeling as though his hand was being crushed as the man shook it vigorously.

'Well met, Thorne, the name's Boulder,' the bald man introduced himself. 'He's Charmer,' pointing at the dark-skinned man by the stove, who nodded politely at Thorne and gave him a reassuring smile. The door creaked open and simultaneously the Hunters' hands flicked to the pommels of their swords. A woman stood in the doorway, with an expression of complete shock on her face.

'Ah, here she is!' Boulder said, as the Hunters relaxed. 'This is Illumina, our very own honorary Regal Hunter.'

Despite the rush of warmth to his cheeks, Thorne couldn't help but look at her. She had long, blonde hair that fell down her back and appeared to shine in the firelight. Slim, but curved. She was clearly not a Hunter; her face was sharp and her cheekbones prominent, her eyes white except for her sea-blue irises and her lips blood red against her pale skin.

'I'm Thorne,' the Warlock stuttered offering a shaking hand.

Illumina ignored it and instead stared at him. And somehow Thorne held her gaze. 'I don't believe it,' she whispered.

The woman broke off into tears leaving Thorne utterly dumbstruck. What had he done? He glanced up at Boulder, who shrugged in return.

'Lumi?' Boulder murmured reaching out for her shoulder.

'Don't!' she snapped, slapping away his hand.

She paused suddenly, her eyes catching Zaine's convulsing body, a look of horror displayed on her face. She mouthed an

243

apology to the bald man, closed the door quietly behind her and ran up to the Hunter, kneeling beside his body.

'Zaine,' she whispered stroking his forehead.

He stirred, muttering something jumbled but did not open his eyes.

'The Banishing,' she muttered.

'Yes,' Dez said, 'it's reaching its final stage, if he doesn't get a new pendant soon…. Well, he won't last much longer.'

'Charmer,' the Regal said.

The man known as Charmer inclined his head, and then left the hut, pulling the door closed behind him. The Regal got up, ignoring Thorne, and walked over to the stove, reaching behind where a stack of bowls were piled. Dez followed and crouched down beside her, whispering something discretely. She replied angrily, pouring water from one bowl to another while sprinkling something into each.

Thorne could only make out a few words from their conversation: '…I should have known… he really is dead…'

Her eyes met Thorne, but this time her expression wasn't accusatory, just rather sad. So clearly so that Thorne felt uncomfortable just looking at her. Illumina returned to the bowls. Thorne was certain he could see tears running down her cheeks.

Dez sighed and returned to Zaine's side giving him a soft pat on the chest. 'Hold on, Zaine… hold on.'

The door opened. All eyes turned to Charmer who held a metallic chain tightly in his hand. Swinging softly at the bottom was a sparkling new pendant. Or rather the two halves of one, attached on a hinge together, revealing hollow innards.

'Gentlemen… lady,' he purred, 'I assume this will do.'

'Yes,' Illumina replied, 'Give it to me.'

He lowered it into her outstretched palm. Illumina nodded her thanks and set about soaking the pendant in the solution she had prepared, then vigorously drying it with a cloth.

She passed Thorne, glancing at him for a second; it was enough to make his heart fly to his mouth, rendering speech redundant.

The Regal then stopped by Zaine's side and turned to Dez.

'Go ahead,' he nodded at her.

'Not yet…' Illumina muttered, 'it would probably help if his pores could breathe.'

'Agreed.'

Thorne looked up. They were going to remove Zaine's bandages? He was going to see his face?

He tried to look around Dez and Illumina but then suddenly Charmer and Boulder were there as well. They almost completely blocked his sight of Zaine. All he could see were his boots.

Thorne heard the sound of a knife being unsheathed, and a satisfying ripping noise, assumedly the bandage.

'That's quite a scar,' Thorne heard Charmer gasp.

'That sounded hopeful,' Boulder laughed, 'finally thinking you can stake a claim to the second most attractive man in camp?'

'Not looking too bad, considering,' Dez muttered, 'maybe could do with a shave.'

'Quiet!' Illumina hissed.

Thorne heard the woman mutter a few words and then silence. The anticipation was killing him, when was he going to see? A cough, and then Thorne heard someone violently vomit on the floor.

'Give him space!' Illumina said sharply.

The men edged backwards but Thorne could still not see.

'Zaine?' Illumina whispered.

Silence, then another cough. 'What? Where am I? Who… Boulder? Charmer? Dez? Illumina? What–'

'Easy, Zaine,' Boulder said, 'you're home.'

'Thorne… Where's Thorne?' Zaine demanded.

The Hunters parted allowing Thorne to pass through. He muttered his thanks, and walked through, coming to a stop by the straw bed where Illumina sat with him rubbing his shoulders.

The floor was red with blood and something darker. Did he throw up whatever was under his skin?

He looked up at Zaine. His new pendant now pulsed green with life. The man had his head in his hands and Thorne could only see the stream of raven black hair that ran down the sides of his hands.

The *stranger* lifted up his head and grinned at the sight of Thorne.

Chapter 22

Thorne was relieved to see that colour had returned to Zaine's skin, and the marks that had occupied the upper portion of his body had disappeared.

Now that the bandages were off, however, Thorne almost felt like he was speaking to a different man. Indeed, he had never imagined that this was what the Hunter would look like. The scar that ran diagonally from his brow to the bottom of his lip was more representative of what he envisioned. But the man was young, with a handsome heart-shaped face, and a stubbled jaw.

Before Thorne could even begin to say anything, the creaking open of the door behind them attracted the group's attention.

'So, the banished one has returned!' a voice sneered, 'so much for the rules.'

The man was Thorne's height, much shorter than all the other Hunters in the room who regarded him loathsomely. He wore a buttoned leather jacket, a bright red scarf, and dark trousers. In place of a sword by his waist were two shimmering daggers. The man grinned and stepped forward, hands held behind his back, his eyes dancing up and down Illumina's body, his lip curling.

'A Regal! Ooh, I must say this is quite a surprise!' the man clapped his hands in delight, and then frowned, 'you're not as pointy eared as everyone makes your kind out to be are you?'

'Aespora toray!' she spat at him, inviting a bellow of laughter from Boulder.

The man shrugged and then his eyes flickered to Thorne.

'Ahhh a Warlock! Goodness me, you know, I was just wondering what this rag tag group of clowns was missing!'

'If you've got nothing important to say, I'd suggest you leave, Bardolf,' Dez gestured towards the open door.

Bardolf raised an eyebrow, his lip curling into a mocking smile, 'my, my, my, a little sensitive aren't we all today?'

Zaine pushed himself off the bed, stumbling at his first attempt to walk but pushed away Dez's offer of support. 'I've had enough of a rough day, and to be completely honest, I'm starting to lose my patience.'

Boulder chuckled, cracking his knuckles.

'Violence, violence, people,' the man wagged a finger disapprovingly, 'it will get you nowhere you know. But I'm here only as an introduction.'

'What introduction would that be?' Charmer asked.

'Not what, but whom,' Bardolf replied, wagging his finger at the dark-skinned man.

'Then whom?' Illumina demanded.

'I,' said another.

A man passed into the room, as quietly as Bardolf before him. He was huge, even bigger than Boulder, who only came up to his hooked nose. It was a wonder how nobody had heard him enter.

The bottom half of the man's face was covered with a red bandana that placed emphasis on his horribly scarred bald head, the scars forming a maze of patterns on his skin. His eyes were sharp and domineering; Thorne found he could only look into them for a few seconds before being unconsciously forced to look away. The man wore an ornate fur cloak, with a beige tunic, and trousers tucked into boots. His footsteps were almost inaudible, despite the sheer size of the man. Thorne knew this man, or rather, had seen him once before.

'Zolft. We should have guessed you'd send your pet in first,' Zaine snarled.

'Zaine,' the man replied with equal distaste, 'it's been a few years since I've had to lay eyes on you, I seem to remember banishing you.'

'And I brought him here,' Dez interjected, pushing past to face the man.

'Oh? And why?'

'The banishing was killing him,' Charmer said, 'Amric would never have allowed a practice as barbaric.'

'Amric was weak,' Zolft's voice boomed, 'I have brought the Hunters into a new age.'

'You have tarnished your own people's reputation, Zolft. That is your only legacy!' Illumina retorted.

The Hunter Lord chuckled gutturally, the noise comparable to that made by a broken coal burner struggling for life. 'You were amusing at first Regal, but you begin to tire me. Bardolf.'

'My lord,' Bardolf bowed his head.

'It has been a while since I heard a Regal scream. Break her arm,' Zolft said.

'No!' Thorne did not know why he was saying it, or where he gained the courage from but, before he knew it, he was standing in front of Illumina blocking Bardolf's path. His hands alight with flames.

Zolft looked at Thorne and frowned, 'a Warlock? Well this is certainly a most interesting gathering.'

'Just say what you need to say and be done with it,' Zaine spat.

'Always to the point, Zaine,' the Hunter Lord said, 'I admired you for that… what a pity… anyway you know the rules, you came when you were forbidden and that means only one thing.'

Zolft turned to leave, his cloak waving behind him, signalling his departure.

'You have until sunrise, Zaine,' the Hunter Lord barked behind him, 'don't keep me waiting.'

Bardolf followed behind, tipping an imaginary hat to them all and bolting before Boulder could reach him.

'Snakes,' Boulder grunted, 'the pair of them.'

Thorne extinguished the flames and stepped away awkwardly away from Illumina.

'Well, that was expectedly unpleasant,' Zaine said, appearing suddenly in front of them before Thorne could say another word. With a heavy sigh he turned to Thorne, 'so, it seems I've dragged you into trouble again, haven't I?'

Thorne grinned, 'I couldn't think of a better person to be in trouble with.'

Zaine snorted, 'well, you may just end up regretting that.'

'So… What's going to happen? Are we going to be thrown out?' Thorne asked, hopefully.

The Hunters looked at each other uneasily; none of them would even look at Zaine who had become visibly sullen.

'At… at sunrise…'

'I'm going to die,' Zaine finished for Dez, abruptly. 'I will be executed when the sun rises.'

The room went deathly silent.

Zaine growled and then headed towards the door.

'Where are you going?' Dez demanded, grabbing his arm.

'Where do you think? I stay, they won't just stop at me, they'll kill the rest of you. Or worse, banish you all.'

He threw off Dez's arm and pulled the door open. Thorne could see the horizon, it had become considerably lighter since they'd last been outside, a blend of colours ranging from amber to dark red.

'Wait!' Illumina shouted, running up to the Hunter.

'Illumina, I cannot, I need to go now,' Zaine growled.

'You listen to me now, Zaine or, Gods help me, I'll execute you myself!' she snapped.

Zaine turned back to her, a bemused expression on his face.

'There is another way,' the Regal explained, 'you were unsuccessful the first time, but you're stronger, you can beat him!'

251

Zaine shook his head, 'I can't, he would… you saw what happened last time.'

'Come on, Zaine!' Boulder growled 'are you telling me you're just going to give up? Give him what he wants?'

'No…' Zaine began, 'I just–'

'Zaine, what would Amric want?' Charmer asked quietly.

'Who's Amric?' Thorne frowned; he'd heard that name before.

'You have not heard of him?'

'No,' Thorne replied. It was starting to annoy him how little he knew.

'He was the greatest Hunter Lord of our generation,' Zaine said, 'but, more importantly, was like a father to us all.'

'Was?' asked Thorne, guessing the answer.

'He was murdered, betrayed, by Zolft.' Boulder said.

'Then why wasn't *he* banished?'

'Nobody would dare challenge Amric's right–hand man, based off a rumour,' explained Dez.

'Especially not after the example he made of me,' Zaine said.

'Everyone knew?'

'Mostly, but he has a considerable number of Hunters on his side.'

'He lied and those idiots believed him!' Zaine said.

'They were scared, Zaine,' Illumina said softly.

252

'They were fools, they should have – they should have…'
Zaine stopped and traced the scar on his face from top to
bottom, 'I'm a fool.'

Zaine slid down and sat by the door, his head in his hands.

'Zaine, what would Amric tell you before a fight? What did
he tell you the first time you picked up a sword and fought me
when we were younger?' Charmer placed his hand on Zaine's
shoulder.

Zaine removed his head from his hands and stood up facing
Charmer with the biggest grin Thorne had ever seen.

*'He's crafty, but I wouldn't worry about him unless you're
playing cards,'* Zaine said.

Charmer smiled, 'yes, he did say that didn't he? Old man
never did get over me beating him in poker… and what did he
say after?'

'Many times in your life you will fail, you will fall.'

'And then?'

*'Never forget, you must rise, and rise again. Your victories
are the sum of all your failures, rise above them and stand!'*

Chapter 23

'So, you have come to make a fool of yourself yet again?'
Zolft laughed.

Thorne saw Zaine's grip on the pommel begin to shake
uncontrollably and his features contort.

'Do you accept my challenge, or not?' Zaine demanded.

A hush fell over the Hunters, who had gathered in a circle
around the pair.

Zolft narrowed his eyes at Zaine and snapped his fingers,
'Bardolf!'

The small Hunter pushed his way through the crowd and
offered the giant his long sword.

Zolft took the sword and Bardolf scurried out of the way as he
took a test swing, the metal screaming as it cut through the
air.

'I accept!' Zolft barked, 'and I choose Bardolf as my second!'

Bardolf bowed and hurried to the Hunter Lord's side with a
wry grin.

'Who is yours?' Bardolf sneered.

Zaine turned back to the group behind him, of Boulder, who
stood expectantly forward, Dez, Illumina, Charmer… and
Thorne. Zaine's eyes finally rested on Thorne and he
beckoned the Warlock to follow.

'Me?' Thorne asked, surprised.

'Him?' Boulder's mouth fell open, 'no offence,' he added quickly, glancing at Thorne.

'Thanks,' Thorne said.

'Yes him,' Zaine replied. 'Do you doubt my choice?'

'No, but this is a Hunter matter. Is a Warlock the right choice?'

'This is my choice.'

Boulder opened his mouth to retort but then stopped and folded his arms, 'fine.'

Dez pushed Thorne forward, 'good luck,' he whispered. Thorne forced a grin, catching a glance at Illumina, who stood staring at him with a mortified expression and then suddenly he was walking along with Zaine.

Thorne smiled weakly and turned back to Zaine 'I'm not going to have to fight right? A second is there to jump in if you fall first right?'

'No,' Zaine shook his head, 'different rules, I'm afraid. You have to fight the clown, while I fight Zolft.'

'You're joking right? Right?'

'I may not have been entirely forthcoming with the nature of this…'

'Not entirely?'

'Anyway, after the blissgiver, he'll be easy, heh?' Zaine gave a wry smile and nudged Thorne with his elbow.

Thorne scoffed.

Then again, he did, on paper, seem to have the better chances in his fight. Bardolf looked far less menacing than Zolft. But he did not like the confident sneer on the smaller man's face. Thorne looked around as he walked trying to ignore the horrible churn he was feeling in his stomach. They were surrounded by Hunters in a large circle. No escape, it was either success or death.

'Oh, and Thorne, before I forget,' Zaine tossed the rod to the Warlock.

Incredulous, Thorne caught the rod and snapped it onto his belt. He'd almost completely forgotten about it.

'The Warlock?' Thorne heard Bardolf snigger, as they approached.

'Ignore him,' Zaine muttered, 'there will be plenty of time to get your own back soon.'

Thorne grinned. They stopped a few metres away from their opponents and Zaine drew his sword and held it up so the edge touched the tip of his nose. 'My weapon of choice,' Zaine barked to Zolft.

Zolft waved his own long sword and Bardolf a pair of daggers. He then pointed at Thorne, 'what are yours Warlock?'

Thorne took a deep breath, this was actually going to happen, he was going to fight… a Hunter. He snapped his fingers and flames emerged in the palm of his hand. Then, without any warning, the Hunters were upon them, the large Hunter's feet pounding the ground with his sword aloft.

Thorne threw his first fireball at Bardolf but the man dodged it, a small circle of flames lying in his wake. That was fine; he had plenty more where that came from.

Thorne closed his eyes and drew on his Majik and gasped.

Nothing... Just nothing. His Majik had suddenly disappeared.

But he had only used a small portion to create that fireball. What was happening? He wiped his forehead with the back of his sleeve, frowning when he saw it come back drenched with sweat.

Thorne felt the rod vibrate at his side.

'What's happening?'

'Oh, now you wake up?'

'Move!'

Thorne jumped back just in time to avoid Bardolf's daggers.

'Do you have a weapon on you?'

'Obviously not!' Thorne thought back urgently, keeping his eyes trained on the small Hunter.

A pause, *'use me.'*

'How?'

'Thorne, you have to– look out!'

With Thorne distracted, Bardolf took his opportunity and jumped in, cutting across the Warlock's left calf with a dagger. Thorne cried out in pain and fell to one knee on the ground, his leg burning.

He closed his eyes expecting the inevitable rain of blows but he felt nothing. Thorne looked up to see the Hunter above him, grinning maliciously.

'Get up Warlock! I'm not finished with you yet,' Bardolf kicked him in the side and jumped back, before Thorne could catch him with the sharp end of the rod.

Thorne groaned and then slowly pulled himself back to his feet.

'Not much fight in you, is there Warlock?' Bardolf giggled, 'pity...'

Thorne snarled and ran at the man, ignoring the painful protests from the back of his leg. However, whatever he tried, he could not land a single blow on the Hunter. Wherever he swung the rod he ended up hitting nothing but thin air, hearing the man's annoying triumphant giggle behind him soon after. He was being toyed with.

'That's not what I had in mind.'

Thorne lowered the rod, his breathing heavy. He was exhausted, yet the Hunter still appeared to be full of energy.

'Are you finished?' Bardolf asked.

Thorne swore at the laughing Hunter and swung the rod again, missing the man by inches.

'Oh, dear me, you almost got me there!' he cackled.

Thorne paused and frowned. He could feel something... something within him... small, but it was there, like a flicker of light from a dying candle flame.

'Thorne! What are you waiting for? Press the attack!'

258

Majik… Thorne thought. Would it do? Perhaps, just maybe it might catch him off guard, but it might go over his limit. He had to try.

He closed his eyes. 'Bardolf?' Thorne said.

'Do you want me to end the game now, Warlock?'

'Burn!' Thorne growled, whipped out his hand and let loose a burst of flames.

The man jumped back but his scarf had caught fire, the flames eating their way up to his neck. The man yelled in surprise trying to beat away the flames. Thorne collapsed on the floor. That had done it… now he had no energy left whatsoever; he'd just signed his own death warrant.

A second later he felt a hand at his robe and his face was pulled close to Bardolf's. 'That was my favourite scarf you idiot!' he spat, his eyes full of malice.

Thorne could feel his consciousness beginning to slip as time slowed with him. He turned his head. Zaine was bleeding from numerous cuts and the larger Hunter had a few as well, but it was Zaine who seemed to be losing the fight, being slowly backed into the crowd. He looked back at his own opponent. He could see the man's daggers rise above his head, arcing straight down into his chest. He felt his blood surge as warmth suddenly radiated around his body. He rolled out of the way and launched his fist into the Hunter's side. Somehow, the punch connected. The man uttered a surprised yelp, as he was flung several yards away, rolling before the feet of the crowd.

The crowd fell silent for a moment. Thorne was as stunned as they. He stared down at his hands, twisting them in front of his eyes, half–expecting his skin to have transformed into rock. Bardolf jumped back onto his feet and slowly advanced towards him whilst clutching his side, flinging a variety of curses at the Warlock. He leapt in the air, daggers raised. Thorne didn't panic, he didn't even think, he just took a step back and knocked the daggers out of Bardolf's hands.

'What Majik is this?' Bardolf demanded.

Thorne grabbed the Hunter by the scruff of his neck before he could manage to scramble for his daggers and smashed his head into the ground. Then as quickly as the heat had rushed to his body, he suddenly felt the bite of the wind around his neck and his legs went weak. A moment later he crumbled, landing beside the fallen Hunter.

*

'Thorne! Hey, Thorne!'

Thorne groaned and groggily opened an eye. His vision was blurred but he could just about make out the outline of the large man in front of him.

'Boulder?' Thorne mumbled.

'Yeah,' Thorne heard the man say, his voice was urgent and strained... emotional.

Thorne turned his head to the side. He could make out another person... no... a body lying beside him. It couldn't have been Bardolf's – it was too big.

Who was it?

260

Wait... Boulder emotional?

No!

It couldn't be Zaine, surely!

Boulder had left him and someone else had replaced him at his side but he couldn't make out who it was.

'–has been decided!' Thorne heard someone shout, 'proving his tremendous valour in battle once again.'

Thorne didn't want to hear this.

'Brothers and sisters! Your Hunter Lord! The worthiest of us all!'

Why Ozin? Why?

'ZAINE!'

*

'Leaving us so soon?'

Thorne turned to find Zaine before him, bruised but well. 'Sorry, the City of Light's calling.'

Zaine's grin suddenly dropped and he adopted a more serious expression and tone. 'I don't like you going up there alone. I've talked with the others and there's something... amiss with that place.'

Thorne smiled wryly.

Thorne looked down at his feet uncomfortably and muttered, 'well... I'll see you later then.'

261

'Of course,' Zaine grinned and grabbed Thorne in a brief, one–armed hug.

'Look, I think, no, I know you'll be a brilliant leader,' Thorne said, 'these people all trust you and will follow whatever you say.'

'Not all of them,' Zaine scoffed, 'Boulder never does anything I tell him to.'

'I never do what?'

Boulder, much like his compatriots, suddenly appeared as though out of thin air. His footsteps not betraying a single sound, despite his hulking mass.

'Nothing,' Thorne snorted.

'Right,' Boulder shook his head and grinned, 'you leaving then?'

Thorne sighed, he really wished he could stay…

Thorne did his best not to look into Zaine's eyes, as he nodded his farewells and then began to awkwardly walk off in the opposite direction.

'Hey!'

Thorne twisted his head, to see Zaine waving something in the air to him.

'Catch!' he yelled.

He then threw the item; Thorne caught it with both hands and opened them to see a small green ruby attached to a thin circle of string. It was his old cracked pendant.

'Bring it back to me,' he said.

Thorne shouted his thanks in reply and continued to trudge on. If he squinted his eyes he could just make out the shape of the City of Light in the horizon. Zakariyanna's words had never left him, plaguing his every thought.

'I saw you being consumed by flames.'

He was almost there. His journey would soon come to an end and quicker than he realized.

Chapter 24

The Hall of Light loomed over Thorne, flames crackling in the middle of the building from torches glaring down at him, like the amber eyes of an enormous beast. This was where Thorne had been told the Steward of the city lived. The Steward apparently governed the city, but of what he was still in charge, Thorne had no idea; the city was slowly crumbling to pieces.

Fissures had formed in the fine details of the magnificent crystal statues that stood near the walls of the city, which had, over time, been worn by rain. Ivy was growing over the buildings and plants were pushing their way through cracks in the cobblestoned streets. If it wasn't for the people running around the city, Thorne would have assumed it had been abandoned. The Hall however, stood completely apart from the rest of the city, its marble walls and steps in perfect condition, unblemished. The doors were gigantic and had swirling patterns indented in the thick wood.

The Warlock sighed and glanced behind him. The Hall stood at the far end of the city on a hill, although the walk had been tiring it was well worth the view. He could see the hundreds of buildings and monuments that towered above the ground and the streets writhing with movement. Beyond the city, Thorne could make out the dark blur of the city's graveyard, where the dark portal resided. He shivered at the memory of passing by it. As soon as he'd come within a hundred metres of it he'd felt a tremor, the sensation was… uncomfortable.

He closed his eyes and breathed in the air, exhaling slowly. I'm not going to die, Thorne thought.

He turned back and walked through the doors and into the Hall, feeling warmth suddenly radiate around him. The Hall was even bigger than the Hall of Majik. The ceiling was lined with golden chandeliers, which swayed in the breeze that had accompanied Thorne through the doors. The walls were bronze coloured with beautifully carved, angelic statues attached to the walls, their hands gripping their candles tightly. Past the marble floor and statues stood a golden throne and, as Thorne approached, he spied at the figure sat stiffly upon it.

The man wore a large white fur coat that fell to his feet and spread from the throne like tendrils. In fact, he was dressed completely in white, from his scarf to his boots. His hands, however, were covered in black gloves. To the right of the man, fiddling with a gleaming medallion was a boy. His clothes were unkempt and ragged, an odd and dramatic contrast, Thorne thought, to the grandeur of the Steward.

Thorne paused before the throne and bowed. The man inclined his head in return and beckoned Thorne forward with a gloved hand. Thorne took a step forward, doing his utmost to maintain eye contact with the man's piercing gaze.

'To what do I owe this pleasure, Warlock?'

Thorne raised his eyebrows, momentarily startled by the soft, almost musical quality of the man's voice. 'Are you the Steward of this city, my lord?'

'Yes,' the man replied, the boy beside him flinched as he adjusted his position on the throne, 'my name is Xalem, I believe you are Thorne?'

'Yes, I am,' Thorne replied in surprise.

He knew his name?

Xalem smiled wryly and folded his hands together, 'so, I will ask again. Why have you come?'

'Forgive me, my Lord,' Thorne frowned, 'but I thought the reason had been made clear?'

Xalem's eyes flickered towards the door behind Thorne.

'The dark point,' he said.

'Yes, my Lord.'

'And they sent a boy to perform this critical task?' the Stewards gaze shot back towards Thorne, scrutinising his dusty blue robes.

Thorne managed to hold his gaze, although not without some discomfort. 'Not initially, my Lord,' Thorne grimaced, 'that was to be my mentor's duty, but he was... killed.'

'I'm sorry to hear that,' Xalem said, adjusting himself on the throne and narrowing his eyes, 'it must have been difficult for you.'

'It has,' Thorne agreed, 'but I'm afraid to say my mentor did not tell me how to destroy it.'

Xalem smiled and then leant over the side of the throne to whisper something to the boy, who stared at the floor, his hands gripping the medallion tightly.

'I wouldn't worry, Thorne.' he said, then turning to the boy by his side and offering a curt nod.

With that, the boy pocketed the medallion and burst past Thorne towards the great doors behind. Indeed, he passed with such speed that Thorne felt his heart jolt. The agility didn't just bely that of a child but seemed abnormal for even a grown adult. This paled in comparison to the show of strength, with the boy alone closing the grand doors through which Thorne had entered, without any apparent difficulty.

'That's… impressive,' Thorne laughed weakly.

Xalem merely smiled and rose from his throne, taking slow steps towards the Warlock.

'So, you have come to destroy the portal?'

'Yes, my Lord,' Thorne said, suddenly very aware of how dark the hall was. Perhaps he was mistaken, but it seemed to be getting darker.

'Why would you ever want to do that?' Xalem inquired, his arms aloft.

As Thorne unconsciously took a step back, he felt the rod vibrate at his side.

'Thorne…'

'Gah!' Thorne exclaimed, still not quite used to the rod's interventions.

'I would not advise remaining where you are.'

'What do you mean?' Thorne replied, his voice coming out louder than he expected.

Xalem grinned at Thorne, and with a whip of his hands the flickering lights above in the chandeliers were snuffed out.

*

'Such a beautiful city,' Illumina murmured, caressing the cracks of a statue with a finger.

'Illumina!'

The Regal looked up to see Zaine, his hand tapping impatiently on the pommel of his sword.

'We need to find him now,' the Hunter said, pulling her away from the statue.

'Sorry,' she replied, following the Hunter across the street.

'We need to keep a low profile, and you going over to admire the scenery isn't helping.'

Illumina glanced around. Thankfully, no–one was paying much attention to the two hooded newcomers. She drew her hood closer, shadowing the bottom half of her face. But when she turned to her right, the Hunter had disappeared. Her heart raced as she looked desperately around the crowded street for the Hunter. Where he had he gone? She pushed herself through the swarm, inviting disgruntled utterings from several passer–by's. Her eyes then caught hold of a hood above the heads of the crowd.

'Zaine!' she bellowed, but her voice was drowned out by the multitude of voices around her.

She finally found the man standing outside one of the derelict shops. Vines almost covered the entire surface of the building, creeping through the windows and bursting through roof.

'What are you doing?' she hissed angrily, 'you just left me walking and–'

Without any forewarning, Zaine's gloved hand flew to her mouth, stopping her from finishing her sentence. She noticed, with surprise, that he had turned pale and that his other hand shook by his side. She followed his gaze, and saw a boy, no older than ten, who stood by the shop staring back at the pair with an inquisitive expression, while fiddling with an odd medallion. Zaine took a step forward and raised his hand. What surprised Illumina was the fact, that, this did not seem a gesture of greeting but rather bordered on the defensive. The boy turned as soon, as Zaine had lifted his foot off the ground, and sprinted away into the crowd, disappearing amongst a sea of bodies.

'Wait!' Zaine cried, dashing into the crowd.

'Athrana's grace!' Illumina groaned.

She followed him through the crowded streets and the darkest alleyways. All the while, he refused to explain to Illumina why this boy was suddenly so important, seemingly more so now than the search for Thorne. However, no matter where they went, the boy was nowhere to be found. Zaine collapsed beside the stairs of the building they had just entered. His breathing was ragged, although this difficulty seemed more influenced by frustration than fatigue.

'Zaine?' Illumina murmured after the Hunter did not move or say anything for several minutes, his face remaining utterly pale, 'who was that child?'

The Hunter took a moment before replying in a shaken voice, 'Thorne is in great danger.'

Chapter 25

The cold wind nipped at the skin of Thorne's face and he awoke to the bright glare of the sun. The Warlock winced and frowned as he tried to push himself up to his feet, but his hand sunk into the ground. He looked down – it was sand, just pure sand. What was happening? He was... Where was he? He could remember creeping darkness, a pale face looking down upon him and then... nothing.

He could feel something nagging at him in the corner of his mind but, no matter how hard he tried, it would not reveal itself to him. Thorne was sure he was supposed to be travelling somewhere but surely not here, to this... desert? However, before Thorne could think further about his rather odd predicament, he was distracted by a low growl behind him.

He whipped around, and gasped.

The alpha wolf stood only a few metres away from him, saliva drooling from its mouth and its eyes hungry.

Thorne took an involuntary step back, tripping over his own feet. Falling over was the stroke of luck that saved him. As soon as he had moved the alpha had pounced; soaring through the air with its jaws open, but its fangs found only thin air to catch.

The Warlock sprung to his feet, not even glancing behind him to see what had happened to his ravenous pursuer, and sprinted in the opposite direction, sand billowing in his wake.

Within a few seconds Thorne could hear the alpha's guttural grunts as it bounded towards him. He looked back. It was directly behind him now, with a single clawed paw raised.

Thorne screamed as it cut into his leg, bringing him crashing into the sand. The beast's head observed him from above, then it opened its jaw revealing a yellowed set of razor sharp teeth. The promise of death hung at the end of every fang.

SHUNK.

Silver flashed before Thorne's eyes. The alpha howled and rolled onto its side, a huge sword embedded in its chest.

'Who?' Thorne muttered, his eyes allowing him his first, and probably final, glance at his saviour.

The sun shone brightly off his golden suit of armour, obscuring the man's face. A golden gauntlet pulled Thorne up from the ground with ease as though he were a rag doll and placed him over a golden pauldron.

'Stay alive, child,' he heard the man say, 'I need you…'

*

'Who are you?' Thorne asked, wincing as he tried to get up from the rock. Thorne felt like he'd seen the knight before.

'I'd advise you to still yourself; that is no small injury,' the knight replied sternly, surprising the Warlock with the power and command held in his voice. There was definitely something… familiar about his voice too but he just couldn't place it.

Thorne shrugged inwardly and turned to his surroundings. He had woken in a cave the size of his old chambers. There was a fire in the middle that warmed the surprisingly cold stone.

The knight placed his gauntlets on the stone bed beside him where the rest of his armour lay. However, when he turned to face the Warlock, Thorne noticed that he hadn't taken off his helmet; it was only piece of armour he had left on. Thorne thought it looked odd with his simple long–sleeved tunic.

'How is the wound?' the knight asked.

'Painful,' Thorne replied.

The knight chuckled.

Thorne frowned, not entirely seeing the what was amusing about his injury, 'so, will you tell me who you are now?'

The knight sounded surprised, 'But surely, Thorne, you already know who. The more interesting question is *why*.'

Thorne was confused. What was it he had forgotten?

'I really can't remember you,' Thorne shook his head, 'or this… place… where am I?'

The knight sighed, stood up and crossed the room to where Thorne lay; his injured leg held up on a slab of stone and his back leaning against the wall.

'I will not be able to show you much,' he explained.

Without warning, he covered Thorne's eyes with his hand and the Warlock was immersed into darkness again. Suddenly, images flew through his mind – his meeting with the golden man, the sparks of different coloured light in a dark sky, a large crowd, a crown, a golden armoured knight. A name burned through his mind and he felt a searing pain erupt within his head. The knight pulled his hand away from Thorne's face before he could shout out and the pain subsided as quickly as it had arrived.

272

Thorne gasped. Tiny lights erupted for several seconds before his vision returned to normal. 'Fierslaken,' he murmured breathlessly, 'Horizon's first king.'

'In the flesh,' Fierslaken spread out his hands.

'But... but that's impossible,' Thorne wheezed, clutching his head, 'you're dead!'

'The Steward is a powerful abomination,' Fierslaken said, stirring the flames with his sword, 'vampires appear to have a knack for storing souls.'

'A vampire? The Steward's a vampire? But that's–'

'Impossible? A myth?' Fierslaken interjected, 'I get the impression, child, that you have been shielded from much of the wonders – and dangers – of this world. Tell me, do you even know what you are?'

Thorne took a moment before murmuring in return, 'what I am?'

Fierslaken snorted. 'Boy, do you still not know?'

'What do you mean?'

'You, boy, are the Phoenix,' Fierslaken whispered. 'I would have thought Vigil would have made that clear.'

'The Phoenix? And who is Vigil?'

'How do you...'

Fierslaken stared at Thorne for a few seconds before putting his head, or rather his helmet, in his hands. 'You old bastard,' Thorne thought he heard the knight mutter.

'That rod you now carry by your side, it was once mine,' Fierslaken said.

Thorne's mouth dropped open, his hand flying to his belt. His fingers did not find his metallic companion.

'You won't find Vigil here, in this realm,' Fierslaken said, 'but you will when you leave.'

'When I leave?'

'You don't belong on this plane and I can set you free,' Fierslaken said getting to his feet, muttering under his breath, 'probably.'

Thorne met the man's gaze, pushing aside the troubling thoughts for the moment. 'How can you do it?' he asked.

'I have my ways,' the man chuckled, 'but I will require you to do something after you disembark from this world.'

'Of course. What do you need me to do?' Thorne asked, leaning forward.

The man jumped off the stone bed, 'I will need you to destroy the artefact that holds me in place here, then I leave the rest to you.'

'The artefact?'

'A painting, it should be very close to you. Vigil will be fully capable of helping you complete this task, I assure you.'

'But… What about the Steward?' Thorne asked, the memory of the man's pale arrogant face surfacing in his thoughts, 'and what about me? What I am supposed to do with this… Phoenix stuff?'

'What the world needs of you, boy, there are dark times ahead. Trust in Vigil.'

'But I–'

The man placed his hand over Thorne's forehead and growled 'Go!'

White light danced before his eyes and Thorne felt an odd tingling sensation. His vision darkened, and he lost feeling in his body as he floated within a black sea – a sea of darkness.

*

A sudden, deep intake of breath, as though he'd resurfaced after a long swim under water, Thorne found himself in a cell. Moss covered the chipped brick walls, and the skeletal corpse of an old prisoner hung from the ceiling by a loop of chains around its arms. Oddly, there was no door, just an arch leading into a torch lit corridor. Only the occasional drop of water and the petrified squeaks of rats disturbed the unsettling silence.

Thorne groaned and slowly got up to his feet, his hand flying to his belt. His fingers closed gratefully over the cool metal of the rod and he breathed a sigh of relief.

'Vigil,' Thorne thought.

'Thorne. You escaped.'

'I had help. I need to find a painting.'

'A painting?'

'It's a... a dark artefact. Don't ask how I know just tell me where it is.'

'Thorne...'

'Yes?'

'Look behind you.'

Thorne swivelled round and smiled in surprise. There before him, untouched and undamaged, was the painting. Thorne could see a vast desert depicted, and on it were tiny moving figures of what looked like animals. Moving figures on a painting!

'Do you know what to do?'

'Majik, of course.'

Thorne snapped his fingers, a flame bobbing at the tip of his finger.

'That kind will not work, this is... powerful, very powerful and resistant as well. Hold on.'

A sound similar to the whir of gears echoed around the cell and the rod's runes began to burn brightly.

'Stab it.'

Thorne did not need telling twice. He thrust the rod with all the force he was capable of into the painting. The result was not as he had expected.

The tip of the rod stopped an inch away from the surface of the painting, some unseen force preventing access the rod's access to it.

'Push! I will do the rest.'

Thorne put all his strength behind the rod and as he did so, dark tendrils suddenly lashed out at him from the painting wrapping around the rod and his arms, burning his skin.

'Arrghhh!'

'Push, Thorne!'

Thorne pushed, ignoring the tightening of the tendrils on his arms. There was a crack and the tendrils were set alight with green fire, releasing Thorne and flailing helplessly by the painting. The rod blazed with green light igniting the painting as well; a black inky substance oozing from the painting and dribbling, sickeningly, down the wall.

The frame collapsed to the ground and then disappeared in a pile of ashes. Gone.

Thorne laughed weakly but the jubilation was short lived, as an ear–splitting scream rang through the corridor, forcing Thorne to cover his ears.

'And we seem to have invoked the Steward's anger.'

'I'm guessing that painting was probably worth something.'

Before Thorne could think of anything else he heard a door slam.

'Run, Thorne!'

His heart pounding loudly against his chest, Thorne ducked under the arch and into the corridor beyond. He ran to the end. To his left stood a closed door; to his right, at the far end of another corridor, he could just see the remains of another door, hanging off its hinges. A sudden gust of wind and the flames of the torches by the door were extinguished. Another second and then the next pair were extinguished, a cold, cruel laugh echoing towards him. Another two, another two, another two, and yet he stood still, fixated by the approaching darkness.

'MOVE!'

Thorne blinked rapidly, snapping out of his trance, pushing open the door to his left and bolting through it. A spiral of stairs greeted him. With the darkness nearing, he sprinted up the steps, ignoring the soreness of his legs. Keep moving. Keep moving. Thorne thought to himself, praying that his haste wouldn't cause him to stumble.

When Thorne reached the top, he found that he could move no further. A brick wall ending his hopes of escape.

'No!' Thorne cried in despair, banging his fists against the bricks.

An odd whirring sound and Thorne jumped back in surprise, as the wall vibrated slightly, releasing a cloud of dust. It began to move back and slowly shift aside, revealing a glow of light.

Once the gap was wide enough to squint through, Thorne could see the back of something. He squinted and quickly realised that it was a throne, the same one in which Xalem had sat. The passage led to the Hall of Light!

He shivered, feeling the bite of a cold wind on the back his neck. He glanced behind him seeing the glow of torches down the stairs extinguishing quickly.

Thorne pushed the slab of the wall, but it refused to move any faster. Only a few more centimetres and he could escape!

'Coming for you,' the cold air behind him whispered.

The pair of torches behind him extinguished, immersing the staircase in complete darkness. Thorne backed against the wall and closed his eyes, praying that his end would be quick.

CA-CHUNK!

Thorne fell backwards through the open section of the wall, tumbling painfully to the floor with a grunt. Quickly gripping the throne, he pulled himself to his feet and began sprinting again towards the towering open doors and the safety of the city beyond. He was almost there, he could virtually feel the air on his face.

A dark shape flew past him and the doors slammed shut. Thorne carried on running to the doors, slamming his fists but to no avail against the thick wood. He slumped to his knees and banged the back of his head against the doors in defeat. So, this was it, this was all his journey had amounted to. This was the end.

Thorne was filled with a familiar sense of dread, as the flames of each mounted brazier and candle was extinguished, one after one, in rapid succession. The entire hall was now immersed in darkness. Again.

'Gods… help me, please,' Thorne muttered under his breath, knowing that no such help would arrive this time.

Thorne took a deep breath and held up his hand. He snapped his fingers, the spark creating a weak flame in the palm of his hand, illuminating a small circle around him. And, sickeningly, the face of the Steward, right in front of him.

Thorne did not scream, but he felt the blood drain from his face and his hand began to shake.

'Boo!' the Steward cackled, before blowing out the flame.

Thorne felt the vampire grab the front of his robes, before launching him into the air. He fell heavily, sliding across the floor, his head colliding with one of the legs of the throne. Lights danced in front of his eyes.

Another cold, mirthless cackle. He heard the footsteps of the Steward echoing around the room, but it was impossible to tell from where.

'It has been so long!' Xalem chuckled, 'so long!'

Thorne turned his head from left to right and back again. It was as though the man's voice was coming from everywhere at once.

'What should I do, I wonder? Kill you now? Quickly? Or slowly? Choices, choices!'

A rush of wind and Thorne could feel the man's icy breath on his neck. 'So many choices,' he whispered, 'but it's so hard to resist... I can hear your blood calling to me, begging me to taste its delights. Perhaps I should indulge myself now just this once–'

BANG!

The Steward disappeared with a gust of wind.

BANG!

'Who dares disturb me!' Xalem growled, 'who dares!'

A door flew open, light flooding inside the hall and two figures burst in. Torches held in their hands.

Hoods obscured their faces, but Thorne instantly recognised one of them, dark hair spilling out the man's hood and across his chest.

'Zaine!' Thorne cried in delight.

The Hunter turned towards him and drew back his hood, as did his companion, long blond hair falling across her

shoulders. Thorne realising with surprise that it was the Regal
– Illumina.

'Thorne stay where you are!' Zaine commanded, drawing his
sword.

'So, you have provided me with a feast. Thorne,' the Steward
chuckled, 'how touching!'

The Steward launched himself at the pair. Shadows whipping
through the air. Before he could watch the ensuing fight,
Thorne's vision suddenly turned white. And, again, the light
faded onto a different scene.

His eyes were fixed on three men, one of which lay on the
floor. Thorne recognised him instantly by his bright golden
armour, Fierslaken.

'Vigil,' Thorne said weakly, 'what's going on?'

There is something I must show you.

The warrior lay unmoving, oblivious to the two men who
stood either side of him. They were talking so discretely,
Thorne had trouble discerning what they were saying.

The man to Fierslaken's left, Thorne recognised as the
Steward, Xalem. He had a bored expression on his face and
his fingers drummed impatiently on his arms.

'So, you wish me to use the artefact to imprison his soul?'
Xalem asked.

'His soul only, nothing else vampire,' the other man growled.
He was a balding man with a squashed sort of face, and a
thick brown moustache that drooped down the side of his
face. Thorne noticed, with surprise, the sparks of a Majik
Master.

281

'The soul?' Xalem repeated.

'Yes. We will keep the body' the man replied.

'And what will you do with his body?' Xalem said, with hunger in his eyes.

'Burn it, we needed the information, not the man.'

'He would not reveal the Old Ones location?'

'No. Evidently taking his own life was a more appealing option. A waste but no matter.'

'Do you seriously believe he will decide to give up this information while he's in the painting?' Xalem said with a sneer.

'Perhaps not, but it is my people's only hope.'

Xalem narrowed his eyes, unfolded his arms and shrugged, 'very well then. And the city?'

'It shall be yours, as you asked,' the man replied, adding darkly, 'providing you control your thirst.'

Xalem's lip curled and then he turned back towards the golden armoured warrior that lay before him.

White light blazed across his eyes and Thorne was thrown back into the normal world. He gasped, breathing in and out deeply.

'Woah,' Thorne muttered.

Bam!

Thorne's eyes darted upwards, seeing the limp form of Illumina slide across the floor to the wall.

'Illumina!' Thorne gasped, jumping to his feet and dashing to the Regal's side.

'Ah Thorne!' the vampire chuckled, 'glad you could join us! Once I've finished with the Hunter, I can thank you personally!'

Zaine leapt forward plunging his sword into a cloud of shadow. The vampire had disappeared. The Hunter rushed towards Thorne and grasped his shoulder.

'Are you alright?' he demanded.

'I'm... I'm–'

'You're what?' Zaine said, glancing around them.

Thorne looked up into the Hunter's eyes, 'I saw Fierslaken... I saw a Majik Master... my people... they made an agreement with that... that thing.'

Zaine's mouth thinned, but he did not stop Thorne mid-speech. If anything, he appeared to encourage Thorne to continue.

'But earlier I saw him Zaine! He was alive! Or at least he seemed to be... He said I was the Phoenix... what did he mean?'

Zaine laughed, albeit haggardly, 'of course, it makes sense now.'

'What does? What about any of this does?'

'Don't you see Thorne? You've been given a gift! You're the Phoenix now!'

'I have shown you the path, Thorne. You must choose to take it.' Vigil spoke.

Upon the words being said, a flash of images burned across Thorne's mind. Two men crouched together on the floor of a small house. One of them held a baby. The other, he realized with surprise, was a Warlock. Not only a Warlock, but Master Farholm, albeit much younger.

'This one is special,' Farholm said, his eyes fixed upon the child.

'Your name is Thorne Grey.'

His vision disappearing in a cascade of flames, Thorne returned to the world, his knees collapsing beneath him. He was the Phoenix.

'Thorne, breathe, the vampire will be back. We need to go!'

A flash of shadow, and Xalem was flying across the air towards them, fangs arching against the corners of his mouth.

And then Thorne understood.

Thorne got to his feet, feeling sudden waves of Majik rushing through him. Now tapping freely into seemingly limitless reserves he thrust his right arm forward and a bolt of pure flame burst from his open palm, slamming into the vampire and sending him flying across the room. The vampire held out his arms like a pair of wings, slowing his descent and then furiously patted against the embers burning on his chest.

Unrelenting, Thorne cast fine streams of white flame, like molten iron, from both his hands, binding the vampire in coils of fire. Thorne raised his hands upwards, in a rapid motion, sending Xalem flying into a chandelier on the ceiling. Then, bringing his hands rapidly down, Thorne slammed the vampire onto the floor; the chandelier following and falling on top of Xalem, with a crash.

284

With a primal scream, the vampire leapt to its feet, grabbed the remains of the chandelier, and hurled it at Thorne. Thorne pushed his hands out in front of him, palms up, and a wall of dense flame erupted from the ground. Each piece of the chandelier disintegrated before it could reach him.

'This is impossible!' Xalem said, staring at Thorne, 'Fierslaken is dead. The line of the Phoenix is dead!'

The vampire whipped his hand in the air and a shadowy tendril smacked against Thorne's chest, throwing him through the air towards the wall. Thorne threw his arms out sideways, cast a wave of flame; slowing the impact against the stone. Dazed and winded but alive, Thorne stumbled to his feet.

'Now, you die!' the vampire screamed, hurling tendril after tendril in Thorne's direction.

But Thorne was ready this time. With a sweep of both hands, flames enveloped and consumed the shadows, their remains fluttering to the ground like ash.

Thorne clapped his hands, and in a burst of flame, he suddenly appeared next to the Steward. Before the stunned vampire could move, Thorne seized his arm and hurled him, as if he were a small rock, into one of the large doors. The force of the impact left a large dent in the wood and the vampire sprawled on the ground.

Xalem pushed himself to his feet, as Thorne approached, and launched a fistful of shadows at him. Thorne waved his hand once and the shadows were engulfed in flames.

'Enough!' Xalem screamed.

More shadows spiralled around the Vampire's arms but, instead of launching them at Thorne, Xalem directed the darkness at the door behind him. With a bang, both doors blew off their hinges and moonlight flooded into the Hall. A hoard of skeletons burst past the cackling vampire, their bones scraping and screeching across the floor. The vampire's cold laughter echoing across the walls.

Thorne glanced at Zaine, and then turned to where Illumina lay.

'Keep them away from her!' Thorne bellowed.

Zaine nodded, his sword smashing a skeleton's skull, as it ran towards the Regal's body.

The vampire narrowed its eyes at Thorne, then sprinted out the Hall. Thorne caught the vampire before he could set one foot into the night, and sent him flying into the door again, with such force the wood cracked from top to bottom. The vampire crumpled to the ground. Thorne crouched, placing his fists on the cold marble, his eyes fixed on the centre of the cracked door. Cracks in the marble slabs spread from Thorne's fists, which had started to glow a brilliant white. The cracked door shook and began to form multiple fissures, spreading from the centre. Then, with a deafening CRACK, it collapsed. The vampire didn't even have time to scream, before massive slabs of wood collapsed on top of him.

Their master defeated, the skeletons paused in unison. Without warning, bones dislocated and collapsed, crumbling to the ground.

Thorne sighed and walked over to the crumbled remains of the door. Thorne was amazed to see that, somehow, the vampire had survived, its head jutting out behind a slab of wood, struggling and failing to prise it away.

Thorne's hands became alive with fire.

'No! Wait!' Xalem pleaded when he noticed Thorne.

'Why?' demanded Thorne.

'If I'm going to burn, then so should he,' he spat.

'Who?'

'Watch,' the vampire cackled.

He took a deep breath and then suddenly he was seeing a room, as though from the vampire's eyes.

The man in front of him wore a black hooded robe and had an aura of command about him. Indeed, there was something familiar about him that Thorne couldn't quite place.

'Your hood, remove it,' he heard Xalem say.

The man's hands reached for his hood, pulling it down to reveal his face and the sparks of his white toga underneath the robe.

'Ah. So, it all makes sense now, Warlock,' the vampire said.

'No,' the man replied curtly, 'call me Master. Master Vey.'

The scene faded and Thorne found himself sitting face level with the sneering vampire lord.

'The Shadow is one of us?' Thorne whispered, shaking his head.

'Of course! So you see, child,' Xalem said, 'even your own kind conspires against you!'

Thorne stared at the vampire in shocked silence. 'They've known I've been here all along!' Xalem said, continuing bitterly 'but it seems they were playing the both of us.'

'What do you mean?'

Teeth thick with blood, the Vampire grinned, 'they knew what you were from the start. Why do you think you, a mere child, were sent here? Looks like I won't be the only one meeting a sticky end.'

Thorne saw the dark tendril just in time and dived out of the way, as it lashed out at him from under a wooden slab. Thorne leapt forward, placing his hands firmly on top of the Xalem's head, and letting the Majik flow through his fingertips and explode into the vampire's body.

Xalem screamed, his eyes and mouth alight with fire. The vampire rose in the air, arms and legs spread out. Beams of light perforated the vampire's pale skin, illuminating the entire entrance to the Hall. Then with one pitiful shriek, he exploded in a shower of shadowy sparks.

*

'Thorne, I–'

'For the last time, Zaine, I don't have time to explain... I need to get back to Dalmarra and... I need to take care of something.'

Zaine opened his mouth to say something but stopped himself and moved aside.

'Thanks,' Thorne muttered.

Zaine didn't reply, shaking his head solemnly as he watched the Warlock stride away. He had changed, it was not just how he acted, the Hunter could see it in his walk as well – how he carried himself with such solemnity, as though he now bore such a terrible burden.

'So, the Phoenix has returned,' Zaine murmured to himself.

Illumina watched Thorne silently, as he clambered down the stairs to the town, and right up to the moment he disappeared within the crowd that thronged the streets.

People stared and pointed at the wrecked entrance to the Hall of Lights. Murmurs slipped from a mass of lips, the air now heavy with rumours. It would not be long before the land was awash with tales.

Chapter 26

He paused, his hand brushing against the marble handle of the door and listened. Thorne could hear the rustle of pages and the sound of a man humming. Thorne took a deep breath, twisted the handle and pushed open the door. The man inside spun sharply as he approached, mouth agape, the piece of parchment he held slipping through his fingers.

'Thorne?' said Master Vey.

'Master Vey,' Thorne replied coldly.

Vey frowned, shook his head and then returned to sifting through piles of parchment.

'I assume your return heralds the dismantling of the dark point?' Vey muttered.

'Yes, that is correct,' Thorne replied.

Vey dropped the parchment he was holding and turned to face him, his arms crossed by his side as his eyes scrutinized Thorne.

'So, he gave you his power?' Vey sighed.

'Fierslaken?' Thorne replied, 'No, I'm pretty sure I always had it, he simply... made me more aware of it.'

'Marvellous, another Phoenix to contend with,' Vey snorted, 'then I imagine you know everything now.'

'You never even bothered to tell me, why?' Thorne demanded, 'were you scared? Why didn't you just kill me before I left?'

'We didn't fear you! Or wish your death!' Vey said, tugging uncomfortably at his collar, 'we had no choice! The fate of our order – the very world – was on the line!'

Thorne narrowed his eyes and took a step forward, 'what do you mean?'

Vey sighed, ran his hands through his hair and took a step towards the window. 'Majik is leaving this world, it's hard to admit it, and even harder to know why, but it's happening nonetheless.'

'What does that have to do with anything?'

'Don't you see Thorne?' Vey span round, hands closed together, imploring Thorne, 'we're becoming irrelevant. Everything about us revolves around Majik! And what is this land without us to protect it?'

'And for that you thought it would be a good idea to sacrifice us both?'

'You survived, did you not?' Vey scoffed, 'as for Rozenhall, well, he should have known better than to risk the Silent Forests.'

With that, Vey made a move for the door.

'Where are you going?' Thorne inquired, putting a hand out before the Majik Master could go past him.

'I have business elsewhere, as I imagine you do as well.'

Thorne bent his head in closer so that the tip of his nose was a few inches away from the man's face. 'It's time to lift away these lies,' he whispered, 'I know who you are, Shadow.'

Thorne backed away, but not before hearing an intake of breath from the Majik Master and a sad sigh.

'Meddling in matters of our order is one thing,' he said, 'meddling in mine is a different thing entirely.'

'I just got back after burning your vampire to ashes, I'm not in the mood for threats,' Thorne said quietly.

Vey shook his head at the floor and began to agitatedly pace around the room, his hands placed firmly together behind his back as he did so. 'There is a darkness rising Thorne, a great darkness, one which will wipe out all life on this land. I did what I did because of this – to stop it!'

'Oh, there was, you gave it a licence to roam around a city of innocent people, and I stopped it!'

Vey smiled wryly and shook his head. 'You fool. If you think the vampire is the worst thing this land has ever faced, you are sorely mistaken. There is a darkness coming, one this world is still recovering from. When it strikes, it will hit with the force of a thousand plagues. It will make the last Shadow War look like child's play.'

'The Necromancers are dead! Fierslaken stopped them!'

'Is that truly what he led you to believe?' Vey shook his head sadly.

Thorne paused and thought back to his time in the painting. He could not bring himself to answer.

'So, what are you going to do?' Vey sneered, spreading his arms wide for Thorne, 'do you dare try to kill me?'

Thorne shook his head, 'I'm not going to be the one to do that.'

Vey frowned, 'you won't? Then who?'

'I SHALL,' Death said, gliding through the door.

Death was the same as Thorne had last seen him, a dark, tattered, hooded cloak, yellowing bones, a skull with numerous cracks on the top, and a large scythe, but the blade's surface was, thankfully, silent this time.

Vey's face fell, and Thorne saw his lip begin to tremble. 'W– who?' Vey stuttered.

Death glanced at Thorne, who shrugged. 'IF IT'S NOT OBVIOUS, IT WILL BE EASIER FOR YOU IF I DON'T ELABORATE,' Death replied.

Death's raised a skeletal hand from his side and extended a single bony finger towards Vey's trembling forehead.

'I OFFER YOU DEATH BY MY HAND, OR BY HIS,' Death said, nodding at Thorne.

'I–I…' Vey snuffled, head twisting rapidly between Thorne and Death.

'EXCELLENT CHOICE…'

*

'That was quick.'

Thorne turned around to face the boned reaper and smiled, although the action did not reach his eyes.

'I AIM TO PLEASE,' Death replied, making an elaborate bow.

'No, I mean, thanks,' Thorne sighed, 'I appreciate it.'

'HM,' Death grunted.

'So. What's your deal?'

'WHAT EVER DO YOU MEAN?'

'You know exactly what I mean,' Thorne replied, 'why would you choose to help me?'

'WHAT? YOU THINK JUST BECAUSE I LOOK LIKE THIS THAT I'M EVIL? HONESTLY... THERE'S NO PLEASING SOME PEOPLE.'

'You harvest the dead.'

Death shrugged, 'NOBODY'S PERFECT.'

Thorne rolled his eyes and then turned to leave.

'YOU KNOW THEY WILL HUNT YOU FOR THIS?'

'Naturally, I doubt they'd believe *Death* was a helping hand in the matter,' Thorne replied, 'well... at least not in any physical sense.'

'BUT YOU KNOW YOUR WORK IS NOT DONE?'

Thorne nodded solemnly, 'yes, I'm aware.'

Death watched him silently for a while. His black tongue probing the vacancies in its mouth where yellowed teeth had disappeared. 'THERE ARE DARK TIMES AHEAD THORNE. THIS WORLD IS NOT PREPARED. IT NEEDS A PHOENIX.'

'But what if I'm not the Phoenix it needs?' Thorne said. Death did not answer.

'Thorne?'

Thorne turned to face the new arrival. It was Fax, Vey's assistant. His eyes flickered between Thorne and the door to the room he'd left with Death, the room where his Master now lay.

There was only one thing he could do... Run.

*

Zakariyanna twirled her fingers around the surface of the lake, her hand leaving soft ripples in its wake. She did not need to hear his footsteps, she could feel his presence from a mile off. But now he was close.

'Thorne,' she greeted him, without looking up.

'Soothsayer,' Thorne replied.

'Whom do I greet?' she asked.

'What do you mean?' Thorne answered, puzzled.

Zakariyanna smiled under her veil, 'on one side of the coin, I see a Phoenix and the other... No amount of flips of that coin will bring you any peace.'

Thorne lowered himself to the floor next to the Seer.

'You have good eyes.'

'Some would say it is a curse,' she chuckled.

Thorne frowned at the water's surface, scrutinizing his reflection and then turned his head towards her. 'I believe you told me that if I went to the City of Light I would die.'

'If I remember correctly, I said you would be consumed by flames,' the seer pointed out, 'but what is fire to a Phoenix?'

'So, your prediction was wrong?'

The seer shrugged, 'right, wrong, what does it matter? Make of my words as you will. The world has no time for narrow minds, and no place for the naysayer. You could have died, or you could have survived. I can only guide. Your fate is your own.'

'Isn't it the Gods'?'

'The Gods' influence only extends so far.'

Thorne glanced briefly at Vigil, tapping the metallic rod thoughtfully.

She smiled at the water, 'what will you do now?'

'I don't know,' he replied honestly.

'I wish you all the luck in the world,' she sighed, 'truly.'

Thorne looked at her briefly, nodded and then jumped to his feet.

Zakariyanna stared into the water. 'Thorne, you know you'll have to make a choice soon – you cannot be both.' Zakariyanna paused briefly before turning to face him, 'Phoenix or Lycan.'

The statement gave Thorne pause. It was the first time he'd heard both titles mentioned in the same sentence.

'What if I can't decide?' Thorne asked.

'Then the world will move on without you,' Zakariyanna replied, matter–of–factly.

*

Thorne was sat in a cellar, his hands resting on a barrel. Rats patrolling the ground in search of leakages and the rotten remains of discarded food. A man sat opposite to him in a creaking wooden chair, moss clinging to the edges by the paved stone floor.

'Have you considered my offer?' MakVarn asked.

'How did you know?' Thorne inquired.

The man smiled and leaned back on his chair, immersing his features in shadow and inviting another long creak from the chair. The sound echoing across the barren walls of the cellar. 'I was contacted,' he said.

'By whom?'

'The Hunter, of course,' MakVarn said, 'he had his concerns and I recognised the symptoms.'

'Symptoms?'

'Pah,' the man waved his hand, 'the usual… mood swings, variances in body temperature, intolerance to silver, etcetera etcetera.'

Thorne nodded, his eyes then left the depths of the flame and returned to MakVarn, 'I've got to make a choice, haven't I?'

'Yes,' he replied, leaning forward 'but the question is, what choice will you make?'

Thorne closed his eyes, took a deep breath and sighed. With every choice is a consequence that could have major or minor repercussions, affecting one or possibly thousands. One choice could condemn or save all. One choice and so many possibilities. It was then that he remembered all those weeks ago in his chambers in the Sorcerers Spire. His first meeting with Death. He remembered the vivid visions that were thrust upon his mind, the roar of flames, the screams of thousands of innocents and the mirror... The mirror with the warped image staring back at him cruelly, slaughter, and carnage burning brightly in his eyes.

'THE FUTURE.' Thorne remembered Death had explained, 'OR PERHAPS ONE OF MANY POSSIBLE OUTCOMES.'

He sighed as he opened his eyes. His choice was made. He had to decide for the future. The man raised an eyebrow at him questionably and Thorne inclined his head. MakVarn gave him a toothy grin, his lips stretching over his abnormally large incisors. He held up his hand next to the candle. Thorne gripped it tightly and shook.

'Welcome to the Brotherhood of Lycans,' the man growled.

TO BE CONTINUED…

I hope you enjoyed reading this as much as I enjoyed writing it. Being my debut novel, it would mean the world if you would take a few moments to write a review on Amazon. Reviews are crucial for authors, and yours will make a great difference! Thank you!

https://www.amazon.co.uk/review/create-review/ref=cm_cr_dp_d_wr_but_btm?ie=UTF8&channel=glance-detail&asin=B07B6C87TN#

Find me on:

Blog:
https://wordpress.com/view/farrellkeeling.wordpress.com

Or join the Facebook group:
https://www.facebook.com/farrellkeelingofficial/?ref=bookmarks

20033611R00172

Printed in Great Britain
by Amazon